Praise for Nadiya Hussain

'Funny, warm and uplifting'
OK! Magazine

'Breezy, funny and winning'
Daily Mail

'A lovely story about family, faith and self-acceptance'
Red Magazine

'Packed with humour and warmth'
Heat

'An enriching, thought-provoking
and – yes – entertaining read.'
Independent

'Proves she's more than just a dab
hand with a piping bag'
Daily Telegraph

Over 14 million people tuned in to see Nadiya win 2015's *Great British Bake Off*. Since then she has captured the heart of the nation. A columnist for *The Times* and *Essentials*, Nadiya is also a regular reporter for *The One Show* and presented a two-part series, *The Chronicles of Nadiya* on BBC One. She is the author of *Nadiya's Kitchen* (Michael Joseph), *Bake me a Story* (Hodder) and has been named as one of the top five most influential Asians in the UK.

Also in The Amir Sisters series:

The Secret Lives of the Amir Sisters
The Fall and Rise of the Amir Sisters

The Hopes and Triumphs of the Amir Sisters

Nadiya Hussain with
Ayisha Malik

ONE PLACE. MANY STORIES

This novel is entirely a work of fiction. The names, characters
and incidents portrayed in it are the work of the author's
imagination. Any resemblance to actual persons, living or
dead, events or localities is entirely coincidental.

HQ
An imprint of HarperCollins*Publishers* Ltd
1 London Bridge Street
London SE1 9GF

This edition 2020

1
First published in Great Britain by
HQ, an imprint of HarperCollins*Publishers* Ltd 2020

Nadiya Hussain asserts the moral right to be
identified as the author of this work.
A catalogue record for this book is
available from the British Library.

ISBN: 978-0-00-819238-9

MIX
Paper from
responsible sources
FSC™ C007454

This book is produced from independently certified FSC™ paper
to ensure responsible forest management.

For more information visit: www.harpercollins.co.uk/green

This book is set in 11.9/16.5 pt. Sabon

Printed and bound in Great Britain by
CPI Group (UK) Ltd, Croydon, CR0 4YY

Chapter One

It was meant to have been the time of Mae's life. It *was* the time of her life. Last night's doner kebab wrapper was still on her night-stand so she scrunched it up and threw it in the bin. Scratching her head she ate another cheese Dorito out of the packet. Crumbs fell on to the jeans she'd packed on top of her bag, but she couldn't be bothered to clean them off. It wasn't as if anyone noticed her. Nor as if she actually wanted to be noticed, she supposed. Not any more, anyway. Whatever. So, she zipped up the bag, mumbled, 'Laters,' as she walked out of her room in the halls of residence, and closed the door behind her.

A slew of students scurried past and she waited at the door, shifting on her feet, glancing at people to see if anyone would catch her eye. There was Marcus who was in her Studying Television class. And Dilek who sat next to him. Dilek would spend the lecture crumpling up pieces of paper and throwing them at Marcus, who'd just spread out his legs, slump further down in his seat and chuckle. The paper ball once bounced off Marcus and hit Mae, who was sitting in the row in front of him.

'Oops. Soz,' whispered Dilek.

'It's all right,' replied Mae, picking up the ball and wondering what to do with it.

She'd wanted to make a joke while handing it back: *More useful than making notes in* this *class. Lucky it didn't hit Buxom Buxton or it'd have bounced off her, straight into her face.* But something caught in her throat. Everything that sprang to mind sounded lame. She picked holes in her retorts before she ever said them out loud and by that time the person had moved on, just like Dilek had, who'd carried on taking notes as Marcus snatched her pen.

Mae eyed them both now as they ambled past, Marcus with his arm casually around Dilek's shoulders. Maybe they'd see her and smile. Maybe even say 'hello'. Except they hadn't noticed her. By the time Mae realised that there wasn't anything lame about her saying 'hello' to them, they'd walked past and the chance was gone.

It was *fine*. She was going back home for Easter and there she didn't have to always worry about words catching in her throat or saying something stupid. Mae wove her way through the corridors, out into the crisp spring air and walked towards the station. True, the Christmas holiday at home hadn't gone as planned. Between two new babies and her mum and dad's gross newly blossoming romance, Mae found herself scurrying from one place to the next, helping out, changing nappies, babysitting, helping her mum in the kitchen. Her mum, by the way, who didn't once ask how university was going.

'Typical,' said Mae to herself as she boarded the train, taking a seat by the window.

She'd expected better of her sister, Fatti, but ... *motherhood*. Mae sighed.

This time would be different because the babies weren't as new any more, and there was a party, of course, because the whole family was getting together after so many months. Her dad had said they were throwing it in her honour. They might not say it very often – or at all – but Mae was sure they were proud of her being at university, even if she was only doing Media Studies. Maybe her family would ask her enough questions about university for her to see that university wasn't that bad. Because it wasn't, really, was it?

A few hours later she stepped off the train on to a small platform under an overcast sky. Ash, her brother-in-law, would be waiting to pick her up so they could drive down to Wyvernage.

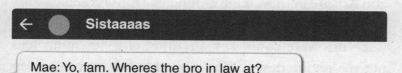

Sistaaaas

Mae: Yo, fam. Wheres the bro in law at?

Mae waited for a response, but after a few minutes, when she saw no one was typing, she called her mum and dad's house phone. It rang twelve times before her harassed-sounding mum picked up.

'Haam,' she exclaimed.

'Whoa, madre. Easy on the eardrums.'

'Oh, Mae. What is it?'

'Er, just waiting here at the station.'

There was a pause.

'What station?' her mum asked.

'Waterloo.'

'What?'

'Sewell station, obvs. Where else? Where's Ash?'

Another pause.

'*Oh my God*. FATIMA.'

Mae pulled the phone away from her ear.

'Fatti, where is your husband?' exclaimed her mum. 'He was meant to pick up Mae at the station.'

'What? Today?' came Fatima's faint but recognisable voice.

'Yes, today. She is waiting now. Okay, Mae. He's coming.'

'He must have forgotten.'

'Adam has been crying so much, ya Allah. Teething. Fatti and Ash are both walking around like those zombies. He's on his way so wait there. Have to go, the fish is burning.'

Before Mae could say anything else her mum had put the phone down. Mae looked at her mobile screen as flecks of rain spattered on it. She would have to take shelter.

'You look wrecked,' said Mae when Ash pulled up outside the station.

'Good to see you too, Mae.'

She got into the car and punched his arm as she laughed, trying to shift her unreasonable feelings of being abandoned. 'Always a pleasure, isn't it?'

Ash looked at her properly and seemed taken aback.

'Yeah. Always,' he replied, turning away and pulling out of the station. 'Sorry about the mix-up.'

'Noz woz. It happens. Hear the little monkey's giving you guys grief.'

That's all it took for Ash to then give Mae a blow-by-blow account of Adam's sleeping patterns, feeding habits, Ash's lack of sleep, Fatti's lack of sleep, Fatti's intermittent crying, Ash's intermittent crying, Adam's not-so-intermittent crying.

'Bloody hell,' replied Mae. 'Lots of crying.'

Ash just grunted then spent the rest of the journey in silence.

It wasn't a fortuitous start to Mae's break but she was an optimist. By the time they were outside her parents' house she had plastered on a smile as she waited for someone to answer the door.

'Ah, my darling bud of Mae has arrived,' exclaimed her dad, pulling her into a hug.

She took in the familiar smell of incense and spices and hugged him back so tightly she felt tears surface her eyes.

'How are you?' he said, looking down at her with such affection Mae thought she might burst into tears.

All the feelings she'd kept buried, telling herself that

everything was okay, that *she* was okay, brimmed to the surface now that she realised that all she wanted to do was cry into her dad's arms. He drew back from Mae and looked her up and down, his face going from proud to perplexed.

'Hmm,' he said, squeezing both her arms. 'You're eating well.'

'What?' she said.

But she was interrupted by the noise of a baby's cry piercing the reunion. Ash cleared his throat as Mae moved out of the way to see him dump her bag in the passage and run up the stairs.

'Fatti stayed here last night so your mum could help her and Ash could get some sleep. But he felt so bad that he came over late and stayed awake with Fatti. He's a very good man.'

'Hmm,' replied Mae.

She entered their living room and it seemed weirdly empty. Perhaps she'd been at university too long but it seemed to her that this house was always bustling with people, and when it wasn't bustling then it was at least familiar. It was the same place she'd spent most of her childhood, but today, for some reason, it felt different. Like she was a guest.

'Where are Farah and Bubblee?' she asked.

'Coming later. You can help your mum prepare the food.'

'Great,' she replied.

'Oh, little Adam,' said her dad as the baby's cry got louder.

He rushed up the stairs, leaving Mae behind, wondering what to do. She took in the magnolia-painted room, the brown carpet, the same they'd had for the past ten years, but there was now a flat-screen television mounted on the wall, a new beige sofa that looked like you could sink into and not come out of for days, and photos of Adam and her niece, Zoya, hung on the walls. There was one with Bubblee, Farah and Zoya. Mae thought it was mad that they were bringing up a baby together – as if the twin sisters were husband and wife – after Farah's husband had died. It seemed impossible that Bubblee had agreed to be a surrogate for them, only for her to now be a co-parent. It just went to show that people could change. Bubblee went from being the free-spirited artist, to being a surrogate for her twin sister who couldn't conceive, to being an actual mother. *Life*, thought Mae. Bubblee had always been the black sheep of the family and now she was daughter and mother extraordinaire, and here was Mae … What was Mae? She'd always trodden on the outskirts of the family and that was all right, she was the youngest, after all. A good fourteen years younger than the eldest, Fatti. At thirty-one years old, Farah and Bubblee were more than ten years older than Mae, and there was an eight-year difference between her and Jay – prodigal son who never quite fell entirely from grace. Of course there were several photos of him.

There was one close-up of him that their mum had insisted hiring a professional for – because he was such a handsome boy and everyone who came to the house should see this, since he was hardly ever there to be seen in person.

She hadn't minded being the observer to the unravelling of each of her sibling's dramas; Fatti finding out that she was adopted and that her biological mum was Mum's sister. The woman still lived in Bangladesh and had no regrets at having given Fatti up when they thought Mum couldn't conceive. It's what family did. The miracle was their mum then having four children after adopting Fatti.

Then there was Farah, who hadn't been able to have a baby, during which time her husband had squandered all their money into one of Jay's hare-brained business plans. Bubblee had some kind of early mid-life crisis because of her lack of artistic talent and came back home, only to end up becoming a surrogate for her sister, and then an actual mother to Zoya (and now emerging curator). Bubblee said she never thought that anything could be as important to her as her art, but here she was, mother and career woman, and she loved both equally.

Then there'd been Farah's husband, Mustafa, who'd taken his own life because of all the money that had been lost. It was amazing that Jay was still seen to be a part of the family after everything he put them through. Mae looked at Mustafa's picture, the one of him and Farah at their wedding – both of them looking so happy – and felt tears prickle her eyes. Yeah, he made some questionable decisions, but he'd been a good guy and Mae missed him. I mean, all of her family's stuff was pretty messed up but she'd witnessed it all, helping in every way she could, while snacking on her stupid celery sticks that thank God she'd now exchanged for some actual food.

Uni was going to be her time to flourish, away from the family's fold, for her to spread her so-called wings and *fly*. Except it soon became clear that, out of the family's fold, Mae wasn't exactly sure what her role was. At university, she wasn't so much flying as flapping.

Mae searched for any pictures of herself and noticed only one, which was the family photo. In it she was laughing because she'd just pinched Bubblee's arm, making her screw up her face.

Her mum came into the room and Mae went to hug her but her mum paused and just stared at her for a while.

'What?'

Her mum simply raised her eyebrows and shook her head as she went around the room looking for the cordless telephone.

'When's everyone arriving?' asked Mae.

'Farah and Bubblee can't make it because Zoya is ill so we do something tomorrow,' replied her mum, finding the phone stuffed between the sofa cushions.

'Oh,' said Mae.

An unreasonable feeling of disappointment washed

over her. She'd had an image of her family shouting out their welcomes as she entered the room. No big deal though. Her mum walked out of the room as Mae sighed and took the photo in her hands.

'Well, Mae. Welcome home.'

Mae woke up the following morning to the sounds of giggling.

'Shhh,' came her mum's voice. 'Mae will wake up.'

Her dad's voice was muffled so she couldn't quite understand what he said, but whatever it was seemed to allay her mum's fears.

'Ugh,' Mae grunted and put her head under her duvet.

← ● Sistaaaas

Mae: O my days!!! Hw longs dis mum n dad weird luvd up phaze gonna last?????

Mae didn't know what was worse – her parents always bickering or always *having sex*. She shuddered. All this family drama had brought them closer together, it seemed. Her mum, specifically, had said to Mae before she'd left for uni: 'I am an old woman, Mae, but I am still a woman! All these years I have cared for you all and worried about everything and everyone and what have *I* got in return? Hmmm?'

'That's sweet, Amma,' Mae had replied.

'Now, I will pay attention to my husband when he wants me.'

'Oh my God, I'm going to *vom*.'

And before Mae's mum could give her any more details, Mae had swiftly left the room and headed for the toilet bowl. She didn't actually throw up, but she had felt pretty close to it. Bengali parents just *didn't talk like this*.

Now, Mae sighed and looked around the tiny room as she waited for a reply. She'd been shoved into the box room because, of course, Jay had moved back in and taken her room and since Mae was not only the youngest, but also a woman, the straw she drew tended to be short. In the meantime, she checked her Twitter account, Instagram, Snapchat and Facebook. Then she spent twenty minutes looking at videos on YouTube about facial contouring. Mae wasn't particularly vain about her appearance, but the way you could change the dimensions of your nose and cheekbones with the stroke of a brush was pretty fascinating.

> Bubblee: Why hasn't uni taught you to write properly?

Mae wondered why university hadn't taught her to do a lot of things properly. It was never going to be easy, being away from home for the very first time, considering she'd never even been on a weekend away without her family. Bubblee always said things were simple for Mae because nothing got to her. And they didn't. Not for the most part. Everyone just assumed that Mae would fit in wherever she went and so Mae had held on to that assumption and thought it was fact.

In the first week of university, at freshers' week, she found that she couldn't just go up to people, put her arm around them and say: 'Yooooo! What's up, old chum?' That would be weird. So, she inserted herself into groups and listened to people talk about their gap year – gap yaaaaaa – the places they'd travelled, the lives they'd led in high school and Mae realised how small her life had been. Still was. Aside from that, she wasn't sure how to achieve the middle ground of small talk; something between familiarity and mundanity. Something to show a flavour of who she was without scaring people off. Instead, she remained a passive listener. The first day she told herself it was to be expected, of course. Throughout the week, when the discomfort hadn't shifted, she reasoned that there was too much hubbub for her to really have a go at the whole 'middle-ground' thing. When it came to lectures though, everyone seemed to naturally get into groups afterwards, as if they'd all known each other for ever. She went to the student bar to see if she could see any familiar faces from class and just sidle up to them, but as soon as she did see anyone she knew she got a sudden bout of anxiety: *What if they think I'm intruding? What if they don't want me to sit with them? What if they don't like me?* The self-assured, unflappable, happy go-lucky Mae of Wyvernage didn't seem to translate in the outside world. Now that she was home, at least she could just *be herself.*

Fatti: It's sweet.

Mae: Think ur mistakin sweet wiv VOM.

Farah: Speaking of. Was going to come over early and help Mum with party stuff tonight but Zoya's being ratty and just thrown up her breakfast all over my hair.

Fatti: Adam's been the same! Did you get that teething toy I told you about?

So it began – the inevitable conversation about babies. Mae loved her niece and nephew as much as the next aunt, but there was only so much chat about baby formula and nappies she could take.

Farah: Bubblee was meant to have got it yesterday but she forgot.

Bubblee: Yes, yes, I know. You've reminded me ten times. I told you I'd pick it up today.

Mae: Ah da happy couple. LOL.

'Are you here to sleep all day?'

Her mum had burst through the door without knocking and was looming at the entrance, wearing a floral print chiffon sari. So, what? Did her mum dress up now? Mae grunted and pushed her head under the duvet.

'Is this what you do at uni? Sleep all day? Your baba didn't give you so much of our savings only to waste it. Come and help me in the kitchen for the party.'

'Ugh.'

And that was the other thing. Her parents were helping her to pay for university, the least she should be doing is enjoying it …

Mae stumbled out of her bed, almost falling over her Converses as her mum opened up the curtains, which let in very little light because of the neighbour's huge tree. She looked around the room – it was crowded enough with just her in it, let alone her mum and her pungent perfume. Still, since it was a party for her, she supposed she could bring herself to help, and she had to remember that having babies wasn't easy. Of course it was going to be hard for her sisters to find extra time to come and see her and hang out the way they used to. It was unreasonable to expect this. Didn't stop it from being annoying though. Mae turned around to notice her mother staring at her.

'What?' asked Mae.

'What are you eating at university?'

'Whatever I can,' replied Mae, thinking this was quite funny.

Her mum didn't seem to share the sentiment though.

'What happened to your carrot sticks and spinach and I don't know what other healthy things you made your abba always buy for you?'

Mae shrugged, putting her hands on her mum's shoulders. 'Realised there was more to life.'

Her mum simply shook her head and walked out of the room, mumbling something under her breath.

'All hail the prodigal babies return,' exclaimed Mae as her sisters and brother in-law, armed with babies, tumbled into the house.

'There she is,' said Bubblee, starting as she looked at Mae. 'Oh. Oh, never mind,' she added before pulling Mae into a hug. 'Good to see you, kid.'

Mae's heart relaxed at the familiarity of the family together. Farah had also pulled her into a hug, rubbing her back and looking at her up and down. (What was up with all her family's looks?)

Farah and Bubblee might've been twins but Bubblee always was the prettier of the two. Now that Mae was here, she thought that actually Bubblee looked even better than she remembered – fresh-faced and … what was it? She stared at her sister for a while when it struck her. Bloody hell. Could it be? Did Bubblee actually look *happy*? It wasn't a characteristic anyone ever associated with Bubblee, and what was even weirder was how Bubblee kissed their mum on the cheek and asked how she was. Motherhood really could bring all sorts together.

'Look how pretty you look,' said her mum to Bubblee. 'When will you find a husband?'

Oh, lord. Not five minutes they're all together and it was all about to kick off. Mae waited for Bubblee's ensuing tirade: *Stop trying to bind me to the patriarchy! I'm happy the way I am. You've never understood me. I don't need a man. I don't want a man ...* etc., etc. But, much to Mae's alarm, Bubblee simply rolled her eyes, a smile playing on her lips, as she said, 'Honestly, Mum ...'

'Look, it's Mae Kala[1],' said Fatti, handing Adam over to her.

'Oh,' said Mae, looking at the chubby face and big brown eyes. 'All right, Ads? What's going on?'

His response was to dribble saliva on to his My Dad Rocks bib, crease his brows into a frown and kick his legs about.

'Don't hold him like that. He's not a puppy,' said Bubblee as she showed Mae how to cradle him.

'Yeah, I *know*. I have done this before, remember? Like, *all* Christmas.'

Which was true enough except Mae still couldn't help her awkwardness at holding babies. And they were bigger now – squirmier and whinier – if that was possible.

Mae waited for Fatti to take her baby back but Fatti was too busy telling Farah that she and Ash managed

1 Kala: 'Aunty' (maternal aunt).

to get four hours of solid sleep last night. Ash joined in on the conversation about the baby that he and his wife seemed to have forgotten.

'Let's not make Zoya jealous now,' said Farah to Mae. 'Sit down.'

Mae sank into the sofa as Farah placed her niece into Mae's other arm. She stared at both babies who looked up at her as if expecting her to say something, anything, to entertain them.

'Weather's a bit crap, isn't it?' offered Mae.

Zoya's response was to spit some milk out of the side of her mouth, but Mae's hands were fully occupied. As she looked up for help she realised that her dad and Ash had gone into the garden, her mum had gone into the kitchen, and Farah and Fatti were still talking as Bubblee was on her phone.

'I've said to Ash, *please*, don't use your phone around the baby,' said Fatti. 'It's not good for them or you. You know?'

'Yes, well, unfortunately some people aren't as reasonable as Ash,' replied Farah.

'Oh, *here we go*,' said Bubblee putting the phone in her back pocket and raising her hands. 'Happy?'

Farah's response was to fold her arms and sigh.

'Er, guys. Yo. A little bit of help here, yeah?'

The three sisters turned around.

'Ah, look at little Mae with our babies. Take a picture,' said Farah. 'They all look so cute.'

'Now you want me to take out my phone?' replied Bubblee, getting its camera ready. 'Smile. Hmm, no. Let's take another one.'

Farah scurried across to fix Zoya's collar that was obscuring her face, managing to wipe the milk off at the same time.

'Mae, look like you're happy to be home,' said Bubblee.

'Of course she's happy to be home,' beamed Fatti. 'It's not the same without you, you know. So, tell us all about uni then. How's it going?'

'What are your lectures like?' asked Farah.

'Have you joined any societies? I hope you've taken up with some feminist movements,' added Bubblee. 'These are your formative years. So much of what you learn now's going to affect your future. Make *memories*, you know? God, I loved uni. It was just the best time. Even though I didn't become quite the artist I thought I would.' She paused. 'Anyway, that's fine, because if I hadn't failed at that I wouldn't be doing all this interesting stuff now. Or "innovative" as one reviewer called it. Not to brag.'

Farah seemed to be ignoring the conversation on purpose but Fatti interjected with an, 'Exactly. This pop-up gallery idea is so brilliant. Isn't it, Farah?'

'Mmm.'

'So,' continued Fatti. 'Tell us about all your new friends.'

'Oh, you know,' said Mae. 'It's mad, isn't it? All those new people. I've not really made that many friends. Just acquaintances.'

None of them responded.

'Like, there are just *so* many people, so I'm all … you know …' Mae shook her head as if crazed. 'Mad.'

Bubblee took some peanuts from the bowl and put them in her mouth, nodding fondly. 'I like the idea of you being a lone wolf. Not being tied down to any one person or group. Good. Well done.'

Why had Mae lied? She got so nervous that her sisters might think she was a loser – not the 'fun Mae' they said she'd be at uni – that she panicked. She wanted to say being a lone wolf wasn't exactly out of choice. That she'd quite like to be a part of some kind of group so she had someone to hang out with during breaks and in the evenings, instead of updating her social media.

'As long as you're happy,' added Fatti.

It was on the tip of Mae's tongue to say that actually, maybe she wasn't happy, when her mum's voice came from the kitchen, asking for help. Much to Mae's alarm her sisters left her with their babies while she heard laughter and chat from the kitchen. That was soon drowned out by Zoya who began to cry, swiftly followed by Adam.

'Yeah,' she said to both of them, trying to rock them at the same time. 'I know how you feel.'

In fact, Mae felt it more acutely than she thought she would when it transpired that this little family gathering had nothing to do with her coming home for the Easter break. Apparently having babies that were teething was more worthy of celebration. What exactly had happened to this family?

'God, I could kill a doner kebab right now,' she said, putting a pakora in her mouth.

Her sisters all looked at her. Fatti cleared her throat and her dad pushed the plate of pakoras away from her.

'I knew the student lifestyle would break you, Miss Kale Smoothie,' said Bubblee. 'Tell me, do students still live on beans on toast?'

Mae scoffed. The irony of the fact that she had been addicted to healthy eating pre-university wasn't lost on her. Moving away was meant to open up her horizons but actually opened up her palate as well. Though some might say it wasn't opening her palate so much as it was destroying it.

'No. Everyone's all organic now. It's mad. You can't go to a café without having something gluten-free shoved in your face. It's such a cliché.'

'So, you're the one who's having beans on toast?' asked Farah. 'Never thought we'd see the day. Speaking of, I made a decent cauliflower and cheese for Zoya but I think the cheese was too heavy for her.'

'Yeah,' added Fatti. 'Adam had the same problem in the beginning but just start with small portions at first and they get used to it.'

'Have some more rice, Jay's abba,' said their mum, getting up to put more food on their dad's plate.

'Sorry,' said Bubblee. 'Have to take this call.'

She got up from the dinner table as Farah watched her go. 'I'm telling you, I'm going to take that phone and throw it in the toilet.'

'You have to understand her work's important to her,' explained Fatti.

'Not more important than a baby,' said Ash.

'Thank you,' said Farah. 'Exactly.'

'The baby's asleep,' said Fatti.

'That's not the point.'

Mae sighed inwardly and got up from the table. Seemed as if the honeymoon period of co-parenting, bringing the sisters closer together, was waning now that Bubblee was concentrating on her work. Mae went up to her room and wondered how long it'd be until someone actually noticed. Somewhere between university and home, her place in the family had disintegrated and it was as if she was taking up space rather than filling the one she'd left behind.

There was a light knock on the door before it opened.

'All right, squirt?'

'Jay!'

Mae bounced off the bed and gave her brother a hug.

'Sorry I missed the party,' he said.

'You didn't miss much.'

He looked down at her and nodded. 'Keeping well then?'

What did all this 'keeping well' mean? Mae asked

about his work. He waved his hand around, saying that it was a delivery job, how good could it be?

'You stole my room,' she said, laughing and pushing him.

Now that Jay was here she didn't mind nearly as much.

'I'm the man of the house. Got to have my due.'

'Ugh,' said Mae. 'That'd be *Dad*, actually, and don't be a loser.'

'All right, squirt. I'm off to bed. Early start tomorrow.'

Was that it? Jay left the room and Mae sat back down on her bed. For some reason she always expected Jay to be this great big brother because that's how she imagined him in her head, but this greatness, even years later, still hadn't emerged. After all the disappointments, and the mistakes he'd made, affecting the whole family, he still seemed untouched by it all. Her thoughts were interrupted by sounds of one of the baby's crying until it was followed by someone shouting, 'Mae, Zoya's woken up. Could you bring her down, please?'

This would not do. This would not do at all.

Chapter Two

The following day Mae woke up to smells of cooking and her mum speaking on the phone at full volume. She put the pillow over her head but nothing short of being in a soundproof bunker could drown her out. Getting out of bed, Mae stubbed her toe, followed by banging her head on the wardrobe because *she was in a box room*.

As she sat at the breakfast table, eating her toast slathered with peanut butter before taking to her Crunchy Nut Cornflakes, she listened to her mum's monologue about Adam and Zoya. Mae could've left the room and she didn't think her mum would've noticed. It was only when her dad came in and patted her on the head, sitting down to have some tea, that she was able to have a conversation about something normal, like the flowers he was growing in his garden. She stacked them up as two of the least boring minutes of her return.

By the afternoon Mae had taken her dad's car and gone to Fatti's, but she was so preoccupied with Adam they couldn't have a conversation without interruption. Mae returned home to find Farah there with their mum, but the conversation was all about, surprise, surprise, Zoya. It did turn, for a moment, to Farah possibly getting married. Farah just looked at her baby and said: 'I don't think I want to any more.'

'What do you mean?' said their mum. 'A husband is good for you. We should start looking for you.'

'No means no, Amma,' said Mae.

'Your turn will also come after uni,' their mum replied.

'No, really, Amma,' said Farah, looking at her. 'I'm happy like this. Really happy.'

Her mum looked confused. 'But what does that have to do with it?'

'Er, kind of everything,' replied Mae.

'What do you know?' said their mum. 'You're still a baby too.'

'A nineteen-year-old, Amma. Kind of done with needing nappies, I'd say.'

But her mum ignored her and continued to press Farah about it. *A woman couldn't live alone her whole life – what would she do when she's old?*

'Amma,' said Farah. 'I tried marriage once, and I don't want to try it again. That's the end of it.'

Eventually their mum just shook her head, said, 'You girls,' and started talking about what to cook for dinner.

Mae felt at a loss. She didn't seem to fit into any space in this family, not one where she could actually be a part of something. It occurred to her that the only reason she had ever fitted in was because she was always dealing with other people's dramas, trying to patch things up between them. Now that everyone seemed self-sufficient, where did she come in? She would've called her high-school friends except one had moved to Edinburgh and had seemed to get so involved with uni life that she no longer had time to return Mae's messages, while the other had gone to Australia, of all places, to study. They'd email, like each other's stuff on Facebook and Twitter, comment on any cool Instagram shots, but hadn't once had a proper conversation since leaving for university.

It was the next day, when Mae came down to the kitchen to see her mum giggling as her dad pinched her bum, that she felt her bile rise again. She went straight back into her little room and stayed in there, watching shows on Netflix, until midday, when her mum began telling her off for being lazy and not helping around the house.

That's when Mae decided to pack her bags and tell her family that she had to go back to university to finish up a project.

'But you only just arrived,' said her dad, who seemed to be the only one genuinely upset by her news.

'Soz, Pops. Life of the uni student, isn't it? Gotta make those grades.'

She felt a flush of embarrassment at this dual lie because she knew her grades weren't exactly making the cut. It was all that time she spent on social media and staring at the ceiling. Her mind refused to focus. There was too much to distract her and nothing to occupy her all at the same time.

'I bought some kale,' he said. 'Maybe you can go back to those smoothies instead of ...' he cleared his throat. 'What you're eating now.'

'Ugh. No, thanks. What was wrong with me all that time? Having soya when I could've been having chocolate? That's bad parenting, that is,' she added, zipping up her bag again. 'Seriously deranged behaviour from a teenager and you thought it was normal.'

She felt tears prickle her eyes.

Fatti: Don't leave! Wanted to come and say goodbye but Ash's at work and Adam's getting a cold I think so don't want to take him out. Message when you get to uni. Love you xx

Farah had managed to swing by but spent the entire time talking about Bubblee's work schedule and how she was never around to help with Zoya. Mae shuddered at the name, haunted by her past obsession with soya and wondering whether this was just another one of her sister's ways of testing her emotional resilience.

As Mae got out of the car at the station, her dad leaned over and beamed at her through the drizzle.

'You have everything? Your toothbrush?' he asked. 'Your amma will be angry if you forgot it.'

'She already asked me twice, Abba.'

'Okay.' He paused. 'You are okay, yes?'

Why did her dad have to choose this moment to ask her? When her train was coming in six minutes, it was raining and the car's engine was running.

'Just fabbo, Pops.' Mae blinked back the tears that really were in danger of falling this time. 'You know. Nothing new's easy, is it?' she added.

What did she hope for? That from just a few words he'd get that things weren't exactly the way she'd hoped they would be? That there was a sadness that had settled itself inside her and no matter how much she tried, she couldn't shift it? She had begun uni feeling passionate about Media Studies but it just didn't last. She seemed to have no friends, didn't know who she was at university, and now she didn't even know who she was at home either.

'You're a very good girl,' he replied.

Mae felt perplexed at this, but her dad clearly thought that was the end of that as he told her to hurry up before she missed her train.

She stepped into the carriage that was full and took her seat by the aisle next to a boy listening to Eminem on his iPhone. The lump in her throat refused to budge because there was nothing she wanted more than to be sitting by the window – to turn her head away from the people shuffling in their seats, reading books, scanning their phones and eating crisps. She didn't understand it.

What did she have to be sad about, exactly? That she hadn't made friends yet? That her sisters, who were all new mothers, were attentive to their babies? That even when they had asked her about university, they didn't really pause to listen to her? It seemed so selfish of Mae. So frivolous. The old Mae would've just got on with things – forget that, these thoughts wouldn't have even crossed her mind. What had happened to her? One of the few times that she had actually mentioned university she'd lied to her dad about her grades. Oh God, her grades. That was another thing that kept chomping at her sadness, turning it into anxiety. To think that her parents were helping her with uni costs, only for her grades to be sub-par. She'd have to do better. *She had to try.* It was when a poodle stopped by her feet and looked up at her with such doleful eyes that the lump seemed to burst and push the tears through her eyes.

'I-I-I'm sorry,' she gasped through her sobs.

The owner of the poodle, a man in his fifties wearing corduroys and a flat cap, sat on the aisle parallel to Mae. He didn't seem to know what to do.

'Would you like a tissue?' he asked.

This just brought on a fresh wave of sobs as Mae nodded and he handed her a packet of Kleenex. She took one, blew her nose, and handed the rest of the packet back.

'Keep them,' he said.

'Th-th-thank you,' she managed to say.

The boy next to her just increased the volume of his music, angling his head towards the window.

'Chocolate?' the man asked, offering her a stick from his Kit Kat.

Mae shook her head as she put her hand out. 'No, thank you.'

The man seemed confused at first, then pierced the foil and handed her two of the four fingers. The train pulled into the next stop and the man made a move to leave. As he got up he looked down at Mae and said: 'Don't you worry there. It'll all be okay.'

With which he tugged on his poodle's leash and left the train, dog in tow. Mae felt the heat on her face from the embarrassing tears that had just exploded and put her hands on her cheeks to try and cool them down. She took out her mirror.

'Ugh.'

She leaned back and closed her eyes, wondering what had come over her. While she was at home she was convinced that everyone was being selfish, but maybe it was Mae who was self-involved? She even considered getting off at the next stop and going back to spend the rest of the Easter break with her family, as she'd first intended. Except she didn't quite like the prospect of being shunted with the babies again. Cute as they were. Mae took a deep breath.

'Pull yourself together,' she whispered.

The boy next to her tutted and got up, walked to

the next carriage and sat down there. Mae would've been offended if she wasn't so glad to get the seat by the window. She shuffled over and got her mirror out again. A lot of people had got off at the previous stop, so the carriage was quieter. There was a man she noticed sitting diagonally opposite her who glanced at her as she took out her lip gloss. He had his phone in his hands, his fingers scrolling down the screen as if he was reading something. She applied the gloss, which didn't really make much difference to her puffy eyes and face and as she decided to put concealer under her eyes she noticed the man with his phone looking her way and she wondered whether this was it. Maybe he found her attractive? Maybe he'd seen her crying on the train and felt sorry for her? Mae did what she'd never done before in her life: she crossed her legs, straightened her back and lengthened her neck in order to seem more attractive to him. He looked in his early thirties, which was old, but he wasn't *bad*-looking. At nineteen years old, Mae had never had a boyfriend. She hadn't even come close. A guy in high school had once asked her out and she was so horrified at the prospect that she told him he was gross and practically ran away from him. It made her feel bad because he wasn't gross, and she did hope he hadn't taken it personally, but he never did look her in the eye again. She blamed her parents and their upbringing. Having boyfriends was *not allowed* and Mae wasn't a rock-the-boat type person. Today, however, felt different.

Today she didn't mind the idea of this random man looking at her. He could've maybe done with a shave and his eyes were kind of beady, plus the grey coat was too big for him but in that moment it was nice to be seen. She took out her kohl pencil and applied it in the rims of her eyes. The final touch was the blusher, which she brushed on maybe too vigorously, but she felt the overall effect wasn't bad. In fact, she looked quite nice. Mae shut the mirror and took a deep breath as she glanced over at the man again. He was grinning now as he tapped on the phone and she felt a sense of unease. She watched as he scratched his head with his finger then looked under the fingernail, scraping whatever had gathered in there under his seat. *Vom.* Mae had to shake her head. First, she bursts into tears in public, then the next man that looks at her suddenly becomes a potential boyfriend. Boyfriend! Mae! As if.

'Gross,' she muttered as the man this time scratched the inside of his ear.

No, Mae had never been like Farah who only ever wanted to get married – and look how that worked out. Then there was Fatti who looked for love and found it with Ash. Despite the fear of her parents, she genuinely thought that she was more like Bubblee when it came to relationships. Just not that bothered. Like, whatever. Mae couldn't help but feel now though that it would be nice to have someone to chill with, relax on her bed. Maybe *in* her bed. Her parents really would kill her if they even got a hint that the thought crossed her mind. Even Farah and Fatti wouldn't approve, they were so traditional. Wasn't that what university was about though? Living life? Doing things – even if you weren't meant to do them? Her dad was right – she'd been a 'good' girl her whole life. Bubblee would scoff at that: *Do you know how damaging it is to put women into these kinds of categories? As if exploring their identity in ways their families don't agree with makes them bad.* Mae knew she was quite attractive, she just never really made an effort, but maybe now it was time. She was nineteen, for God's sake! She looked over at the man and realised now that actually he was kind of creepy. It didn't matter, because the more she thought about it, the more it made sense: she would get back to university and make an effort to find a boyfriend and have a relationship. Somehow the idea of it felt easier than just making friends. People hooked up all the time at student bars so she'd just give that a go and see where it led. She imagined it was far easier to snog someone than have a conversation with them, so whatever. The fact of the matter was that she did not want to be alone any more, so she was going to buck up, stop complaining and make some changes. The train pulled into the next station as the creepy man got up and looked at her again, but this time there was disgust on his face and Mae's heart thudded, unnerved by a look of such loathing. *What the hell had she done to him?* It took her a few more stops but she shrugged it off, told herself it was nothing, and anyway, who cared? Now she had a plan for university and it would change everything.

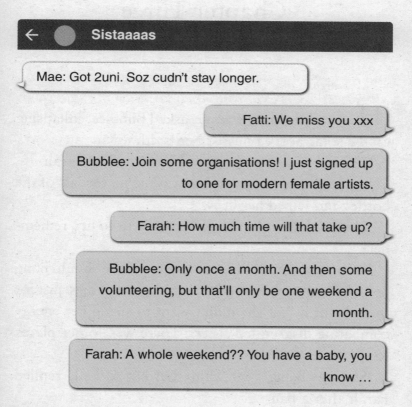

Sistaaaas

Mae: Got 2uni. Soz cudn't stay longer.

Fatti: We miss you xxx

Bubblee: Join some organisations! I just signed up to one for modern female artists.

Farah: How much time will that take up?

Bubblee: Only once a month. And then some volunteering, but that'll only be one weekend a month.

Farah: A whole weekend?? You have a baby, you know …

Ugh, Mae thought. Whatever she decided to do had to be better than what her sisters were doing, at least.

Chapter Three

'How was the baby today?' asked Bubblee, collapsing on the sofa. 'Sorry I missed her bedtime.'

'The baby has a name, you know,' replied Farah.

Her back was turned as she washed up the last of the bottles and wiped her brow.

'I know,' sighed Bubblee. 'I gave birth to her, remember?'

For a moment, Bubblee wondered if she should hang on to her annoyance about Farah's constant digs, just for the sake of it, but she didn't want to spend her energy combating disgruntled sisters. There were other places to spend it.

'She was being a bit whiny but not so bad,' replied Farah after a pause.

She came and sat down on the sofa opposite Bubblee, put her head back and closed her eyes. Bubblee was on her phone and swiped right. It was a match. Bubblee had heard plenty of dating disaster stories – she'd even seen some of the romcoms that Farah liked to watch in the evenings when Bubblee was in and out, working. The idea of dating, and men in general, had always filled Bubblee with a powerful sense of contempt. Watching her twin sister get married and set up a house with a man who was – she was sorry to speak ill of the dead – not Farah's equal, even made her marginally disdainful of her own sex. It had all seemed so mundane to her when she was at university, then later, when she was honing her artistic craft, it didn't get any less dull. The idea of someone being a part of her daily life, watching her, interfering with their unsought opinions, made her angry enough to not want to even give it a chance. Men, in her experience, hampered things. And women, she witnessed with increasing annoyance, more often than not allowed it. Bubblee would never be one of those women, and the only way she was sure not to become like that was to not date at all. Then along came Zoya. Little, monkey-faced, chubby, cranky, saliva-spouting, inquisitive-looking Zoya. What had begun as a favour for her sister – and considering Bubblee was a virgin, the favour wasn't to be taken lightly – had become a new life for Bubblee. She realised that life could take twists and turns and that some of the things you couldn't control could still work out pretty well.

When Bubblee pushed their baby out into this world she didn't realise she'd also pushed out a part of her cynicism and a whole load of reluctance. She had doubted her decision to carry her sister and brother-in-law's baby, and that doubt had turned into her biggest source of happiness. So, Bubblee rethought her whole approach to life. It just so turned out that dating was actually *fun*. Yes, it was pretty problematic as a social construct given that women often seemed to be the ones who had to wait for men to make the first move, but it was what you made of it that mattered. And Bubblee never did wait for the men. She'd drop them a message as quick as she'd drop them when they were rude or obnoxious. As she tapped a new message to her latest match, she wondered at the irony of the fact that it took having a baby to be bothered with a man.

'What are you smiling at?' asked Farah.

'This guy – listen: "biggest turn-ons: a woman who stays in shape and knows what cryptocurrency is." What a loser.'

She hadn't looked up at Farah, but if she had she'd have seen her swallow hard with a mild look of panic on her face.

'Do men think we're meant to find that attractive? "Oh, yes, please. Thanks for appreciating my body and my intellect." Get a lobotomy, please.'

When Farah didn't answer Bubblee looked up at her. 'Not the way it was in your day.'

Farah managed a forced smile.

'You should give this a shot at some point,' added Bubblee. 'If you feel up to it.'

'No. I'll leave that to you.' With that Farah got up and stretched her back. 'I'm so tired. I'm going to bed.'

Bubblee looked back at her phone. 'Night.'
With which Farah left and went to bed.

Farah *was* tired. She *did* want to sleep. She had checked up on Zoya before getting into bed, made sure the baby monitor was on, checked the house temperature was between eighteen and twenty degrees and closed her eyes. Half an hour later she still hadn't heard Bubblee come up the stairs and go to her room. It was ten o'clock so she guessed it was too early for her. Nowadays Farah was ready to go to bed by seven o'clock if she could but there were always chores waiting, days to map out, online grocery shopping to do. Even when Zoya had gone to sleep there was no guarantee that Farah could do all these things uninterrupted, and often she'd spend up to an hour trying to put the baby back to sleep, especially when she woke up in the evenings. It was, of course, part and parcel of motherhood. Sometimes Farah looked at her baby's face and was so overwhelmed with love for her it brought tears to her eyes. Fresh anxieties would occur to her as well: what if the blanket suffocated her at night? Is that red mark just a rash or something more sinister? Why is her poop coming out so dark today? Farah would be writing an email to Mamas & Papas about their out-of-stock fleece onesie and she'd have to rush up to make sure Zoya was still breathing. Her mind, she found, was not her own any more. Now, lying in bed, Farah missed her husband. She wished he could've seen the way their baby snatched at her toy giraffe, how she settled on Farah's chest and went to sleep; she wished he could smell the top of Zoya's head. But the idea of dating! What was Bubblee thinking? Why would Farah want a man to come into her life and disrupt her already frantic days? It was the last thing Farah needed, and certainly the last thing she wanted.

Except that she couldn't help but be surprised that Bubblee *did* seem to want it. When she had first mentioned it to Farah, Farah had looked at Bubblee as if she wasn't her sister at all. She had written it off as a glitch and pushed down any worry that Bubblee might actually be serious, because Farah had other things to worry about, like Zoya's new baby formula. But now the worry was back. And it had no right to be. Farah took a deep breath and told herself that she should not overthink things, that life had a way of working itself out. She reminded herself of her baby, sleeping in the next room, and a wave of gratitude came over her. It was with thoughts of her itinerary the following day that Farah drifted into sleep, only to be woken up by crying at one in the morning. She put her hand out for the baby monitor and tumbled out of bed, managing to drag herself into Zoya's room. Without putting the light on, and being careful to stay out of Zoya's view, she patted her baby's chest lightly. Zoya continued to cry for a good ten minutes before she began to settle as Farah managed to open her eyes. It was when Zoya had drifted back to sleep that Farah realised Bubblee hadn't got up, even though Zoya had clearly been crying for a while. Farah crept out of the room and quietly opened the door to Bubblee's room only to see that she was fast asleep, sleeping mask on and, it seemed, ear plugs in. Despite the fact that it was the middle of the night and Farah was exhausted, she found she still had the capacity to be annoyed. She would've slammed the door behind her if it wouldn't wake the baby again. Instead she switched on the light.

'Huh, what? who?'

Bubblee sat up and patted the bed with her hands before taking off her mask, only to have to shield her eyes from the glare of the light.

'What? Are you okay? Is it Zoya?'

Bubblee sprang out of bed to rush to the baby's side except that Farah hadn't moved.

'It *was* Zoya, she's probably been crying for ages, did you even hear?'

'Oh.' Bubblee blinked hard and rubbed her face. 'She okay?'

'Obviously,' replied Farah.

Bubblee flopped back into bed and was putting her mask back on when Farah said: 'Is that it?'

'Hmm?'

'Do you even have your monitor on?'

'What? Yeah, no. Why?'

'No?' asked Farah.

'No.'

'So it's always up to me to get up when she cries?'

'Huh? We don't live in a mansion. It's not like she's in the East Wing,' replied Bubblee.

'Nice ear plugs.'

'I went to sleep late.'

'So?' Farah resisted the urge to ask whether it was because she was working or swiping through whatever latest app she was using to find dates.

'*So*, I have to be up at six to drive to Addersfield for a nine o'clock meeting with a potential donor for the next project.'

'And I'll be up at six to feed the baby and start my day.'

'You went to bed at ten,' replied Bubblee.

'Because I was exhausted.'

'So was I, and now I'm even more tired thanks to you disturbing me.'

Rage bubbled inside Farah. *Disturbing* her? What about Farah being disturbed? Bubblee had only got up twice at night during the whole week, and that was because it was the weekend.

'I can't believe you,' said Farah.

She was too angry to even stay in the room. Instead she walked out, this time without thinking, slamming the door behind her. Right on cue Zoya began to cry.

'You can see to her this time,' she shouted out to Bubblee.

The following morning both were indeed up at six in the morning and both refused to speak to one another.

Bubblee greeted Zoya with a kiss and cuddle, Farah asked the baby how she was, pointing to the day outside, describing the weather, speaking, in Bubblee's view, so much that she was sure Zoya would tell Farah to shut up if she could talk.

'There's a cloud,' Farah said. 'There are lots of those today, aren't there? Is it going to rain? Rain is wet, isn't it? Like the water when you take your bath. Shall we take a long bath today? You'd like that, wouldn't you?'

'Right, Monkey,' said Bubblee to the baby. 'I'm off. Behave.'

Bubblee kissed Zoya on the head and headed out of the door. Farah had waited for Bubblee to turn around and say something. Anything. Just a goodbye to show that she felt bad for the way she spoke to Farah last night, but she didn't.

'I just can't believe her,' she said into the phone to Fatti as she put some more porridge into Zoya's mouth.

'You don't want her falling asleep at the wheel,' said Fatti.

'What if I fell asleep while feeding Zoya and she, I don't know, fell off the sofa.'

'You put her in a chair.'

'That's not the point,' replied Farah.

Fatti sighed. 'Ash doesn't always wake up with me.'

'No, but you take it in turns, at least.'

Farah knew Fatti didn't have anything else to defend Bubblee with or she'd have said.

'Ever wish we were young like Mae, swanning off to uni and living a life of no responsibilities?' said Farah.

Fatti paused. 'Not really.'

Farah smiled, wiping porridge from Zoya's face. 'No. Me neither.'

'Would be nice to have a break now and again though. Not that I'm complaining,' added Fatti. 'But I just found out that Ash's children are going to be staying with us all summer.'

'What?' exclaimed Farah.

'You know his ex is getting remarried? Well, she and her husband want to go on honeymoon and so we're going to have the children the whole time.'

'Oh God.'

'It's fine. They are his kids,' said Fatti.

'Yeah, but his son …'

There was a long pause.

'He's a little older now,' said Fatti.

'What? Fifteen, right? Still holding a grudge against the world?'

'And me.'

'Oh, and his daughter. She's a real piece of work.'

'It's fine,' said Fatti. 'It'll be nice even. Maybe. I'll get to know them properly.'

'Fatti, your eternal optimism is a lesson to us all,' said Farah.

'So, are you going to call and say sorry to Bubblee?'

'Ha. No. But if she calls to say sorry to me, I'll accept it.'

Except Bubblee didn't call. Not only did she not call, but she sent a message to say she'd be home late. At first, Farah read the message in disbelief. No apology, not even a *reason* as to why she'd be out. That evening, Farah decided she wouldn't go to bed until Bubblee came home. Unfortunately, Farah's mood wasn't helped by the fact that her sister walked in at midnight.

'Oh. You're up,' said Bubblee.

'Where were you?'

Bubblee sighed. 'I had a date.'

'Right. Don't you think you should've told me?'

'I didn't think you were my mother.'

'No, but *you* are a mother. Or had you forgotten?'

'God, your nagging never stops.'

Farah had to take a deep breath and swallow her sense of being wronged. 'You know, for all your feminism, I hope you realise you're behaving like the worst kind of husband.'

'Maybe that's because I'm not your husband,' said Bubblee.

'That's not what I meant, and you know it. "Man", "husband", whatever you want to call it. It's fine when you're spouting your high ideals but are you actually living up to them? If you don't want to be in this then don't be, but don't make *me* feel like I'm the one being unreasonable.'

Farah waited to see the effect of her words on Bubblee. She noticed the look of incredulity and confusion on her sister's face. Without waiting for her to respond, Farah walked out of the room, up the stairs and into Zoya's room.

'I love you, little one,' she whispered, stroking her hair.

With that, she went into her room, closed the door behind her and fell straight to sleep.

> **Fatti:** Any ideas on how to entertain two teenagers over summer?

> **Bubblee:** Netflix.

> **Farah:** All you need to do is be organised and plan something fun to do outside the house. Don't worry about Adam, I can look after him now and again.

> **Bubblee:** Mum called telling me that Jay didn't come home until three in the morning and that we should find him a wife. Hahaha. As if I'd knowingly ever get some poor woman mixed up with him.

> **Fatti:** He's very good with Adam.

> **Farah:** Don't get me started on Jay …

Chapter Four

Mae looked at her sisters' messages and wondered what it'd be like to have their problems. It hadn't taken more than forty-eight hours for Mae's sense of optimism to collapse into a heap. The day she got back to university had been normal enough, even that evening and night passed without much happening. Mae had gone out to the student bar but there was hardly anyone there since most people were away for Easter. Still, sitting there on her own, she felt a sense of confidence expand in her and was certain that if someone fairly normal sat near her she'd go over and say hello. It was a shame the opportunity hadn't presented itself.

The following day Mae had gone about the business of having a doner kebab and then sitting in a coffee shop to figure out which assignments needed to be done so she could come up with a sensible plan to do them all. She'd chosen Media Studies because she'd been passionate about it in high school so she was going to reignite that passion. It had to still be there somewhere. If she could find it again then she'd have something positive to focus on. In any case, handing her assignments in late now was not an option – not if she wanted to actually pass the year. Of course, Mae got slightly distracted by her usual social media addictions. She wasn't even sure how she ended up on this Facebook page. Maybe it was someone on Twitter that had mentioned an obnoxious man, typically shaming a woman who had been minding her own business, that made her click on the link they'd added. These things always disgusted and fascinated her in equal measure. Before clicking on the video that had been uploaded she skimmed through the comments section.

Who cares if someone's putting their make up on in public? What's it got to do with you?

Ugh. Hate this shit. So gross. Seen her face? She should've put her make up on before she left the house n done us all a favour.

Are you crazy? Shes so pretty. Doesn't even need the make-up.

Thank you. I'm not the only one who hates this!!!!

Mae rolled her eyes, mostly because she didn't get why people wasted their time on something like this. Did they seriously have nothing better to complain about?

'Losers,' she mumbled as she went to the video and clicked on it.

That's when her heart fell to her stomach. She watched the video, looking at herself, sitting on a train, taking out a mirror and applying lip gloss.

'What?'

Then she continued to watch as she relived the routine of her putting on kohl pencil, blusher, mascara, all the while hearing sniggering from the person who'd been recording. It couldn't be. This wasn't real, surely. Had Bubblee put this up as some kind of practical joke? But Bubblee didn't have time for this kind of thing. And Farah and Fatti definitely wouldn't be so creative. They weren't even the sort of sisters who thought practical jokes were funny – especially not Fatti. Mae watched the video until the end and sat for a moment in disbelief. It didn't make any sense. She was only putting make-up on. What was the big deal? She clicked on the profile of the person who'd uploaded the video and that's when she realised: it was the same man who she, stupidly, for a little while, thought was actually admiring her. She noticed he'd posted a comment with the video:

People are making this about the colour of her skin, or being a woman and overweight, but not everyone appreciates having to look at someone slap on the cake while getting to work. Have some respect for other people on public transport. I don't shave or cut my fingernails in public, why do I have to look at you women put your make-up on? #doublestandards #equality

Mae's heart was thudding fast as she looked at the number of people who'd watched the video. One thousand and fifty-two. *Geez.* It wasn't great, but she guessed that it could be worse. And anyway, who cares? *It was only make-up.* Mae went back to the comments section and couldn't believe what she was reading.

H8 stupid bitches like this. Wish youd punched her in the face. C if she cud put make up on that. LOL

Why had that loser got so many likes? It didn't end there. It went on and on about how women who apply make-up in public should have unspeakable things done to them. Mae sometimes forgot how depraved people who hid behind fake profiles and pictures could be.

That fat cow needs more than make up to help her looooool

That's when she put her phone down, her heart thudding so fast she thought she might have a heart attack. She took a few moments before she opened up her laptop to have a look at her class notes, ignore what she'd just seen, but she couldn't get past the first few lines. How could she concentrate on anything when she knew that people were saying such things about her? That people were watching her, judging her, ridiculing her … for *what*? Yeah right, this guy wasn't sexist. She bet he'd never have done the same if a man had been combing his beard or something on the train. She went back to the video and watched it again. Was this a bad dream? Mae pinched herself to see if she'd wake up, but that didn't work, obviously. It was just so absurd. It wasn't just that the video had been taken, uploaded and then *shared*, it was the venom with which people had commented. Mae couldn't quite get her head around it and the only thing she knew was that she had to speak to Fatti. She picked up her phone again and tapped on her sister's name.

'Fatti?'

'Hang on – one second, Mae …'

Adam was whining in the background but Mae waited. Then she waited some more.

'Don't hang up! I'm coming.'

Eventually, Fatti did come back to the phone.

'Sorry, he'd done a massive poo and it got all up the back of his Babygro. I was just washing him. How are you? Oh God. Just *one* minute, okay? Adam! You're fed, changed and clean, why are you whining? Right, sorry. All this baby wants is to be held, it's not as if I can resist, is it? I'd say that you know how it is, but luckily you don't – not yet. All I can say is enjoy the life you have as much as you can. Farah and I are actually kind of jealous.'

'Fatti …'

'What is it, darling? Are you okay?'

It was the softness in Fatti's voice that almost broke Mae. She bit back her tears because she suddenly felt so far removed from the lives of her sisters – as if they wouldn't understand.

'Yeah, yeah, fine. Just calling to see what was going on.'

If Fatti had insisted, asked her whether she was sure there was nothing wrong, perhaps Mae would've given in and told her, but she didn't ask. After a few minutes Fatti's house phone rang and she said she had to go because Ash needed her.

'Send us pictures,' said Fatti before she put the phone down.

They always said this to Mae, and the few times she had sent pictures of her lecture theatre, or lunch in the canteen, they hardly commented on it. Mae looked back at the video and played it again. Every time she watched it she convinced herself it was fine. Until she read the comments again. More likes for the video now, more comments, more shares. The ones of support didn't quite lift her spirits in the same way the negative comments sank them. She shut the laptop again and looked around the coffee shop – as if someone might recognise her. A girl, Mae noticed, had been looking at her. Mae's face flushed, wondering if she was staring because she'd seen the video. Before daring to look around any more, Mae stuffed her things in her bag and made her way out of the coffee shop, to her dorm room.

> Bubblee: I've found a great nursery in town that does singing classes for babies. Have booked Saturday afternoon for the kids – let's all take them. Xx

> Fatti: Great idea! Will tell Ash.

> Bubblee: Okay. Maybe I'll bring my date, see how easily he scares ;)

> Farah: Can't we just keep it as a sisters thing?

> Fatti: Thing is, weekends Ash likes to spend time with both of us because he says he misses us during the week …

> Bubblee: Farah, you can stay home and I can take Zoya alone. You can then have your *me* time.

'You haven't picked your phone up for three days,' blared Mae's mum's voice through the mobile.

'What?'

Mae stuck her head under her duvet since the curtains

weren't proving sufficient protection against the sunlight flooding her room.

'Where have you been?'

'Busy,' said Mae.

'Your abba and me need to throw your things away.'

'What things?'

'In your room.'

'Why?' asked Mae.

'What does it matter why? For the babies when they come and stay, of course.'

Of all the things in life that were going on, why did this have to be a discussion?

'Can't you just put them in the attic?'

'Where is the room?'

'You can't just throw all my things away without me checking them first.'

Her mum gave a deep sigh. 'I'm not storing them for ever. Oh, I have to go, your abba and I are going for a walk in the park.'

Her mum giggled and put the phone down.

> Fatti: Morning, kalas!

With the message was a picture of Adam, spitting out what looked like apple puree.

> Farah: And morning from me too!

And there was Zoya, lying on her jungle gym, furrowing her brows at the elephant dangling over her head. Mae lifted the covers and stared at the ceiling. She'd missed morning seminars and knew if she didn't get up in the next two minutes to get ready for her afternoon class, she'd miss that too. She had an assignment that was due the following day, which she hadn't even started, and reasoned that the only way she'd make the deadline was if she bunked Introduction to Moving Image and Sound. Except that she lay like that for two hours, looking at her phone and that video that had now been watched more than four thousand times. She had tried to ignore it, shrugged it off and pretended it hadn't happened. Only every time she tried to forget, she'd be reminded by a new message from a random person on Twitter or Facebook. How many people that looked at her knew who she was? When she went out and someone stared, was it because they were as disgusted by her as the man who made the recording? The one class she had attended someone looked at her and said: 'You're that make-up girl.' And that was it. No, *sorry you've been getting so much flack online, it wasn't bad at all, don't take it personally*. Just an identifier and then gone. By eight o'clock that night the only time Mae had left her bed was when she needed to use the toilet. Her paranoia had confirmed itself as fact so her only refuge was her room and the walls that protected her from the outside world. But why was the world dictating her actions?

She couldn't stay in her room for ever. (God, how she wished she could.) Who the hell was this creepy man to stop Mae from living her best student life, though? As if she wasn't making it difficult enough for herself. A slow, burning, anger began to bubble, turning into a feeling of uncharacteristic defiance. At nine o'clock Mae swept her duvet cover off her and jumped out of bed.

'That's enough, Mae. Get a *grip*.'

The problem with feeling sorry for yourself was that once you started, it was easy to spiral into despair. No, if she was going to reignite her passion in her studies then the same should be said for her life in general. A video was not going to ruin her or her sense of self. Whatever that self was. So, she rummaged through her wardrobe, got into a short black skirt and white T-shirt, washed her face, brushed her teeth and put on some make-up (feeling like she should look over her shoulder in case someone was watching her), ready to head out.

She put her hand on the doorknob and took a deep breath as she opened the door and stepped into the hallway. It was empty. Mae felt her heart pump faster, along with her breathing. For a moment she wanted to turn right back around and get back into bed, but wouldn't Bubblee have shaken her by the shoulders and told her to let no man bring you down? So, Mae walked on, out of the doors in her halls of residence and into the outside world. There was a definite sense of spring in the air as she only needed a jacket. With each step she became more resolute and assured. It helped that it was night-time. She walked to The Crypt, the club where all students headed to at night, where she had never gone because she never had anyone to go with. She guessed that there were some things you just had to end up doing alone. It was either that or not do them at all, and that wasn't exactly life-affirming.

When she got to the club the doorman took one look at her and opened the barrier. There were people dawdling outside, smoking, laughing, in groups and couples, no one paying attention to her or recognising her. She walked into a dimmed arena that was lit with a red hue, lights flashing, Rhianna blaring, crowds and crowds of people and suddenly Mae felt more in command of who she was. There was a comfort in being lost in a crowd. Everyone was so consumed with dancing, laughing and drinking that it helped Mae to shed her layers of self-consciousness.

She walked over to the bar and hesitated, looking at all the alcoholic beverages behind the bar. If Mae were quite honest, life all felt *a bit much*: never being able to speak to her sisters because of the babies, university, *that video*. She felt her face flush anew with the shame of it.

No friends.

Not one. Mae wasn't just lonely, she was *alone*. The knowledge of it settled in her stomach and chest. There was no one she could talk to, no one to share the misery of her online shame with, no one to even come to a club with. What kind of a loser was she? Why hadn't anyone told her that being out in the world was hard? That making connections with people was even harder? And yet, she looked around and no one else seemed to be having trouble with it. She stared at the people to her left and right, ordering drinks, laughing with their friends and the desperation to just *be* one of them gripped her. She had never touched alcohol before but right then, there was nothing she wanted more. How could you crave something that you'd never had?

What would her sisters say? But they weren't there, were they? Mae had nothing but an empty room to go back to. And knowing that her video was being watched by people even as she sat there. All those comments, all that *hate*. And no one to share the pain with.

'What can I get you?' asked the bartender.

Mae gulped, took a deep breath. 'I …'

What was she doing? This wasn't like her. It went against everything her parents had ever taught her.

Her parents, who never even ask about her life at uni. The bartender was staring at her … did he recognise her from the video too?

Before she could find out she blurted: 'Vodka shot. Please?'

For a moment her heart beat faster, as if the bartender would raise his eyebrows and say, *You're not allowed to drink*. By the time she'd had these anxieties the shot of vodka was already in front of her. What if her dad ever found out? What if someone here knew her and reported back to him? She didn't think she could bear the look of disappointment on his face.

Mae glanced from side to side, unsure of what to do with the drink. Was she meant to just knock it back the way she saw people do it in films? Or was she meant to get salt and a lemon as well? No. She couldn't do that – she'd feel too ridiculous. At first, she was going to just take a sip, but knew that was also ridiculous. So, Mae took a deep breath, put the shot glass to her mouth – thinking of that creepy guy on the train, the humiliation she was suffering because of him – and knocked it back.

The strength of the shot surprised her, burning down her throat as she coughed and spluttered. She absorbed the weird grainy taste, still spluttering as people looked at her. It took some time to get over the burning as she tried to clear her throat and pretend that this wasn't the first time she'd ever had a shot of vodka. Was she meant to feel different? She *did* feel different. She felt quite … pleasant. Who cared if it was a placebo or not? If it meant she didn't care what people around her were thinking, then it could only be a good thing.

'Good sir,' she said to the barman. 'Another, please.'

So she took another shot, this time prepared for the burning, although the effect of it still surprised her and she coughed again. Her senses seemed to relax, the anxiety that had settled itself in the pit of her stomach had somehow dissipated. Mae wondered why it had been there in the first place. What exactly had been the big deal? Sure, she had no friends, got publicly shamed, random strangers were spending their time taking a dig at her, getting personal – just being *mean*, Mae thought with disdain. This shouldn't stop her from doing things, though. She was still her own person, after all. When you're your own person, what do you do? You be adventurous, that's what. This time, when Mae asked for another drink, she said to the bartender that she'd take anything he thought she'd enjoy.

'Maybe some orange juice for you,' he said.

'Ugh. You can give me that for breakfast,' Mae replied.

He looked amused although Mae wasn't sure why.

'First time drinking?'

'How did you know?' Mae said, looking at him in fascination.

Was there a sign on her head? Did she make it that obvious? Or was he a mind reader?

'Magic,' he replied. 'Here, have this.'

Mae looked at the glass filled with ice and lime and a drink that looked too much like Coke.

'Are you tricking me? I'm a grown woman, you know. I can handle more than a Coke.'

'With rum,' he replied. 'The special ingredient.'

Mae liked this bartender with his shiny skin, big hair and white teeth. A friendly face.

'Rum and Coke?' she repeated with giddiness. She

raised the glass to him. 'Well, cheers to you. Cheers to everyone.'

Mae took a sip and felt her throat burn a little, a pleasant taste of buttery Coke in her mouth.

'Well done,' she added to the bartender who nodded to her, smiling. 'I've decided you look like a trustworthy person. Did you know that?'

'No, but thanks.'

'More people should have friendly faces like you. Honestly. The world would be a better place.'

Mae took another sip of her drink and felt that the world perhaps *was* a better place. She turned around to a group of girls next to her and admired one of them who had long blonde hair.

'God, I wish I had hair like yours,' she said to her.

The girl looked at her for a moment before she decided to smile. 'Yours isn't so bad.'

'Oh no, it's short, isn't it? Yours is like, *long*. And blonde. Even if I grew mine out it'd never be that colour, you know? Where's your necklace from? They real pearls?'

The girl laughed. 'No! They look it? You're so cute.'

Mae *was* cute. She was also funny and charming. And she had a brain, which wasn't always a given when you had cute looks and a personality.

'Bartender, friend!' Mae exclaimed. 'A round of drinks for the girls. Especially my blonde friend, here. Doesn't she have the best hair you've ever seen?'

Mae took the liberty of stroking it as the group of girls Mae had never before met exclaimed how she was the coolest. She could add *that* to the list of her personal attributes. Each girl in the group stood in front of Mae, waiting to be complimented for something or the other and because Mae was cool, she didn't fail to find something nice to say. They each hugged her as they trotted off and for a moment Mae wondered why they hadn't invited her to come along and dance with them.

'Hit me up with another rum and Coke,' she said, raising her voice over the din of the music, even though her glass was still three-quarters full.

'Take it easy. And no need to buy more drinks for people you don't know.'

'Ugh, don't be such a killjoy. And I am *easy* as they come,' she replied. 'Easy-peasy. You know I'm famous, right?'

His response was to raise his eyebrows.

'Like, *famous*.' She nodded, knowingly. 'That's right. Not just a cute face. A *famous* face.'

She raised her glass to him.

'I mean, don't get me wrong, there's good famous and bad famous and I guess if you were to ask, then I'd be bad famous, but you have to take what you get. If you know what I mean. There's a video,' she added, leaning forward. 'Some sexist jerk recorded me putting make-up on, on a train. It's like, so bloody what? Right?'

'Right,' the bartender replied, pushing several shots of vodka towards another group of students.

'Then he had the nerve to put it on Facebook and it only went viral.' Mae fiddled with the straw in her drink, staring into space. 'People can be horrible,' she mumbled.

The bartender pushed a packet of crisps towards her. 'Lesson one: don't drink on an empty stomach.'

'Sound advice.' She opened the packet and finished the crisps so quick even he was impressed.

'Don't sweat it,' he said. 'The video, I mean. Tomorrow it'll be something else.'

'Exactly!' Mae exclaimed.

With which she spun around with her drink and made her way on to the dance floor. She felt her hips swaying to the music before she got enveloped in a crowd of people. Dancing was *fun*. Why had she never wanted to do this before? Why had she always felt self-conscious at the idea when no one even cared? It was a few minutes later that she felt someone behind her. She turned around and looked up to find a sweaty guy smiling down at her and, for some reason, his hands were on her hips. She shifted slightly but when he didn't move she thought, well: this is the university experience, isn't it? That's what Bubblee was talking about. And Mae was getting some attention. Maybe this guy would turn into her boyfriend? He wasn't bad to look at, though she supposed she'd have to check that in proper daylight. Whatever he looked like though, right now, this was exciting. So, she let him keep his hands on her hips and they danced. Even when he leaned in closer she didn't move. It was when she felt something distinctly weird against her hip, as if poking her, that she turned around.

'I'm Mae,' she said.

'Huh?'

'*Mae*.'

'Cool,' he replied, getting closer.

The blue and purple lights flashed over his thin face.

'What's your name?'

He leaned into her. 'Steve.'

His hot breath against her ear made her queasy and she wasn't sure why. She put her hand out for him to shake, which he held on to with his own clammy hands.

'Let me get you another drink,' he said. 'What'll you have?'

Mae looked at her glass that was still half full but what the hell. You had to live a little and Steve might be a bit clammy but he was buying her a drink.

'Rum and Coke,' she replied.

He came back ten minutes later, two drinks in hand, and she'd already set her old glass down.

'You're a nice guy, Steve.'

'Thanks,' he replied. 'You're a nice girl.'

'You think?'

'Yeah.'

'How nice?'

'Hot nice.'

Mae put her arm on his shoulder and looked up at him.

'You're hot nice, too,' she replied.

This was a lie, obviously, but sometimes you had to lie to be nice. Steve's features were too pointed to be hot. His eyebrows too pale. But it seemed that people *weren't* all horrible. There were Steves in the world and she felt so elated to have found this out that, without thinking, she went and kissed him. The first kiss she'd ever had and it felt weird. His wet lips against hers. Was this how it was meant to feel? So sloppy? Then he pushed his tongue into her mouth and it made her giggle.

'Whoa, easy there, Steve,' she said, spilling some of her drink as she wiped her mouth.

Before she knew it he was kissing her again, but she liked the feel of his hand on her waist, squeezing it, pulling her towards him. The music seemed to get louder and she heard cheering from one side of the club. Lights flashed faster and brighter and she opened her eyes to see Steve's own eyes shut tight, his brown hair pasted to his forehead from the sweat. Mae had the uncontrollable urge to laugh.

'Something funny?' he said when she couldn't contain it any more and moved back.

'*Yes*,' she said, laughing. 'I mean, no, but it is kind of funny, isn't it?'

'What?'

He looked serious and she wondered if she'd done something to offend him.

'Nothing,' she said, taking a sip of her drink.

'Have some more,' he said, tucking his finger into the waist of her skirt and pulling her forward.

So she did. 'Rum and Coke is good, isn't it? In fact, I think it might be the best thing I've ever had to drink. Like, *ever*.'

'Yeah. It's all right. You wanna get out of here?'

This, to Mae, seemed to be the best idea anyone had ever come up with in the whole world.

'Yes!' she said, knocking back most of the remainder of the drink. 'Let's get out of here. Woohoo!' She grabbed Steve's hand and put her glass down as she danced towards the exit. 'We are outta here!' she exclaimed to the doorman. 'Thank you, of course, for your duty as a bouncer. Godspeed, my man. Godspeed.'

'You're wasted,' said Steve.

His face had got blurry and she felt herself sway on the spot. Mae tried to focus on him. Steve with his brown hair now swept back, his pointy nose and dark eyes.

'Bloody hell, Steve. I think you're right.'

Which only made her laugh again because *wasted* was a bloody funny word.

'*Wasted*,' she repeated, still swaying as he caught hold of her shoulders.

'Let's go back to mine. I've called an Uber.'

Steve had grabbed her wrist a little too hard and was hurting her, but she didn't want to be a wet blanket.

'*Yours?*' she said, feeling the urgent need to sit down. 'Why is everything spinning?'

'I have that effect on girls,' he said, holding her wrist tighter, pulling her towards the pavement.

His voice was distorted though and Mae felt she might faint.

'You all right, love?' came a voice, but it wasn't Steve's.

Then someone shouted. The world got fuzzier and darker as Mae felt Steve release her wrist from his grip. She stumbled and held on to a lamp-post. She wanted to say that she couldn't focus, that everything was turning to a blur. That she would throw up.

'Look at her,' someone shouted.

That's when Mae fell to the ground and everything went black.

Chapter Five

A brick house had clearly landed on Mae's head. It was the only explanation for how she felt when she woke up. Where was she? What time was it? For a moment she thought she was in Wyvernage, until she opened her eyes, just a fraction, to see that she was in a room quite foreign to her. Except it wasn't foreign. It was a dorm room. *Her* dorm room. How did she get here? Mae tried to recall what had happened but no memory of anything came to her except the first day she started university and entered this place. She let out a low moan, pressing her hands against her eyes, feeling dizzy, even though she was lying down. After a while, she tried to open her eyes again. As she squinted she saw a white T-shirt and black skirt flung over the back of the chair at her study desk. A vague recollection of wearing it began to filter through her mind. A club, a bartender ... *drinking*.

'Oh God,' she murmured as she went to pull the duvet over her.

The stress of the activity was as if the brick house had smashed itself against her skull. Without warning, a wave of nausea swelled up in her chest and Mae had no choice but to take her smashed skull and leap out of bed. Luckily, she tripped over a bin. She grabbed it and emptied the contents of her stomach into it – each heave feeling as if it would make her head explode. The vomiting didn't stop until she was heaving out nothing but phlegm. Mae collapsed into her bed again, holding on to her head with a desperate need for water but no energy to get any. Then she heard her door creak open and if she was in her right mind she'd have jumped out of bed or something. Instead she just moaned some more.

'You're awake,' came a woman's voice.

Someone had slid their hand under Mae's head, lifting it up, and put a bottle of water to her mouth.

'Sip slowly, or you'll throw it all up.'

She did as she was told.

'Here take this. It's a paracetamol. For the headache.'

The idea of putting anything else in her mouth made Mae want to reach for the bin but she was too weak to argue. The woman popped a pill into Mae's dry mouth, which she tried to gulp down with some more water.

'How are you feeling?' the woman asked.

Mae ventured to open her eyes again to a blurry image of a pale face and black hair. 'What's happening?'

Before the woman could answer Mae retched again; this time the woman brought the bin out in front of her just in time. She rubbed Mae's back with soothing sounds, telling her it was okay. That she'd be okay.

'Oh, God, I'm going to die,' mumbled Mae.

'No, you're not. Not this time.'

With which the woman made Mae rest her head against the pillow once more and Mae drifted into a restless sleep.

The next time Mae woke up it was dark outside and she was still dizzy and confused. Looking at the bin, she remembered the random woman. Who was she and how did she know Mae? Maybe she was a hallucination in the guise of a guardian angel? Mae really didn't need to add hallucinating to her troubles. She looked at her bedside table and there was a plate with dry toast on it, along with a note of some sort, only Mae couldn't focus her vision enough to read it. The brick house that had smashed her skull earlier seemed to have lifted a little as Mae tried to get out of bed to use the bathroom. She took a moment, her legs dangling from her bedside, and tried to get up. It took a few attempts without her wanting to hurl again. It was so dark that there was nothing for it but to switch on the bathroom light. As soon as she did she felt as if the light had shot an arrow to her brain. She squeezed her eyes shut and fumbled around to sit on the toilet, just about managing to get to the tissue roll to wipe herself. Each activity took up so much energy she had to rest between them. Eventually, she managed to pull up her pyjama bottoms but then wondered how she'd got them on in the first place. A face drifted into her memory, white and sweaty, and she wondered who it was. Mae washed her hands and looked at her face in the mirror.

'Oh God.'

Her black liner had smudged down her face, her eyes were bloodshot, lips smeared a faint red. She ambled back into her bed, curling up in a foetal position while she checked her phone. Lots of messages from her sisters' WhatsApp group, but she didn't have the will power to read them. That was when the door to her room opened again, the shadow of the same woman who'd been there earlier, appearing.

'Hey,' she said, sitting on the side of Mae's bed.

The familiarity in the voice of a stranger felt odd to Mae – so odd, she couldn't quite reply.

'Still dazed?' she offered.

Mae hadn't switched the light from the bathroom off, so she could see the woman's face more clearly – her porcelain skin and straight, black, shiny hair. Why did she look so familiar?

'Who are you?' asked Mae. 'What's happened?'

'You should eat that toast.'

She handed the plate to Mae who couldn't quite grasp it, so settled it on her duvet over her chest as she lifted herself up. The woman, though in the light she was clearly a student too, got up and put the pillow against Mae's back. Her hair smelt like coconuts. Mae took the toast and bit into it.

'Mmmm,' she said. 'Soggy.'

The woman looked at Mae as if she were about to tell her off.

'Sorry,' added Mae.

'Don't be.' She shook her head. 'I've seen this too many times.'

'Soggy toast?'

'I'm Ji Su.'

'Mae.'

'Yeah. I saw from your ID in your wallet.'

A panic ran through Mae. What kind of a person went through another person's wallet? Who was this woman and why was she bringing Mae all this stuff? What the hell happened last night?

'I had to know your name – figure out any details I should know about you. In case I needed to call an ambulance or something.'

Mae gulped, the dull throbbing in her head bringing with it another bout of nausea.

'How much do you remember about last night?' Ji Su asked.

Mae tried to think. She remembered her first shot of vodka. A bartender. Blonde hair and strobe lights.

'Ugh,' she said. 'I think there was a boy there. But I can't be sure. I'd had a bit to drink,' she admitted, feeling a flush of embarrassment mingled with a sense of being a normal student. Just like anyone else.

'Do you remember where you were?'

'It was The Crypt, right?'

Ji Su nodded. 'There was a boy there. Can you remember his face?'

Mae thought hard for a few moments, trying to piece together the fragments that were floating around in her head, which she couldn't quite grasp.

'I don't know. It was dark, and the lights and music. And, you know, the drink.'

A few moments' silence passed between them as Mae stared at Ji Su. She was sure she'd seen her somewhere before, but she couldn't quite pinpoint where. Did Mae have selective amnesia? She recalled her birth date, her sisters' names, her brother's name and all their birth dates, where she'd gone to school ... It all came to her apart from the past twenty-four hours, which were lost in some sort of fog.

'Were you there?' Mae asked. 'Last night?'

Ji Su nodded.

'Did we speak?'

'No.'

'Why do I feel like I've seen you somewhere before?'

Ji Su smoothed out the crease in Mae's duvet and looked at her, smiling. 'In a coffee shop. Some days ago.'

Mae furrowed her brows.

'Skimpy's,' added Ji Su.

The memory came to her with a thud. Of course. It was *her*. She was the one who'd been in the coffee shop when Mae discovered the video of her online.

'Oh.'

'I've seen you around the campus a few times,' said Ji Su. 'But you always have your head down.'

An ironic laugh escaped Mae. 'Well …'

'I get it. That video was awful.'

Tears stung Mae's eyes as she tried to stay focused on her white duvet.

'And all those comments …' added Ji Su. 'I'd have liked to have talked to you but you always seemed to get away.'

Mae bit back her tears, tried to level her voice but it still came out thick. 'Oh, it's nothing. It's fine.'

'Are you kidding me?' exclaimed Ji Su.

Mae was taken aback at the rise in her voice and leaned back, the pain in her head expanding.

'It is *not* bloody okay. Nothing about anything of this is okay. Do you get that?'

Mae was too scared to do anything else but nod in agreement.

'No, don't just nod like that,' said Ji Su. 'You have to know that whatever's happened – none of it's okay. Not for you, not for *any* woman.'

Ji Su's eyes flashed with anger, the colour in her cheeks had risen and she looked so agitated Mae could do very little but offer her toast.

'The last thing you should be doing is blaming your-self. You're not, are you?'

Mae shook her head. Of course she felt that if only

she *hadn't* put make-up on in the train, no one would've taken that video and she wouldn't have been so miserable. But she dared not voice this to Ji Su – she didn't want to appear weak to her. Why it mattered what Ji Su thought of her Mae didn't know, but it did.

'Are you sure?' asked Ji Su, boring into her eyes.

Mae noticed how thick her eyelashes were.

'I'll never put my make-up on in public again, that's for sure,' said Mae, trying to laugh.

'What? Well, not just that … you really don't remember anything from last night?'

'I don't know. It'll come to me, I guess. I've never really …'

God, it was so hard to explain to people who weren't Bengali or Muslim that drinking just wasn't something you did. Not when your family was so traditional. It seemed so *sad*. As if, just because you didn't drink, you didn't really live. But then Mae looked at Ji Su and felt that she could tell her anything. That maybe she would understand.

'The thing is I've never really drunk before,' finished Mae.

'No kidding,' replied Ji Su with a sympathetic smile.

Was it that obvious? There was no end to all these embarrassments. And then Ji Su put her hand on Mae's and gripped it tight. 'Some guy tried to drug you.'

She paused, as if wanting to let the weight of this sink into Mae.

'What?' said Mae. 'No. No, that can't have happened.'

'No?' said Ji Su. 'You said you thought you remembered some boy?'

Mae shrugged uncertainly. She thought she did and then she got a flashback of someone putting their tongue in her mouth.

'Oh God,' said Mae as she lunged for the bin.

She wiped her mouth and took another sip of water.

'I need another paracetamol.'

Ji Su readily took the packet from the table and popped one into Mae's hand.

'Yeah,' said Mae. 'There was a guy. We were just messing around.'

'He got you a drink?'

'I don't know. Maybe. I guess.'

'Well, I can tell you. He got you a drink,' said Ji Su.

'So what?' said Mae. 'I've never drunk before. It just hit me hard, I guess.'

'I'll tell you what happened. You were dancing, in your own world, when this guy – this *jerk* – came up behind you. And you, being a bit tipsy, turned around and didn't push him away. I don't know. Maybe you like that kind of guy. The ones who just do what they want without asking if it's all right with you.'

It was Mae's turn to flush red. She *did not* like that kind of guy – but isn't that just what happened in these places? Isn't that what people expect, especially when you're a carefree, *fun*, cool, student? Who wants to be the loser who kicks up a fuss?

'Anyway, he took advantage of the fact that you didn't say anything and even then you were laughing so I thought maybe it's not what I think. I thought, maybe she's all right and anyway, it's none of my business, right? But his face …' Ji Su's features were etched with disdain. 'He just looked so full of it. I don't know, I've seen men like that and once they get started, they don't care.'

Mae felt that this was a bit judgemental of her, but let her continue, trying to recognise anything from Ji Su's version of events – given that Mae hadn't enough recollection to come up with her own. It was a shame to have to rely on someone who was little more than a stranger.

'Then you seemed to have an idea, took his hand and made your way out of the club. I don't know … call it instinct or whatever. Or maybe what was going on with that pathetic video.' She paused and softened her voice. 'It makes you vulnerable, doesn't it? That kind of stuff. It gets to you even when you try not to let it.'

What was it about this girl that made Mae well up every time she looked at her? It was if she could see into Mae's soul and it was just plain weird.

'So, I followed you out, just to make sure. Just to *check*. And I'm so glad I did.'

'Why?' whispered Mae.

'It might've been the first time you'd ever had a drink,

and yeah, maybe you had overdone it, but you looked as if you were going to pass out. You could barely stand straight without that jerk holding you up. Anyway, as soon as I asked if you were okay, jerk-face piped up, "She's fine, all right?"' Ji Su scoffed. 'I've seen that arrogance before. "Then let her tell me she's fine," I said to him. Bouncer didn't care. Just thought you were another wasted girl, leaving with her boyfriend, or ready to hook up with someone.'

A strange tightness took hold of Mae's chest – she'd put her hand on it without realising.

'Turns out that guy was as idiotic as he looked and started getting rowdy with me. They get annoyed when they realise they've haven't got away with something. They're so stupid they aren't even subtle about it. A bunch of girls came out and some blonde-haired one shouted out that you were her friend, but when she saw this guy – Steve, apparently – she started shouting at him. I mean, *shouting*. She said all kinds of stuff: *What the eff are you doing here? You're a creep. Why don't you piss off?* That kind of thing. Seemed like he'd gone out with one of her mates and didn't exactly treat her well. And that's when you collapsed. We got you in a car and I had to go through your bag to see where you lived. Anyway, blonde-haired girl helped me get you to your room in the end. God, she was loud. But helpful, you know. In the end. I wanted to take you to the hospital, but I checked your breathing and you dipped in and out of consciousness so I figured you were all right. Anyway, I stayed with you during the night, just in case. Then I had to go to class in the morning, but kept coming in to see how you were. Then you woke up and I have to say, it was a relief.'

It took a while for Mae to process all this information. So much had happened and she had no recollection of it whatsoever. It put the fear of God in her. How wrong things could've gone. What if Ji Su hadn't been there? What if she hadn't been looking out for Mae – a complete stranger to her? Would she even be lying in bed right now with soggy toast and a head that throbbed? It was beyond belief and yet there was no reason for Ji Su to lie. And she remembered the blonde-haired girl with the pearl necklace. Mae felt a flush of gratitude towards her. She wished she could find her to say thank you. But first she should thank Ji Su. Except Mae's mouth was dry and the words seemed to catch in her throat.

'I ... I don't know what to—'

'Hey,' said Ji Su. 'Don't say anything. I know it's a lot to take in.'

'But I—'

'Yeah, I know.'

'What if—'

'But it didn't, did it?' said Ji Su, as if reading Mae's thoughts. 'You're safe.'

The words that seemed caught gave way to something completely different as a sob rose in Mae's throat and she burst into tears. Ji Su came forward and put her arms around her, enveloping her into the comfort of her sweet-smelling sweatshirt. Once Mae started she couldn't stop. She couldn't stop thinking about the past year, and then the past few months, and now *this*.

'I ... I ... I,' she sobbed, but she didn't even know what she was saying.

'Stop it,' said Ji Su. 'No one deserves your tears.' She pulled Mae back and looked at her. '*No one.*'

How could Mae tell her how much everything was bothering her: how lonely she felt, how she wasn't keeping up with uni work, how she hated being here? Instead she just nodded.

'Now, get some more sleep, okay?'

'Okay,' replied Mae.

'And let's get some coffee tomorrow? When you're around?'

Mae nodded again. She felt like a child, as if Ji Su was one of her sisters or her mum and it comforted her. Perhaps she'd been looked after a little too much at home and she was more used to it than she'd ever imagined. She'd been a big fish in a small pond and didn't realise that the world was an ocean full of unknown and possibly dangerous beings.

'Thanks. Oh God,' said Mae putting her face in her hand.

'What?'

'What day is it?'

'Thursday,' replied Ji Su.

'My assignment,' replied Mae. 'Shit! It was meant to be handed in today.'

Ji Su looked at her watch. 'It's eight thirty. Just email your tutor telling them what happened. They *have* to understand.'

'No. I hadn't … I haven't even finished it.'

Mae wanted to be sick again, but it had nothing to do with her hangover.

'Oh. Well, maybe we can get you an extension, given the circumstances? Don't worry, I can be a witness for you. They can't take this stuff lightly.'

Mae didn't want to tell her that she hadn't even started it. What had she been thinking? What a mess.

'Don't panic,' said Ji Su. 'We'll sort it out.'

Ji Su looked so sweet, like Fatti, but there was a steeliness to her that reminded Mae of Bubblee and even Farah.

'Why are you being so nice to me?' asked Mae.

'We sisters got to stick together,' she replied with a laugh. 'I've put my phone number into your mobile. Ji Su. And I've given myself a missed call in case you don't message me,' she said with a smile.

'I will. Trust me. I owe you—'

'Nothing.'

After Ji Su left, Mae's mind fluttered with what had happened. She got her phone out.

Mae: Yo peeps. Whats hangin?

Apart from Mae's head in shame. She waited for a response, but none came. If only Fatti were here, Mae could've cosied up into her arms. Farah would've brought her tea, Bubblee would've been calling the police and filing a complaint and probably leading some kind of movement. Mae sank back into her bed and thought of Ji Su. Of course she owed her something. She practically owed Ji Su her life.

Mae had disturbed sleep and when she woke up the following morning there was still a dull ache in her head. Before she got ready she messaged Ji Su to see if she was free around midday. The least Mae could do was buy her lunch. She went to her first lesson but spent the entire time checking her phone and began panicking that Ji Su fed her number incorrectly into Mae's phone, but of course that wasn't possible, not if she'd given herself a missed call. Mae hadn't realised that she was of a paranoid disposition until she'd started university. She needed to buck up and stop thinking the worst. If there were Steves in the world there were also Ji Sus and there was no reason for Mae to think she wasn't genuine. It was around eleven o'clock when she got the message from her:

Ji Su: 12pm, Skimpys. It's a date xx

Mae's spirits rose, which was just as well because when it came to seeing her tutor for Studying Television class she felt she might just throw up again. She knew Ji Su was right – all she had to do was explain the truth – except that Mae was aware that it wasn't as if she was on top of all her work in the first place. It turned out that the teacher was sympathetic when Mae told her the story. She guessed it helped that she ended up crying in the teacher's office, and not because she wanted to either – it was so embarrassing the way she welled up at the drop of a hat. But she was only given a forty-eight-hour extension. Still, it was better than nothing. She'd work all night for it. This was where caffeine came in handy. And Red Bull. Mae would have lunch with Ji Su and then go straight to the library to work. She could only try her best now to scrape through that assignment before beginning revisions for her end of year exams.

It was weird walking into Skimpy's and seeing Ji Su in public, sitting with her head bent low over a book, her sleek, black hair falling over her face. She was wearing a red T-shirt and baggy ripped jeans, plaited bracelets and other bands around her wrists. Mae felt unaccountably shy. And nervous, though she didn't know why. There was something about Ji Su which made Mae want her respect. She looked down at her black leggings and wondered whether this black and red chequered shirt made her look too *normal*. Mae got the impression that Ji Su liked things that were different, and people who set themselves apart from the norm. Ji Su looked up and Mae attempted a smile. She seemed to consider Mae for a moment. Did she not recognise her? What had Mae expected, a flourishing welcome? Why not? Mae decided it would help if she actually moved so she walked towards the table.

'Hi,' she said.

'You came.' Ji Su put a bookmark in the page of her book and snapped it shut. 'I'm glad.'

'Why wouldn't I?' replied Mae, putting her rucksack down and taking a seat.

Ji Su merely shrugged. 'Did you get an extension for your assignment?'

'Forty-eight hours.'

'What?' she exclaimed. 'Is that it? After all you've been through? That's outrageous. Who's your tutor?'

'No, no, it's fine. It's fair, if you think about it.'

'Fair? *Fair?* You've got to be joking. Nothing about what happened is fair, and the least your tutor can do is give you some time to recover from your ordeal before you having to give in this stupid assignment.' She shook her head in agitation. 'Your tutor a man or woman?'

'Woman.'

Ji Su scoffed and folded her arms, leaning back in her chair.

'No, really, she was sympathetic about it.'

'Yeah, really sympathetic. Give me her name,' she said,

this time coming forward. She had a look in her eye that told Mae that Ji Su would always fight for the things she wanted, that no one crossed her, and if they did, they'd be sorry. Mae instinctively put her hand on her arm.

'Seriously. It's all right. I just have to deal with it, don't I?'

'You're too nice for your own good. Next thing you'll say is that you'd have deserved what happened to you if you'd got into the car with that jerk.'

'No,' exclaimed Mae. 'Of course not. But, well ... it was stupid of me, wasn't it? To get so drunk.'

A steely look came across Ji Su's face. 'And what about him?'

'He just saw an opportunity, I guess.'

'And that's okay?'

'No, I'm not saying that ...'

Mae was getting tongue-tied; she wanted Ji Su to like her but she couldn't help feel that she *was* partly to blame for the whole thing. That the way life seemed to be spiralling out of control had at least something to do with Mae. She was, after all, the common factor in everything.

'Tell me,' said Ji Su. 'What are you saying? Because it sounds like you're blaming everyone but him.'

Mae went quiet.

'I'm sorry,' continued Ji Su, 'but this is just typical for a woman to feel she has to make excuses for a man's behaviour.'

'I'm not making excuses,' mumbled Mae.

'Then what are you doing?'

'It's just …'

'What?'

'It's fine, don't worry,' said Mae. 'I don't even know you. You don't need to hear it.'

This time Ji Su put her hand on Mae's arm and held it there. The sunlight came through and settled on her face, bathing it in an angelic hue. How was it possible for a person to have such beautiful skin? Mae now noticed the plumpness of Ji Su's pink lips, the contouring of her cheekbones and felt a sense of her own physical inadequacies in comparison.

'Why don't you tell me and I'll be the judge of that?' said Ji Su.

So Mae did tell her. She told her everything about the hardship of adjusting to university, how she didn't feel herself here, not like the old Mae back in Wyvernage who was carefree and had a joke for every situation. Uni was meant to be the place where you found yourself, but Mae was just losing herself instead.

'I don't know,' she said. 'Maybe it was being brought up in such a close household where I never really saw the outside world or knew how to act in it. Not really.'

'Were you home-schooled or something?' laughed Ji Su.

Mae laughed too. '*No*, but thanks for that. High school was different, like whatever. Everyone knew each other and it was just an extension of the family, I guess. Everyone here seems to have already come with like a *life* before, you know? They've all got these crazy stories and things they've done and I'm just like *whoa*. Where have I been all these years?'

Ji Su let out a laugh. 'Oh, please. This lot? They all think they've lived and they go on about their gap yaas, but they don't have a clue. Privileged idiots, the lot of them.'

'Oh, God, I'm being such a whiny cow. *Poor me, I'm losing who I am.*' Mae rolled her eyes at herself. 'Sorry. Ignore me. I'm as bad as the rest of them.'

Ji Su gave a half smile and considered Mae. 'I don't know. You're not so bad.'

'Give it five minutes and you'll see I probs am. Seriously. Run now. Take cover.'

But Ji Su didn't say anything. They both sat in silence for a few minutes before she said, 'You think we should get some food before they kick us out?'

Mae nodded. 'But I can't stay for long. Assignment, remember?'

'Oh, I know, but before that we're going to the police station and filing a report.'

'What?'

'Yes.'

Mae gulped. Wasn't this taking it too seriously? 'Can't we just forget it happened?'

'So … what? He can try to do it again to some other

poor girl? We have a first name, and trust me, his face is etched into my memory.'

Mae groaned. She just wanted to forget the whole thing ever happened. 'I don't want to go through it.'

Ji Su paused. 'You know that he might do this again? This time there might not be someone to stop him.'

Mae felt the weight of this possibility. Wouldn't it be nice to go back to her room and eat a doner kebab? Ji Su was still staring at her.

'What about my assignment?' said Mae.

'I've got work to do too, so you and me are going to the library and we're not leaving until you're done. All right? But this is just as important. More important, in fact.'

There was nothing for it. Mae would have to go through the indignity of admitting she'd been drinking and was stupid enough to have got drugged by a random man. So, they sat and had lunch before heading over to the police station. Mae let Ji Su do most of the talking as the police officer kept looking over at her, eyeing her as if she was the suspicious one. They asked her to make a statement, took Ji Su's description of Steve and said they'd look into it.

'How?' Ji Su asked, folding her arms.

'There's very little we can do without a full name. You say you don't know if he was a student or not, and the lady you said that recognised him ... well, unless we can get her in here, there's not much else to go on.'

Ji Su exhaled rather loudly. 'Right. Great help you guys are.'

'We can only work with what we have,' he replied, looking bored, as if he'd had this conversation a hundred times before.

'Ugh, come on, Mae,' said Ji Su, taking her hand. 'Shouldn't have even bothered,' she added, looking back at the police officer and glaring at him.

They walked out of the station as Ji Su began to rant about how students' problems are never taken seriously.

'He didn't have a lot to go on, though, did he?' offered Mae.

'Oh God,' said Ji Su. 'We're going to have to do a brainwash reversal on you.'

But she said it with half a laugh as they made their way to the library, ready for an inevitable all-nighter.

Chapter Six

Mae wasn't sure if Ji Su stayed with her both nights because she actually had an urgent assignment due too, or because she was keeping an eye on Mae to make sure she didn't give up. The project had been completed as best as it could in the timeframe, but Mae didn't feel good about it when she emailed it over to the tutor. If only she'd begun it when she received it. Even if she'd begun it a week ago, got her head together and focused, it would have had a bit more substance. *Shoulda, woulda, coulda.* Although, if Ji Su hadn't herself been focused those two days at the library it could've gone very differently. Mae was amazed at how many guys ended up sitting at their table, eyes flitting towards Ji Su, asking if she had a pen they could borrow or some other lame excuses. She'd just look up at them, straight-faced, and say, 'No.'

One tried to engage Mae in conversation and she found herself fidgeting and bumbling over her words, as if her brain and mouth had been disconnected. Why did it always feel so hard to talk to men? Anyway, it became clear that he was only talking to Mae to get information about Ji Su. Mae looked at her from the corner of her eye. She was acting as if nothing at all was happening.

'Your friend shy?' he asked Mae.

Ji Su turned to him and replied, 'No, just really bored by your banal chat.'

Mae was sure he muttered something derogatory under his breath as he walked away.

'He might've been nice if you gave him a chance,' offered Mae.

'What? With how he just spoke when he left?' Ji Su shook her head. 'You really do have a lot to learn.'

The following few months dissolved into a blur of study sessions, coffee breaks and long chats with Ji Su. Mae found out that Ji Su's parents came to England when she was five. They settled in a town outside Manchester where she went to school and finished high school – with straight As, of course. Her mum was a social worker, specialising in women's care, and her dad was the head of a charitable organisation that specialised in helping men from East Asian backgrounds with depression.

'You can imagine all the fun chats at our dinner table,' said Ji Su.

She also had an older sister who was an archaeologist – currently abroad in Jordan on a dig – and a brother who was doing a PhD.

'I always tease Eun Jung about the fact that she's

abandoned women's rights to go looking for fossils. Mum wanted her to do something meaningful, but she had her mind set, and trust me, no one can change her mind.'

'Must run in the family,' replied Mae. 'If I'm honest you all sound like you're overachievers, but whatever.'

Ji Su laughed. 'Hardly. Anyway, you can imagine Mum's over the moon that I'm an officer at the Women's Union here. Trailing in her footsteps. Just as well it's what I want to do too, otherwise that would've been awkward.'

It all sounded so perfect to Mae. She couldn't help but compare it to her own parents: a mum who was a housewife and a dad who had worked as a security guard at the shopping centre in town for most of his life. It was so uninspiring. Except when Mae alluded to this, Ji Su flashed her a look.

'Don't do that. Don't belittle what they do to try and make life work. That's better than any high and mighty CEO or whatever. Trust me.'

Mae was immediately embarrassed and wished she hadn't said anything, but Ji Su carried on as if nothing happened. That was the thing about her: she believed so strongly in what she felt. She'd make you question what you were thinking – you might feel bad for a moment – but she explained things in such a way that just made sense. Mae had hung out in her dorm room and people would come in and out, borrowing stuff from her, bringing stuff back and Ji Su was always friendly but there was also a distance to her – as if she never really let people too close to her. Mae felt privileged that she was spending so much time with her because there wasn't a day that went by when they didn't see each other and she could hardly be seeing other people at the same time. A few times she'd gone to a meeting at the Women's Union where they'd talk about what was happening; which female student was having problems with a male professor, dates gone wrong and Mae was horrified at how often these things happened. It was as if she'd been living in a bubble, completely unaware of the kind of stuff women had to put up with. She'd think again and again about how lucky she'd got that night at The Crypt, and what if Ji Su hadn't been there, what if she'd become a focal point of discussion in this very union? *If* she'd have come forward and actually said something, which of course, so many women didn't.

'And that's what I'm here for,' said Ji Su, smiling.

They'd often study together in the library, but while Ji Su's head would be down, Mae found herself gazing at people, fiddling with her phone, checking her social media. She found herself looking at other uni courses online and came across some random things: *Ethical Hacking. Viking Studies. Equestrian Psychology and Sports Science.* Weirdly, her university offered that last course, which probably said something about the uni. What was wrong with her? Why couldn't she concentrate?

They both did their assignments and took their exams. Even though Ji Su's parents lived close by she'd moved into a new flat, saying that she felt too crowded at home and needed to be alone with her own thoughts and live her own life. Mae's mum kept asking when she was coming back for the summer, but why would she want to do that – spend it in that dingy room she'd been relegated to – when she now had all this time, without the worry of classes and studying? She'd get a part-time job. Ji Su said she could stay with her once they'd got their results and Mae had to vacate her dorm room. Ji Su's flatmate wasn't moving in until the new term, anyway.

It had already been a month of picnics and films, hanging out and giggling until late into the night about the latest ridiculous fashion. All the while this was happening Mae noticed how sometimes Ji Su would take her hand and not let it go for a while. She'd put her arm around Mae and Mae would feel a flush of excitement and happiness. One night, Mae was lying in bed after they'd had dinner and watched a film and she wondered what it'd be like if Ji Su was lying with her. The thought brought about a panic. That was silly. She'd never thought of women in that way before. Never. Mae wondered back at any crushes she'd had in high school – they were all fleeting but they'd always been crushes on boys. Yes, she would sometimes admire a girl, think one was pretty or another had nice hair, but that was normal, right? Plus, it was just so easy to be around Ji

Su. She made Mae a more interesting person simply by being friends with her. Tomorrow, she was going to move in with her for the summer and things would be even better than they had been.

Mae was packing up her stuff when her phone rang.

'Baby's asleep finally and I was just waiting for Bubblee to come home so I thought I'd see how you were,' came Farah's voice.

'Oh, hey. Yeah, fine.'

'You're getting all your work done?'

Which showed how much her sisters knew.

'I'm getting my first year results tomorrow,' said Mae.

'So soon? Where does the time go? How are you feeling?'

'Oh, you know …'

It was the first time Farah had called in about a month. Last time Mae had been with Ji Su so couldn't really talk, but now that she had her sister on the phone again with her full attention Mae didn't want to talk about uni. She wanted to tell her what had happened at The Crypt. But where would she start? At the point where she was already fairly drunk because of a couple of shots of vodka and two and a half glasses of rum and Coke? Farah would probably give her a lecture about that. And even if Mae left that part out – she'd never admit it to Ji Su – she *did* feel ashamed. Embarrassed that she'd been in a position of weakness. That due to her own idiocy someone tried to take advantage of her. No matter how much she listened to Ji Su's point of view, no matter how much rational sense it made, Mae couldn't help feeling this way.

'Enjoy it while you can,' said Farah. 'When you're married or have kids it'll all change.'

Mae had to clench her jaw. It was becoming really boring listening to people with babies or families hash out the same old line.

'Yeah, first time I've heard that,' replied Mae.

'That's because it's true.'

Farah really didn't get sarcasm.

'Right, yeah,' said Mae.

'So … what else is new? Give me some fun gossip. Who was that friend you mentioned? Ji Su? What is she? Korean?'

'What does that matter?' asked Mae.

'Doesn't. Just wondering. Any nice Bengali girls there? I find it's helpful to be around people of the same culture.'

Mae found her annoyance rising. What was her sister talking about? What difference did Ji Su's cultural heritage make? That's when she realised how different she was to Farah, and even Fatti. How small both of their lives had always been. Such a thought wouldn't even occur to Bubblee. Or at least the Bubblee she used to know.

'That's not really what uni's about,' said Mae.

'They might have nice brothers or cousins for you.'

Farah had basically turned into Mum.

'What?' said Mae, her voice terse. Most unlike her.

'I'm just saying,' replied Farah.

'Kinda helpful if you don't.'

There was a long pause. 'Just because I never went to uni doesn't mean I don't have opinions,' said Farah.

Mae moved the phone from her ear, looked at it, confused. What the hell was her sister on about?

'Er, all right.'

'Suppose you uni-goers don't care what non-uni people have to say.'

'You okay?' said Mae, genuinely perplexed.

'Fine. Anyway, I'll leave you to it.'

Farah said goodbye and put the phone down and Mae wondered if her sister had always been this, well ... uptight.

'Thanks for the good chat,' said Mae to herself. 'Geez.'

That's when her phone beeped.

Ji Su: Good night, babe. Xxxxxx

Mae smiled. It was useless thinking about the annoying things that her sister had just said. Farah was just Farah. She thought instead about the following day, when she'd get her results. At least Ji Su would be there, so she could cry about her crappy result and then go and hang out. Maybe watch a film in the flat that night, to christen it. The idea softened the inevitable blow of a poorly graded year, and even though Mae felt bad, she didn't feel *that* bad.

For the first time since she left home Mae felt hopeful and her loneliness had all but disappeared. Things were finally panning out. It'd all be fine in the end, despite her results, because what was the worst that could happen?

'Oh God, oh God, oh God, oh God. Why, why, *why* did I have to leave it all until the last minute?' exclaimed Mae as she and Ji Su went to collect her results. 'Like, am I stupid?'

'I didn't want to say …'

Mae pushed Ji Su as she laughed and put her arm around Mae's waist. 'You'll be *fine*. I promise.'

Mae stiffened slightly, suddenly very aware of the feelings Ji Su's hand gripping her waist evoked in her. Did she want Ji Su to keep her hand where it was or not? Before Mae could answer her own question, Ji Su removed her hand to look for something in her bag. They went into the administration office to collect Mae's envelope and she held it for a while before giving it to Ji Su.

'I can't do it.'

'*Do it,*' said Ji Su.

'It's all right for you, brainbox. You got a first.'

'I worked hard.'

Mae sighed. 'Let's talk about that. How'd you manage to do that?'

'Nice try with the deflection,' replied Ji Su, shoving the envelope in Mae's hands again. 'Open it.'

'Can I just … can we just have one last day of fun and no worrying? *Please?*' asked Mae.

Ji Su looked at her and shook her head. 'Just get it over and done with.'

'Pleeeeease?' said Mae.

Ji Su sighed. 'You know part of your problem is always wanting to bury your head in the sand?'

'What do you mean?' asked Mae, feeling that Ji Su was probably right.

'You know what I mean. You never want to face up to things. *Things*, by the way,' she added, looking at the envelope, 'that will still be there when you get your head out of the sand.'

Mae gave Ji Su her most pathetic look. Her friend looked at her for a while and just sighed.

'*Fine*,' said Ji Su. 'But I don't get how you can wait to see your results. I'd go mad.'

'Yeah, well, I think we've established we're both a little different when it comes to this stuff. Most stuff.'

'No. Not most stuff.'

That's when Ji Su took Mae's hand again and didn't let it go, all the way to Skimpy's. After lunch they sat in the park, reading and talking about moving Mae's things to the flat until they realised they should stop lazing around and go and actually collect them.

Ji Su didn't hold Mae's hand this time when they got up and it was as if they could both feel the lack of it. Silence seemed to fall between them, and not the natural ones they were used to. Something had shifted but Mae wasn't sure what. She kept on trying to fill in the quiet with inane comments like: 'Do you think I should get that sweater from H&M?' Or, 'Nice day, isn't it?' She hated herself for that last one. Who knew that one day she'd turn into the kind of person who talked about things like the weather. When she put the key in the door, she could feel Ji Su behind her, watching her, and Mae's heart beat faster. She wanted to tell her that she couldn't come in, that she should go back to her flat, because this feeling that Mae was having was overwhelming her and she didn't know what to do about it. And at the same time, she knew she didn't want Ji Su to leave. As Mae opened the door to her room, she wondered what other kinds of doors she might be opening. Each action, each step, felt charged with something like change, though Mae hardly knew why.

'Room's a mess, obviously,' said Mae. 'How'd you feel about that when we're living together?'

'I'm used to it. And any time I get annoyed I'll just beat you with a stick, of course.'

They entered the room and unfortunately the silence was only made worse by the lack of people around them now. It was just the two of them.

'Can't put it off for ever, you know,' said Ji Su.

'Huh?'

'Your results.'

'Oh.'

Why was there so much life happening right now? Mae wasn't sure what to do with so many feelings. She looked at Ji Su and thought how beautiful she was and without even thinking about it, went to touch her face. Her skin was as smooth as it looked and Ji Su moved towards her, there barely being a few inches between them.

'What am I doing?' whispered Mae.

'Whatever you want to.'

Mae swallowed hard before she closed her eyes, unable to do anything but just stand there until she felt Ji Su's lips on hers. The second set of lips she'd ever felt on hers, and she couldn't even remember the first. This was wholly new and yet didn't feel weird. Mae kissed her back, thinking how warm and comfortable it was, and how nice it felt to have Ji Su's arms now wrapped around her, and then she opened her eyes, just a little, to see Ji Su's face, her eyes closed, and the feelings that she was having began to drift away. Perhaps she needed more time to get into it, so she closed her eyes again, kissing her even harder.

'Ow,' said Ji Su.

'Oh God, sorry.'

'It's okay.' Ji Su tucked a strand of hair behind Mae's ear. 'Just, you know, take it easy.'

Mae nodded, but this time became so self-conscious she barely opened her lips, let alone her mouth. Ji Su's hands that were now in Mae's hair felt uncomfortable. She pulled back.

'Is it okay?' asked Ji Su.

'Yeah, no, it's fine.'

'Fine?'

Mae nodded. Oh God! What was happening? It had felt so right up until that moment. Mae had felt *something*, she was sure of it. How could she not? All you had to do was look at Ji Su to get it. Mae took both her hands in hers.

'What is it?'

'Nothing,' replied Mae.

Ji Su went back in to kiss her but this time Mae pulled back.

'Is something wrong?'

'No, no …'

How was she meant to explain it? She hardly understood it herself.

'I really like you,' began Mae.

There was a pause. 'Right …'

'But maybe we should stop.'

Another pause. 'Why?'

'Dunno. Kind of weird, isn't it?'

Mae saw Ji Su stiffen. 'Weird?'

'Oh no, not like that. You're amazing, you know?'

'But?'

'It's not a *but*. Well, I guess it is when you put it like that. It's just … I thought I felt something. I *did* feel something. I mean, look at you. You're bloody beautiful.'

Ji Su just looked at Mae with her discerning gaze.

'I mean, it's ridiculous how hot you are. Can't believe you'd even look twice at me.'

'Shut up.'

'I don't know …' said Mae, wishing it didn't have to be so complicated. 'Something doesn't feel right to me about it. Do you know what I mean?'

Ji Su took her hands out of Mae's. 'I see.'

This was it. This is what happened when you opened your stupid mouth and tried to be honest about something. Mae panicked. What if Ji Su left and never spoke to her again?

'I *do* like you,' said Mae. 'You're amazing.'

'Mhmm. I think I'm going to go.'

'What? No. Stay, let's talk about it. Please.'

Ji Su looked at her. 'I don't want to talk any more.'

How could this be happening? Just a few hours ago they were in the park, plucking daisies from the grass and flicking them at each other, sipping from the same can of Diet Coke.

'Don't you care about me?' said Mae, sounding more pathetic than she wished.

She didn't get why Ji Su looked so angry. Wasn't she always the one who said that you should be honest with the person you're with? Didn't she tell Mae she should never feel like she has to do anything physical with anyone? When Ji Su didn't speak, Mae couldn't help but blurt it out: 'You're the one who says you should feel comfortable in any physical relationship.'

That's when she noticed there were tears in Ji Su's eyes. 'I didn't realise this was *any* relationship.'

It took a moment for the weight of these words to hit Mae. 'What? No. That's not what I meant.'

Ji Su just shook her head and grabbed her bag. 'Hey, listen, it's fine. You've said enough for the both of us.'

'Hang on. I'm moving in with you.'

'I don't think that's a good idea.'

Mae's heart sank. 'What? Why are you overreacting?'

'*Overreacting?* I'm not the one who made the first move here, Mae. *You did*. Yeah, I had feelings for you, but I didn't know what you were about, so I just went along with being friends, because that's fine. *You're* the one who decided to change things.'

'So? Can't we just change things back?'

Ji Su shook her head as if in disbelief. 'Do you think things are that simple?'

'It was only a kiss,' Mae exclaimed.

'Oh, right. Is that all it was?'

'You know what I mean.'

'No, actually,' said Ji Su. 'I don't. Even you don't know what you mean half the time.'

'It's uni, we're students. Isn't this what students do?' said Mae.

'Jeez, I knew you were naive, but this … Uni isn't the fulfilment of this idea you've built up in your head, Mae. It's not some box-ticking activity.'

'I know that.'

'Do you? Doesn't sound like it. Sounds like you wanted to mess around with me, then you changed your mind and you know what? That's fine. You can. But you can't have it all your way. You can't be friends with someone for months, kiss them, change your mind and think it's all right to go back to the way things were because, oh, look, *that's what students do.*' Ji Su threw her bag over her shoulder. 'You need to grow up.'

The words hit Mae like a small knife, just below her left collarbone.

'I am grown up,' was all she could manage to respond with.

'Yeah, you sound it.'

'But—'

'I'm done here, Mae. All these months I thought we could be friends and then this happened. I don't think I do want to be just friends with you.'

'Do you … do you have feelings for me? Real ones?'

Ji Su let out a small laugh, but not because she found what Mae said funny. 'You're something else. Here I was, buying this whole innocent charade.'

'What charade? I didn't— I couldn't tell.'

'Yeah. Right.'

With that Ji Su opened the door and slammed it shut behind her.

Mae sat on the edge of her bed for ages after Ji Su left, playing the entire scene back in her head. It didn't make sense. She had wanted to kiss Ji Su, be close to her, until of course she didn't. She retraced the steps of her emotional change and of course it all came to the point where she'd pulled back from the kiss. She *had* been attracted to Ji Su. Hadn't she? Well, Mae knew she'd admired her. Perhaps she'd mistaken admiration for attraction. How the hell were you meant to tell one from the other? Especially when someone was being so kind and friendly and listened to everything you had to say? Mae was embarrassed to have dumped everything on Ji Su and then not been able to give her what she wanted in return. The conversation felt unfinished though and Mae was meant to be moving out of her room today. Where would she go? Things couldn't be left like this, surely? She picked up her phone.

I dont wanna lose you. Plz lets talk? Xxx

It was a bit desperate, but then Mae *felt* desperate. It only took a minute for the response from Ji Su to come:

You feel how you feel. But don't message me. If and when I'm ready to speak to you, I'll message.

Mae put her head in her hands. Was that it? She wished she could call one of her sisters to ask them what to do. But none of them would understand. How could they?

She flung her legs on to her bed to lie down and stare at the ceiling when she brushed against an envelope. Her results! One problem had overtaken another potential problem. She wished she could leave it for one more day, but what was the point? Maybe there'd be some good news in there for her? She slid her finger through the flap and took out the transcript, turning it over to the blank page.

'Deep breaths, Mae. Deep breaths. How bad could it be?'

Her heart felt as if it had leapt from her stomach into her throat and a dull thud began to take place in her head. Turning the transcript over she looked at the breakdown of marks, trying to find the crucial detail of her final mark. Then she found it.

'What?' she whispered as she swallowed hard.

She flipped through the pages to see if she'd read it wrong. Maybe that was the result for just one of her modules. That couldn't be right. It didn't matter how hard she looked though, there was no other mark to be found. She looked through the breakdown of each module, the mark for each coursework assignment and every exam she took. She had barely scraped by in some and in others she'd failed so badly that it meant … she couldn't quite believe it … she'd failed completely. How could this be happening? Mae wanted to be sick but instead reached for her phone to call Ji Su. Her finger hovered over her name, but Mae couldn't be that selfish, not when Ji Su had said not to contact her. She put the phone back down and stared at the piece of paper again, as if doing so would change its contents. What did this mean? It was too late to go to the office and ask what happened. Could she sit the exams again? Would she have to retake the whole year? What about the money her parents had spent for her to be able to actually study? What a waste. Mae got up and paced around her room, asking questions to which she had no answer and could get no possible answer. She went out for a walk, wandering the streets, the air warm with summer. People were out in their skirts and shorts, laughing and gossiping in groups. Why couldn't she be one of them? She had no choice but to eventually go back to her dorm, crowds of students celebrating their end of year results as she locked herself up in her room. Would someone come knocking and throw her out? No one new would be moving in and where else could Mae possibly go at this time? She had to speak to someone in the office the following morning. She didn't even bother to change her clothes as she lay down in bed and spent the entire night tossing and turning.

The following day she went straight to the office, not bothering to wash her face or change out of yesterday's clothes.

'Right, well, looks to me you'll have to retake the year,' said the administrative assistant.

'No, come on. Can't I speak to someone else? Isn't there a chance to retake?'

'If you've failed one module and passed all the others, then yes. But looking at your results, I'm afraid that won't be an option.' She must've seen the distressed look on Mae's face. 'Are there any teachers who'd vouch for you? Help you out maybe?'

It was useless. 'No,' said Mae quietly. 'No one.'

She left the office and tried to register the fact that not only had she lost her one friend, but she'd have to repeat the same year all over again. When she got to the dorm there was a notice to say she'd have to leave that day. Things had changed too much too fast and there were no other options for her now.

Mae: Guess wot guys! Im comin home. Get the red carpet out.

Her own fake chirpy message made her cringe, but there was no way she could let on what had happened. How would she be able to look her parents in the face? How could she tell them all, with any dignity at all, that not only had she failed, but that she was, in fact, a failure?

Chapter Seven

Mae tried to come up with all sorts of places she could hover for a while before having to catch her train in the hopes of bumping into Ji Su. She even considered going to the Women's Union to see if she was there, meeting up with any of its members, but then thought it might come across a bit stalkery. She had some pride. Even though it felt pretty battered.

You need to grow up.

Innocent charade.

Charade?

Mae *was* grown up, though. What did Ji Su mean by it? Just because Mae didn't have life experiences she was somehow less of an adult? And *innocent charade*? That was offensive – as if the whole time they'd been hanging out somehow Mae had been deceiving Ji Su. This felt like a gross injustice against her. The more Mae thought about it, the more her sadness turned into anger. Ji Su had thrown accusations at her and she'd been too shocked to even register them, let alone respond. Why *wouldn't* she ask whether Ji Su really had feelings for her? Could she not see the disparity between them? It wasn't long before Mae lost the energy to be angry. She carried her heavy cases, with an even heavier heart, to the station to go back home.

This time her dad came and picked her up.

'My darling bud of Mae has come home at last,' he said. 'What was this staying away all summer? Hmm?' He looked her up and down and cleared his throat. 'You're having too much fun in the uni, aren't you? You are behaving, though, yes? Being my good girl?'

Mae had flashbacks of taking shots of vodka, almost going home with a random man … *kissing another girl.*

'Obvs, Padre.'

Mae tried to give him her most convincing smile, covering her lies and sense of guilt that she'd wasted her parents' money. Even she didn't feel very convinced by it but her dad didn't seem to notice. She sank down in the passenger seat.

When they got to the house everyone was there. All Mae could think was, *great, this is actually Groundhog Day.* They all seemed to pause when they looked at her. Did they know something? Was *failure* written on her forehead? Her dad cleared his throat again – did he have a throat problem or something? – and breaking whatever spell that had them staring at Mae.

'One year down, two to go,' exclaimed Fatti, rocking Adam in one arm. 'I'm so proud of you. Excuse me, I think he's done a poo.'

There was no way she could explain this one to her family. Failing university was one thing, but failing the first year, and for Media Studies? Her dad would be baffled and everyone would know she was incapable of succeeding at anything on her own. She'd always been the baby of the family and it had become clear she couldn't fend for herself. Ji Su was right. She wasn't a grown-up.

Everyone bustled around her, just like they had during Easter, so she went to go to her room. That's when she remembered her room was a shoebox.

'Why do I have to live like this?' exclaimed Mae, stomping back down the stairs into the living room.

'What do you mean?' said her mum. 'He's your brother. Have some respect. And don't you care about your niece and nephew? That they should have a room to stay and be looked after by their grandparents.'

'Hello, I thought adults got dibs on stuff like that?'

'What dibs?' said her mum. 'Behave like an adult then.'

Argh.

'Anyway, you won't be here long, will you? You'll be going back to university so what does it matter?'

'Jay's hardly ever at home, why can't he have the box room?'

'Give your *brother* a box room? He's a man. He needs his space.'

God, if Ji Su could hear her mother now she wouldn't be so quick to defend her whenever Mae complained about her. She looked at her dad for support, but he merely shrugged.

'Men do need space, Mae.'

'*Abba*,' interjected Bubblee. 'That's ridiculous. You know it is.'

'*Thank you*,' replied Mae.

Their mum pointed to both of them. 'See?' she said to her husband. 'This is what happens when you let girls go to university.'

'Maybe we should let Mae be here for more than five minutes before we all start arguing,' replied Farah, giving Zoya to her returning sister.

Zoya started crying. 'What do I do with her?' said Mae.

'Don't worry, she'll get used to you,' said Bubblee laughing, but Mae couldn't deal with someone crying on the outside the way she was crying on the inside so handed her to Bubblee.

'Just going to put my stuff away. In my *hole*,' Mae added, flashing a look at her mum.

She sat in the room, with its curtains still drawn, and looked around the tiny space. She rested her elbow on her suitcase because there was room for little else other than the single bed and a small table next to it. *How is this happening?* She took out her phone, hoping she might have a message from Ji Su, but there was nothing. What had made her want to kiss her? Was it actual attraction or because Ji Su was the only one who seemed to understand Mae? She just made her feel so comfortable. So *understood*.

It was almost time for dinner so Mae decided she'd just get into the pyjamas she'd left at home last time she was here. As she put them on it became a bit of a struggle to get them past her thighs.

'What the ...?' she mumbled, trying to shift them past what was now bulging flesh. '*What* is going on? Seriously? On top of everything else?'

'Why is it so dark in here?' said Bubblee, charging into the room and stretching over the bed to pull the curtains back. She then pressed herself against the wardrobe because of the lack of room for her and a struggling Mae.

'What are you doing?' she asked.

'My stupid pyjamas.'

By this time Farah and Fatti were at the door as well, though unable to come into the actual room. Mae pulled her legs out of the pyjamas and threw them on the bed. 'Mum's only gone and shrunk them in the wash. I loved that pair as well.'

There was a collective pause as Mae rummaged for the leggings she'd just taken off.

'Are you actually joking?' said Bubblee.

'What? Something wrong with leggings?'

'Mae ...' began Farah.

'*Yes?*' said Mae, getting increasingly agitated with all these people around her and now her favourite pyjamas being ruined.

Everything was ruined.

'Do you think it might be something else?' said Fatti.

'What are you on about?' said Mae. 'Fats, do you think they can be stretched back to their normal size? Ugh. I really do love them, you know.'

'Mae,' exclaimed Bubblee, almost letting out a laugh. 'Your pyjamas haven't shrunk, you idiot. You've only gone and gained ...' Bubblee looked at her up and down, 'like, fifteen pounds.'

Mae's face fell. 'What? Shut up. I have not.'

She looked around to Farah and Fatti for support but it didn't seem to be coming. Fatti looked a little distressed. Farah had her 'mum' look, not saying a word, waiting for Mae to come to her own conclusion.

'You guys are idiots,' said Mae. 'Except for you, Fats, obvs. How have *I* gained fifteen pounds?'

Bubblee picked up the discarded pyjamas. 'These are *not* shrunken. And nor are you, quite frankly.'

'*Bubblee*,' said Fatti. 'You still look great, Mae. Don't worry.'

'Except that's not the point,' said Farah. 'You're the last person I expected to fill your body with junk. You were always so conscientious with your kale smoothies and spinach concoctions.'

'That was weird,' replied Mae. 'I didn't know what I was missing out on.'

'Yeah but ...' began Fatti. 'You were *so* obsessed with it, Mae.'

Mae recalled the carrot sticks she'd offer to her sisters when looking at them in disgust as they put another onion bhaji in their mouth; the way her dad would stockpile the necessary fruits and vegetables for her; how keenly she looked for gluten-free products. That Mae and that lifestyle felt like another's. Almost as soon as she got to uni it all fell through. She'd been out one night, on her own, feeling so hungry and despondent at her lack of friends, when she passed a kebab shop. Her stomach had been growling and she thought: *one doner kebab won't hurt*.

And it didn't.

'Are they always this delicious?' she asked the Al-Kebabish's owner in wonder, who in turn looked at her, confused.

After that day, she never looked at another bag of kale.

'And now …' continued Farah.

'You've gone completely the other way,' Farah finished. She paused. 'Are you okay? I mean, are you happy?'

That's when it dawned on Mae as she looked down at her body. Had she really gained so much weight? She wore leggings most of the time, and most of her skirts had elastic waists. Her tops were never fitted.

'Oh my God, are you saying I'm fat?' exclaimed Mae.

'Not *fat* exactly,' replied Farah. 'Just, you know, healthier than you were before.'

'It's fine,' said Bubblee. 'Chill out. Fatti's not the only chunkster in the family now.'

'I mean, *are* you chunky?' wondered Farah, tilting her head sideways and taking in the view of Mae's bare legs.

'*No*,' added Fatti, having gone a shade of red. 'There's nothing wrong with some extra curves, anyway.'

Mae dropped down on her bed, but ended up sitting on the lid of the suitcase. 'Does that mean I have to chuck out the pyjamas?'

'I'll take them, don't worry,' replied Bubblee, picking them up. 'They are quite fun.'

'It's all those doner kebabs I've been having,' replied Mae.

'Guess you'll have to give them up,' replied Farah.

Mae snorted. 'As if.'

'That's my girl,' said Fatti, pushing past Bubblee to give Mae a kiss on the head.

Despite her sisters' looks, Mae didn't care that she'd gained weight – aside from the fact that her clothes weren't fitting her. Ji Su had liked her, after all, just the way she was. Perhaps Mae's attraction to her was for this very reason: she saw no need for Mae to change or be something other than what she was. And it was a relief. Mae leaned her head against Fatti's and wanted to cry and tell her everything that had happened.

'Oh, Adam's crying. Time for his feed.'

With which Fatti manoeuvred past Bubblee, almost elbowing her on the way out – by accident – and went to check on her baby.

'Come on then, chunky,' added Bubblee. 'Let's celebrate

your return and end of year success.' Mae managed to get up as Bubblee put her arm around her. 'I really am proud of you. You survived the jungle that is the first year. Now you can survive anything.'

Mae wasn't quite sure that she'd survive the summer with her family when she woke up to the sounds of babies crying.

'Ow,' she exclaimed as she hit her head on the shelf above her when she got up.

No space was safe in this room. It was eleven o'clock in the morning but she pulled the duvet over herself. Five minutes later the door opened and her mum exclaimed: 'Do you know what time it is? Your abba and I have to go shopping. Fatti has gone to pick up Ash's children because he's working and Farah has a dentist appointment so they've left the babies with me. You look after them.'

'What?' Mae reared her head from her refuge.

'You think you'll just sit around all summer and not help? Mae, university has made you selfish. Think about the family.'

Oh, *now* her mum was talking about helping the family? What about the fact that her mum and dad had kept Mae awake with all the noises coming from their bedroom? Mae couldn't help but let out a reflexive moan at the memory.

'Don't make that noise.'

'I could say the same to you,' mumbled Mae.

'What?'

'Nothing,' said Mae, pushing her duvet to one side, reminding herself that her parents had funded her first year at uni and she owed them now. Big time. 'What could I possibly have to say?' she sighed.

She went downstairs and looked at Zoya and Adam on their playmat.

'What do you do with these babies then?' she asked, putting a piece of generously buttered toast in her mouth. 'Can't they just lie there and, like, *chill* for the rest of the day?'

'Here,' said her mum, shoving a piece of paper into Mae's hands. 'Instructions from Farah and Fatti. You girls and your modern ways. We never had to give people lists before.'

Then her mum spouted off a list of things that had to be done: feeding times, when to change the babies' nappies, where the nappies were. Zoya had a sore bottom so extra Sudocrem. Adam keeps throwing up after food so feed him slowly. On and on the list went until her mum's words became white noise.

'Are you listening?' said her mum.

'With rapture,' replied Mae, slumping on the sofa. 'Are you going shopping or leaving the country?'

'We are having lunch out.'

'Excuse me?'

Their parents never ate out. They just didn't believe

in paying money for food that was made by a stranger when they could prepare something better at home. And cheaper. Mae's dad had meandered down the stairs, kneeled on the floor to kiss both the babies, taken his wife's hand and left with her, giving Mae a vague wave goodbye. She watched in disbelief as she heard the front door shut.

'The world has gone topsy-turvy, kids,' said Mae, bending over to look at their blank faces. 'Sorry you have to see all this.'

Zoya apparently was also sorry because she scrunched up her face, turning red, before she let out a wail. This set Adam off so Mae had to abandon her half-eaten toast and pick them both up.

'This,' she said, barely able to hear herself beyond the cries, 'is my life.'

Nothing much changed over the next week and Mae found herself not only becoming a babysitter – without pay – but also a chauffeur to Ilyaas and Aima, Fatti's stepchildren. Aima was only a few years younger than Mae but seemed to think she had the answer to most of the world's fashion problems.

'You know leggings *aren't* flattering, don't you? *Just* saying.'

Most of Aima's statements were signed off with 'just saying' and there were times when Mae wished she could respond with *just shut up*. She came pretty close to it a few times. Ilyaas, a year and a half younger than Aima, was less offensive because he tended to stare out of windows and usually just grunted in response to questions.

'Hey, cool sweatshirt,' Mae would say, walking into Fatti's house, and he'd stare at her before shrugging and walking away.

'Verbose, that one,' said Mae to Fatti when the teenagers were in their respective rooms, watching things on their laptop or listening to music.

Fatti gave a deep sigh, shaking the baby monitor to check it was working. Adam was napping. Mae could've done with a few of those herself, what with her parents keeping her up most of the night.

'It's not easy,' said Fatti, looking rather exhausted. 'They're good children, really.'

Mae raised her eyebrows.

'They *are*. I mean, I'm sure they are. Deep down,' added Fatti. 'But it's hard to know what the boundaries are. Ash's at work most of the time and I'm with the baby and they hardly leave their rooms. When they do, they walk around looking so bored I try and suggest things for them to do. Aima has a problem with anything I come up with and Ilyaas just says, "Whatever".'

'Yeah, Aima-loser,' said Mae.

Fatti flicked Mae's arm. 'Stop it.'

'And s-ilyaas.'

'Mae …'

'*Just saying.*'

Fatti laughed despite herself. 'She never finishes a sentence without it. What is that?'

'Idiocy,' Mae replied.

She sat and listened to Fatti's mounting woes: what if Ash blamed Fatti if the children weren't happy? How could she get them to like her? What was a stepmother's role when the children were grown up? It'd be nice for Adam to have a good relationship with Aima and Ilyaas but they hardly looked at him, let alone played with him. Mae nodded where necessary, interjected where appropriate – and sometimes where it wasn't appropriate – and all in all tried to listen to her sister's problems without thinking about her own. *Do not think about the disaster that is your own life; instead concentrate on others* had become her motto.

Mae had no idea what to do about her results, Ji Su – or *anything* – so she tried not to think about it. It was easier said than done. She still found herself tossing and turning at night, waking feeling groggy and anxious, not realising why, until the reality of her life hit her each morning like some kind of recurring nightmare. As Fatti talked, Mae waited for her to ask her questions about how being at home felt, but, as if on cue, Adam started to cry, just as the phone rang. Mae answered it since Fatti was preoccupied.

'Oh good, Mae. Just the person I wanted actually. Where's Fatti?' asked Ash.

'Tending to the baby. Making sure it's alive, et cetera.'

Ash paused. 'Anyway, would you mind driving Ilyaas and Aima down to the office? Thought it might be nice for them to hang out here for a bit – see how a driving school operates.' These adults, they really had no idea about what teenagers wanted to do during their holidays, did they? 'And then I'd take them into town for a bite to eat.'

'Sure, bro-in-law, sounds riveting. And it's not as if I have anything better to do.'

Ash was too distracted by another call to detect the sarcasm. 'You're a star. So good to have someone to help Fatti.' He paused again. 'Has she said anything? To you?'

Mae took a deep breath. 'What would she say to me? It's Fatti. She's worried about everyone but herself.'

Or me.

'Hmm,' said Ash. 'Thanks, Mae. Got to go. I'll see you later.'

Aima refused to go. When Mae entered the room she looked up at her, phone in hand, as if Mae had just done the most socially unacceptable thing by interrupting her conversation.

'Driving school? Really? Not exactly the height of excitement,' said Aima. 'Just saying.'

'Of course you are,' replied Mae, bowing out of the room, closing the door and sticking her finger up at it.

She turned around to see Ilyaas standing there, watching her.

'Oh. That was ...' Mae brought her middle finger to her face as if inspecting it. 'Just scratched myself.'

'On a door?' he said.

He so rarely spoke Mae forgot his voice was that of a man's rather than a boy's.

'Splintery,' she replied.

They stood like this in the passage until he said: 'I have to go with you to Dad's office.'

Ilyaas didn't have to roll his eyes for the disdain to show.

'New trainers?' asked Mae, looking down at his luminous Nikes. 'Nice.'

He shrugged. 'Whatever.'

'So, last year of school next year?' said Mae, stopping at the traffic lights. 'Free to go crazy then.'

'Yeah, real crazy,' muttered Ilyaas.

Mae gripped the steering wheel harder. 'Want to travel or anything?'

He scoffed and looked out of the window. 'What, like everyone else?'

Mae nodded. 'True words, my friend. True words.' It took a few moments before Mae realised he was actually looking at her. 'I mean, it's hardly original, is it?' added Mae.

Ilyaas turned back to look out of the window again. 'Exactly.'

Fatti: Good luck with the date tonight Bubs.

Mae: Poor guy. tell him 2 say l8rs to his self-worth.

Farah: You forgot your keys. Don't ring the doorbell when you get back, you'll wake the baby.

The following day Mae had to first listen to Farah complain that Bubblee was acting like a dad that babysits, then to Fatti that Ash had clearly said something to Aima who came down in the afternoon and sat in the living room, on her phone, pretending she was listening to Fatti, while simultaneously rolling her eyes. Followed by Bubblee's account of her third date that week.

'To be honest, he was too good-looking for his own good. Doesn't leave much room for the imagination, does it?' said Bubblee.

'Mmm,' replied Mae, lying in her single bed, scrolling through Twitter.

'That's not to say he wasn't good at other stuff.'

Mae put her phone down and looked at her sister's face with an emerging smile.

'*Just saying*,' added Bubblee.

Mae laughed. 'How's Farah feel about this gallivanting, young lady? Also, I'm telling Mum on you.'

'I never thought dating would be fun. No strings attached, just random conversations, other stuff, and now and again I even meet people worth listening to.' Bubblee paused. 'You dating anyone? At uni?'

Mae's heart began to race. If anyone was going to understand, it was Bubblee. She paused and wondered where she would even begin. Ji Su's hands in Mae's hair and lips on her mouth. How nice it had felt until it didn't and how confusing it was. How Mae had lost a friend because of it. But too much time passed and Mae's courage eventually failed her. It was one thing speaking to Bubblee about boys, but about a *girl*? Mae wasn't sure that even Bubblee would be prepared for that.

'Nah. Who has the time?' Mae replied.

'That's right. You work your arse off and do something with your life,' said Bubblee. 'Relationships and distractions can wait.'

As Bubblee left the room Mae looked at Ji Su's updated WhatsApp picture. She was wearing a yellow T-shirt that said: *You Don't Own Me.* Mae listened to the hubbub downstairs until, inevitably, someone called her name to help with the babies. She had little choice but to go and answer.

Chapter Eight

It turned out that Ilyaas liked spending time with his dad more than anyone – even Ash – could have predicted. Of course, the duty of ferrying Ilyaas around had fallen on Mae. *You don't have babies. You don't have a full-time job. Take Dad's car. Shouldn't he enjoy being retired and spending time with Mum?* It was a mug's game being a student. It transpired that your time wasn't your own, whether you wanted to spend it in bed, on your phone, or just walking aimlessly around, didn't matter.

On the plus side, these journeys to and from town with Ilyaas weren't as bad as Mae had thought they'd be. Being out in the fresh air, she supposed, was better than rotting away in a box room. Plus, there was only so much she could check her phone for messages from Ji Su or pretend to coo over her niece and nephew before being lumbered with looking after them.

'Oh, this song!' exclaimed Mae, putting the volume up on her car.

'You like it?'

'Kidding me? *Love* it. Suppose you're too cool for it,' said Mae.

'Nah. It's all right, actually. You don't have bad taste. For a girl.'

Mae pointed her finger at him. 'Don't go making those sexist comments in front of your aunt Bubblee. She'll shred whatever of yours comes into reach to pieces.'

It was the second time Ilyaas had laughed at Mae, although he tried to hide it.

'Well, at least you like to work with your dad,' said Mae. 'Could be worse. You could spend your time driving people around. Wink, wink.'

'You're a geek,' said Ilyaas.

'And proud.'

Mae turned right at the pedestrian crossing, admiring the way the sun shone through the clouds, bathing the green hills in its light. What was she doing with her life? She'd been home for over a week already and no clarity had come to her about what to do or what to tell her family. How to tell her parents that she'd wasted their money. Mae felt her stomach clench, a bout of nausea hitting her. Whenever her family mentioned how simple it must be to be a student, a wave of anxiety would well in the pit of her stomach. How was she meant to move forward? Every time she thought of it she was faced with nothing but a brick wall, and that just made her want to bang her head against it.

'If a little adrift,' she added out loud without meaning to.

Mae went to change radio stations, trying to pretend that slip of the tongue hadn't happened. They approached Ash's office and Mae parked up outside it, settled between a post office and a coffee shop.

'Well, Godspeed for another day, my friend,' said Mae.

Ilyaas went to get out of the car but paused. 'There are jobs and stuff.'

'Hmm?'

'You could help out with Dad. Here.'

'Oh. Well, I don't think he needs any more help.'

Ilyaas responded with another shrug and stepped out of the car.

On the drive back home Mae wondered whether it was time to stop moping around, doing things for others, and maybe get out of the house and start doing something for herself. None of her sisters really did summer jobs, not even Bubblee unless it was something at an art gallery, but if Mae carried on like this she might actually go mad. More than that, it was time for her to make some money to at least try and pay her parents back. The panic in her chest was rising, but then she caught a sign for the stables that she often passed. The horses that were trotting around the fields with people riding them always pleased her. For some reason or another she decided to pull into the stables because the alternative was to go home and sit around, brooding, trying to push back the anxiety that seemed to be the most constant thing in her life.

Getting out of the car, she saw a woman tending to a horse. Mae stood for a while just watching the way the horse's mouth would twitch, and the woman would calm it with the palm of her hand; or he'd move his hooves, his tail swaying gently. It was when the woman turned around that Mae realised she'd been staring at her.

'Sorry, didn't see you there. Can I help you?' the woman asked.

'Oh, no, I just … I saw the horses and thought they looked nice, you know?'

The woman smiled and Mae noticed how broad her shoulders were. She was almost envious of them.

'Don't know many people who don't like them,' she said. 'And I judge the ones who don't. Do you ride?'

'Oh, me? No,' Mae laughed. 'I mean, I wouldn't say no, but I don't think I've got the, you know, grace for it.'

'That's what learning is for,' replied the woman.

'Can I …?' Mae walked towards the horse with her hand out.

'Of course. Ginger's a little feisty, but doesn't mind people, as long as they don't annoy him.'

'I know how that feels,' said Mae. 'Hey, Ginge,' she added, patting him on his muzzle.

''*Er*. It's Ging*er*,' the woman replied. 'And I'm Alison.'

'Oh, sorry. I'm Mae.' She turned to the horse again. 'All right, boy?' she said, looking at Ginger's wide, clear eyes, the flecks of white on his forehead.

There was something so calming about him as she

stroked his shoulder. The beating of her heart seemed to calm down and Mae understood why some people might feel that animals make better companions than humans.

'Do you want to take him for a ride?' the woman asked.

'What? Oh, no, thanks. I mean, yeah, but don't I have to book and stuff?'

'Why don't we call it a free trial run, and if you like it, you can come back?'

'Really?' asked Mae. 'Just like that?'

'Just like that,' Alison replied.

There wasn't much else to think about.

'You'll need proper boots.'

Alison went into the stable and came out with riding essentials, which Mae put on, feeling both excited and nervous. Getting on the horse was a little trickier than she thought it would be. Whenever she'd watched it on television they made it look so simple, but she was clearly as graceful as she had imagined, and she hadn't imagined much.

'You just need to pull yourself up,' said Alison.

I am pulling myself up, Mae wanted to say. It took a few more tries and a push from Alison to help Mae get her leg over Ginger. She slid her feet into the stirrups and felt a little steadier.

'There you go,' said Alison, showing her how to hold the reins and adjust the stirrups and then leading her into a gentle walk.

Mae had to grab on to the reins as she pressed her legs to the horse's sides, surprised at the force of the animal, but once she got into her stride she felt more secure, more in control.

'Just give him a little kick if he slows down, pull back the rein if he's too fast,' said Alison.

Moving through the open fields seemed to open up Mae's senses as she took in the fresh air. She felt a rush of love for this animal she'd known for about five seconds. She patted Ginger's shoulder, whispering to him, telling him what a good boy he was, feeling instinctively when to pull the rein, when to press into him.

'Do you live nearby?' asked Alison.

'Not far.'

'What do you do?' asked Alison.

How to answer a question to which Mae barely knew the answer? So much of what a person did was attached to who they were, so did this mean Mae was nothing?

'I'm at uni,' Mae finally said.

She couldn't bring herself to tell the truth. Alison began to ask questions about it: which uni, what did she study, how did she find it, what did she want to do with her life? It occurred to Mae that had her family actually asked her similar questions, she'd have very little to say – perhaps, right now, she should be grateful for their indifference. They'd made a round with Ginger and Alison was leading them back to the stable. Mae wanted it to last longer, to go around the fields on her own, to maybe get Ginger to go a bit faster and be lost in the comfort of her own thoughts.

'Here we are,' said Alison.

Getting off the horse was almost as stressful as trying to get on, but Mae managed to stumble to the ground and turned to face Ginger.

'Thanks, boy. That was good going, I reckon. Fancy it again some time?'

Ginger let out a snort, which made Mae laugh.

'I'm going to take that as a yes, because otherwise you've hurt my feelings.'

'You're welcome to come back whenever you want,' said Alison. 'If you're interested in finding out more, I'm around. Or there's George who works Wednesdays and Fridays.'

'Yeah, I'd really like that,' replied Mae. 'How did you get into it?'

Alison explained how she grew up on a farm in the Highlands. Her whole family were riders and when she moved here she worked towards opening up a stable.

'Oh, you own this?'

'Yep. My pride and joy,' replied Alison.

Mae looked around the stable and thought what a remarkable achievement it was – to have had a family like that and then for it to inspire a whole lifestyle.

'You did this all on your own?' she asked.

'Well …' Alison said. 'My vision, but I had help. As you usually do. But the nuts and bolts of it was me, yes. Wasn't easy, but nothing worth anything ever is.'

They stood around talking for a little longer as Mae had so many questions, questions she never thought she'd have about horses, but eventually Alison had to go and do her job.

'Well, I hope I see you again,' said Alison, shaking Mae's hand.

'Me too.'

It occurred to Mae that she wasn't really doing anything during the summer – wouldn't it be nice to help out here? Make some money as well as do something she enjoyed? The idea filled her with excitement – doing something *useful*.

'Do you have any jobs here? For me? I don't even mind cleaning out stables, if I have to.'

'Afraid not. I'm always happy to give new people a go, but all the jobs are taken right now.'

'Oh,' said Mae, barely able to hold back her disappointment.

Alison looked at her with sympathy. 'Before you go … wait there.'

She left Mae and came back minutes later with a book in hand.

'This is one of my favourite books about horses,' said Alison, showing a copy of something called *Heads Up – Heels Down*. 'It's old but very good. Take it.'

Mae hesitated. 'You're giving it to me?'

'Well, I'd like it back, but it's always nice to see young people take an interest in horses. More people should.'

'Thanks,' said Mae, taking it. 'I promise I'll bring it back.'

'Good,' replied Alison. 'I hope it means you'll be back for another go on the horse.'

Mae nodded. 'This time with a proper booking.'

They shook hands again and Mae left, her heart feeling lighter than it had done in a long time, her legs feeling weirdly exerted. Odd how just sitting on a horse was so much work. When she walked into the house she saw her mum and dad pull away from each other, flushed with embarrassment. *Oh God*. That was it. Mae couldn't stay in the house and do nothing for the rest of the summer. That was enough moping about. If you wanted things to change then you had to change them. She had to find a job, or else she'd quite literally die of nausea.

'And how do you feel about babies?'

Mae squeezed her hands together, looking over the madcap desk at the woman opposite her. There were all types of coloured papers strewn over it, pens and pencils scattered everywhere, a box of plain white mugs in the corner that looked in danger of toppling over.

'Great,' exclaimed Mae. 'I mean, I love them.'

White lies were essential when it came to interviews, of course. The woman ran her fingers through her brown, frizzy hair. Mae noticed there was blue and yellow paint on her fingers.

'We've got an assistant but summer's a busy time so

we need some more help. Can you handle them?' she asked. 'Because we get all sorts in here. And mothers need to feel that their babies, the fruit of their daily efforts, are looked after, not just because they're paying you, but because you genuinely *care*. It's a joyous thing, to imprint your baby's foot or hand on a mug like this and sip from it for the rest of your life.'

Not being sure how to respond to this, Mae nodded with as much passion as she could. 'Yeah. Of course.'

Maybe her mum had a point. Maybe modern living was weird.

'But if they know the baby's been distressed while it's happened, it mars the experience. Quite rightly.'

'Mhmm. Totes. I mean, *totally*.'

It was when the woman opened the door to several screaming babies, paint all over a mat and the walls, and a bedraggled-looking assistant, that Mae said she realised that she was late for another interview and ran out of the place as fast as she could.

The next interview was for becoming a promotional jockey. It wasn't working in a stable but she'd get to hang out with some horses, at least. She'd learn things and be around people who might know more than her. Except when she went in, the man who opened the door stared at her for a while.

'The ad was for someone petite,' he said.

Mae looked down at herself. 'I'm five foot two.'

He sighed and let her walk in. 'So, er …' he shuffled

around some papers, not looking up at her. 'Any experience?'

'Being a promotional jockey?' she asked. 'Yeah, loads.'

Mae laughed, but he didn't return the favour.

'What hours can you do?'

'Whatever you want. I'm on uni summer break, so …' she spread out her hands, 'free as a bird. Or a horse. Although, horses aren't really free, are they? But I love them. Horses. They're like, amazing, right?'

He glanced up at her and sighed again. 'Listen, you seem nice and all, but the uniforms are small, and I think you might, let's say, struggle.'

'Why?' asked Mae.

'We mean petite in height *and* weight.'

Mae had to swallow hard. 'Are you saying I'm fat?'

'No, no. It's not that, I'm not a sizeist.' He looked at her in horror as Mae just stared at him. 'My wife's a little on the large side,' he continued, stuttering. 'I don't mind it at all … Important to have a woman with curves. Not that I'm suggesting anything here.' He went red as he stumbled over his words.

Mae wasn't sure whether to be annoyed at him or to laugh.

'But the uniforms are already in and we won't have anything that fits you.'

'Right.' Mae looked at her hands, feeling ashamed of her weight gain. If she were still clean-eating she'd have got this job. But then she thought what Ji Su would have to say about it and blurted out, 'So, you just thought everyone who applied would be skinny?' Mae sucked in her cheeks to show her point. 'And it's not like we ride the horse, is it?'

This was interesting. Perhaps Mae did let too many things go. Perhaps she should be more assertive.

He cleared his throat. 'No, but, well, like I said, the uniforms are already in. You understand what a jockey is, don't you? They're diminutive in frame and—'

Mae couldn't believe it. She was being *mansplained* to.

'All right there, Jock prof, I know what jockeys are, thanks.' She got up, grabbing her shoulder bag from the floor. 'You know where you can stick your small-minded, fat-shaming jocks.'

With which she stormed out of the room, slamming the door behind her.

It had been a good enough story to tell her sisters that evening and at least they laughed.

'Poor guy,' said Fatti, her arms free of Adam as Ash was changing his nappy.

Bubblee looked proud. 'Well done, Mae. Told him what was what. Uni's making you feistier.'

Bubblee's phone buzzed as Farah stared at her typing a message to someone. Somehow sensing something, Bubblee looked over the phone at Farah and raised her eyebrows.

'Someone new or old?' asked Farah, feigning indifference. And not very well, in Mae's opinion.

'Someone irrelevant,' answered Bubblee, getting back to her phone.

'But relevant enough to message?' replied Farah.

Bubblee shrugged. 'If you say so.'

Fatti and Mae exchanged looks.

'What other jobs could I do?' said Mae. 'I seriously need the money.'

Bubblee looked up from her phone again. 'Why seriously?'

Mae hesitated. 'Oh, you know. Fund the student lifestyle. Everyone works, isn't it?'

'I'd take advantage of Mum and Dad helping you with money and concentrate on your studies. Don't get me wrong, working is good for you, but make the most of what you're getting,' Bubblee added, getting back to her phone.

Mae swallowed hard and tried to smile.

'God, can you put that thing down for two minutes?' exclaimed Farah.

Then they heard Zoya crying and Farah raised her eyebrows towards Bubblee.

'I'll go then, shall I?' said Bubblee, getting up and leaving to check on their daughter.

'Maybe we should pay you to look after the kids,' said Farah, still looking towards the door from where Bubblee had left.

'Not enough money in the world,' mumbled Mae.

What Mae really wanted to do was tell Ji Su about

what had happened. That night when she lay in bed she went through Ji Su's Facebook page, feeling a twinge of envy at anyone who was getting to spend their time with her, while Mae was lying there, feeling her brain rot with every day she spent at home. She knew she shouldn't but maybe enough time had passed? She tapped on Ji Su's WhatsApp.

> Hey. How ru?

It was impressive that Mae only spent seventy-two minutes staring at the phone, waiting for a response. Finally, she decided it was time to go to sleep. Tomorrow's job interview had to go better.

Mae had got the bus, taking her over an hour with waiting time and changes, and walked towards the booth to enter the amusement park. *A World of Adventures* was written in yellow and pink, overarching the entrance and flickering with lights. She noticed three of the bulbs were broken. There were only two glossy red booths so she chose the one with the shortest queue.

'Heyyyyyy!'

Mae took a step back from the curly-haired blonde, waving a pamphlet in her face. The gloss of the paint on the booth, she noticed up close, was looking kind of worn.

'All alone? No worries! We've got loads of animals to keep you company while you wait for your rides.'

'Huh?' said Mae.

'Not *real* animals. Duh.' Crazy Curly rolled her eyes, which seemed to have a knock-on effect on her breasts, which rolled about in unison. 'There's Brave Brian the Bear, Zippy Zebra, Playful Pig and more.'

'I'm here for a job interview,' explained Mae.

Crazy Curly's face dropped. 'What? Ugh. Could've said. Oi! Bri! Another interview.'

Bri, an acne-ridden teenager, was in the booth next door, which was next to a wooden hut. He pointed towards it without looking up at Mae.

'Do I go in?' she asked.

He looked up at her. 'No, you just stand outside.'

For a moment Mae thought he was serious.

'Course you go in,' he said, looking at Crazy Curly and rolling his eyes.

'Oh, right.'

God. What nice people, thought Mae as she knocked tentatively on the door.

'Come in,' someone barked.

She stepped into the hut with its wooden beams that didn't seem to go with the plain white desk the man was sitting behind.

'Mae Amir?' he said.

She nodded as she took a seat opposite him.

'What kind of name is Amir?'

'Bengali.'

'Hmm.'

He made a note on a piece of paper.

'Experience?'

'Er … I'm a people person,' said Mae, hopefully.

She was getting good at lying in her quest for a job. Anyway, how could you get experience if no one employed you?

His eyes flicked through the limited information Mae had provided on her CV before he turned the piece of paper over to see that it was blank.

'Summer job, eh?'

Mae smiled her most radiant smile and nodded. 'I learn quick and I love the amusement park here. Family-friendly and all.'

'Hmm, yeah. You people are keen on that stuff, aren't you? Very well. And you can work weekends? And during the day as well? Do you get sick a lot? Can't abide by sickness.'

'I can work whenever, and no, I'm as healthy as anything.'

He made a few more notes on a piece of paper.

'When can you start?'

'Soon as you ask,' replied Mae, crossing her fingers under the chair.

He paused and looked at her. 'All right then. You've got yourself a job.'

Mae couldn't believe it. That easily? 'Really?'

'You want it, don't you?' he said, eyebrows knitted.

Mae nodded vigorously. 'Yes. Of course. I can't believe it,' she exclaimed, barely able to contain her joy.

'No pissing about, eh? And smile,' he said, showing a set of nicotine-stained teeth. 'You get fired for wearing a mug like it's January, okay? See Leanne out there? At the booth? Curly-haired blondie? That's what we want for our customers.'

Mae wanted to say that Leanne was kind of terrifying, but perhaps it wasn't the time for that.

She nodded. 'Yeah, of course.'

'Got a shift for you tomorrow, nine thirty to six thirty. We open at ten. *Don't be late*. You'll need to change.'

Oh God. The bus into town where she had to change over only came once an hour. It meant she'd have to leave at like seven in the morning. He opened a drawer and asked: 'What are you? Medium? Large?'

'Medium. I think.'

Taking out some clothes wrapped in plastic, he threw it at her. 'You'll wear that when you're not in costume.'

'Costume?'

He stared at her. Mae waited for him to answer. Had he heard her?

'Well?' he said. 'I've got a park to run now. Does it look like I have time to answer inane questions?'

'Oh, right. Okay.' Mae was unsure for a few moments before she got up and walked to the door. 'Well. See you tomorrow then,' she added, looking back. 'Sorry, I didn't catch your name.'

'Barry,' he said, without looking up. 'And you'll do well to remember it.'

Ha! Who'd have thought that getting a job could be that easy. Mae felt rather uplifted at this success so on the way home she decided to stop by Ash's driving school.

'Young man,' she said to Ilyaas, who was doing some filing in the back room. 'I owe you an ice cream. Or whatever you crazy kids eat and drink nowadays.'

'You're only a few years older than me,' he said.

'Whatever. Congratulate me, please, I got myself a job.'

Mae went to high five him and he put his hand up to her.

'Oh, good,' said Ash, walking in.

Ilyaas went back to his filing.

'What's the job then?'

Mae filled them in and Ash said to Ilyaas: 'Maybe you and Aima could spend the day there?'

'Bro-in-law, I don't think it's exactly their idea of cool, you know?'

'Nah, nah. It sounds all right,' replied Ilyaas.

Ash couldn't have beamed more had Ilyaas just announced he'd decided to become a brain surgeon. He left the two in the room as Mae chatted about the park and threw a packet of Skittles towards him.

'Hope you brush your teeth before bed,' she said.

'You don't have to sound like my mum,' he replied.

'Of course I do. Or my sister'll get blamed for your rotting teeth.'

She opened her own packet of Skittles and popped

several in her mouth. Ji Su hadn't messaged her back, but now, at least, she wouldn't have to dwell on it, stuck in a dingy room or babysitting. Now she had a job.

When she left the office to go back home she had a spring in her step as she got on the bus, feeling that the cloud of failure was still hovering, but at least it wasn't raining down on her quite as hard.

Chapter Nine

The following morning Mae changed into her uniform, which was a bit on the snug side, and made her way to the park in her dad's car. He'd agreed she could use it when working. Her mum had looked at him, as if in doubt. She never had liked the idea of any of her daughters working – said it gave them too much independence, but they'd been through three daughters and Mae was able to get away with things Fatti, Farah and Bubblee only dreamt of. Her dad, however, always had been more amenable and handed over his car keys as he whispered in Mae's ear: 'Because I trust you.'

She felt a rush of love and affection for her dad as she said thanks and took the keys.

Mae got to work half an hour early to show how conscientious a worker she was going to be. Unfortunately, Barry was ten minutes late and Mae found Leanne and Bri a little hard to communicate with. The other people working there hung about, sitting on the brick wall, tapping away on their phones and they didn't look like they were in the mood to be disturbed, while Leanne and Bri were both engaged in the kind of flirtation that Mae found nauseating.

'Go get me a Coke from the machine,' said Leanne.

'Get it yourself, and get one for me too,' replied Bri.

'I got you one yesterday.'

'So? I'm the king and you're my servant.'

It went on like this until Barry came bounding towards the entrance, walking past a few customers who had got there before opening time.

'Damn car,' he exclaimed. 'None of you numbnuts know how to open this place?'

'You've got the keys and codes, 'member?' Leanne rolled her eyes.

'You're lucky you're good with the customers or I'd fire you.'

Leanne looked over at Mae. 'Whatever. He's been saying that every year for three years straight.'

Leanne and Bri took up their posts in their booths, while everyone set about to do their respective tasks.

'So?' said Mae, following Barry into the wooden hut. 'What do you want me to do?'

He looked at her, as if surprised that she was in there.

'What do you think?'

I don't know. That's why I'm asking.

'Oh, for God's sake. Am I going to have to handhold you the whole time?' he said.

'But you—'

'Where the hell is that Henrietta? I swear I'd kill her

if she wasn't going to burst into tears every time I spoke to her. Here, take this.'

That's when Barry took out two furry brown items. Mae would've been confused if she hadn't seen the distinct horse's head attached to one of them.

'What—'

'What do you think? You're the back end of Happy Horse.'

'What?' said Mae.

Barry looked at her. 'The. Back. End. Of. Happy. Horse.'

'Oh.'

He threw both pieces to her and she almost fell back from the weight of them.

'Find that bloody Henrietta and tell her if she doesn't sort out her time-keeping I'll fire her before she can whimper her way out of it.'

Mae was too disconcerted, both by the horse and Barry's manner, to ask any further questions. Where was she meant to go? What was she meant to do? Who the hell was Henrietta and where was Mae meant to find her? She dragged the horse's costume to Leanne's booth and asked who the other half of her horse might be and where she might find her.

'Probably crying in a toilet somewhere. Look in the ladies' room.'

The sun had begun to press down upon the day and Mae was feeling the heat of both that, the task ahead, and the polyester outfit she was wearing, not to mention the horse's costume she was carrying around. It took her twenty minutes to find the ladies' room, and just as Leanne had said, there was indeed a girl, wiping her eyes in front of the mirror.

'Henrietta?' said Mae.

She looked over at Mae then at the costume and burst into a fresh set of sobs. Another ten minutes was spent trying to calm her down.

'You're so nice,' said Henrietta after having recovered somewhat. 'That-that-that *pig* Barry. Don't let him bring you down.'

Mae was too distracted by the fact that Henrietta was about as tall as her so wondered how this was going to work.

'Do you think we should go?' she asked, handing Henrietta the back end of the costume, hoping to get away with it.

'Oh no. I'm always the head,' she replied, taking it from Mae.

'Right.'

Henrietta put on the horse's head as Mae took the remainder material and slipped it over herself, sliding her legs into the back end of the horse.

'Am I just meant to stay bent over?' said Mae, distressed already at how dark and uncomfortable it was.

'Yep. Can you shift back a bit? God, it's so hot. I get really faint when it's hot. Do you have any water?'

Henrietta then took something out of her pocket and Mae heard the twisting of a wrapper. 'My sugar gets really low so I have to keep boiled sweets with me. In case.'

'Right.'

Without warning Henrietta then strode towards the bathroom's exit, forcing Mae to trot behind her, almost losing her balance.

'You're going to have to keep up, you know,' said Henrietta. 'I bruise really easily.'

By the end of the day, Mae stank, her feet ached, and she thought she might be on her way to being the hunchback of the amusement park. Although, apparently, how Mae felt wasn't nearly as bad as Henrietta's eczema, coupled with her low blood sugar and her nerves that were put on edge every time Barry's name was mentioned.

'Oh, calm down,' said Leanne as they were waiting to be told they could leave. 'You know his bark is worse than his bite.'

'The material on that horse really makes my skin worse.'

Leanne squinted at Henrietta's forearms, bare legs – anywhere her skin was exposed – and asked, 'Where?'

'Just because you can't see it, doesn't mean it's not there,' said Henrietta.

When Barry marched out of the hut he said: 'She whining again?'

Mae noticed Henrietta's eyes fill with tears but was finding it hard to be sympathetic.

'Right. Good job today. Now get out of here so I don't have to see your mugs any longer.'

Mae did wonder whether there was an HR department for the park.

'Oh, and before you go …' Barry threw a plastic bag to each of the employees who caught them. Apart from Henrietta, whose bag fell to the floor.

No one bothered to look inside as they all said 'Cheers' and goodbye to him. Walking towards her dad's car, Mae saw that Barry had stopped Henrietta and was talking to her with his hands on his hips, his face going red as she burst into tears and ran away. He looked after her and shook his head before he went back into the hut. For a minute Mae considered going after Henrietta but she was so tired all she could do was think of her bed. She sat in the car and took a deep breath.

'From uni student to horse's arse.'

She put her head on the steering wheel when there was a knock on the window that startled her. It was Barry. She wound down the window and attempted to smile.

'Here's another one for you,' he barked. 'First day dibs.'

With which he gave her another plastic bag and walked off. Mae opened it up and looked inside to find an array of pick 'n' mix. She picked up a sour coke bottle and smiled before putting it in her mouth.

'Thanks,' she called out from her window.

Barry simply waved without looking back.

There was no way Mae was telling her family exactly what she was doing at the amusement park. The following day she and Henrietta took up their normal positions except Henrietta refused to talk to anyone. When a boiled sweet dropped from Henrietta's hand, Mae tried to make a joke – about it going in one end and coming out the other – but this didn't seem to amuse her. The day after that Mae suggested they take being a horse's arse in turns.

'Didn't I tell you about my fainting?' said Henrietta, exasperated.

It was all Mae could do to not push her into the teacup ride. A few hours into her fifth shift she thought she heard someone say her name.

'Neeiigh,' replied Henrietta. 'I'm Happy Horse – I don't know a Maeeeeee.'

Mae rolled her eyes as she wiggled free from her costume to see who it was. It was Ilyaas. *Oh God.*

'Oh, hey. What are you doing here?' she asked. 'How'd you get here?'

That's when she looked behind him to see her parents, Ash, Bubblee, Farah, Fatti, Aima and Zoya and Adam in their prams, behind him, all looking some version of confused or amused. Mae felt her face flush, resisting the urge to get back into her costume and never come out.

'Well,' said Bubblee. 'We always knew you were a bit of an arse.'

Fatti hit her on the arm as her parents looked too horrified to say anything.

'This is what you're doing all summer?' said her mum. 'Jay's abba, are you seeing? What is this?'

Mae's dad just shook his head, shrugging at the sight before him. Henrietta took off her horse's head and looked at Mae. 'You know family time isn't allowed when you're not on your break?'

'Henrietta, please shut up,' said Mae.

'I'm glad someone's taking their job seriously,' said Bubblee, hardly able to hold in her laughter.

'I do, as a matter of fact,' replied Henrietta. 'Despite all my ailments.'

Henrietta gave Mae a look of disdain as she flicked her head and put on the horse's head again.

'What are you all doing here?' asked Mae.

'We thought we'd surprise you,' replied Farah. 'It was Fatti's idea.'

'Ilyaas mentioned you might like it,' added Fatti.

Mae could see that even Fatti was finding it hard to suppress her smile.

'Whatever,' said Mae. 'I'll get fired if I stand around talking to you losers.'

'All right then,' said Bubblee. 'Glad you're not horsing around.'

'Shall we wait until the end of your shift so you can tail us back home?' said Farah.

Mae slipped the material over her head as she heard Aima say: 'That *cannot* be good for her skin.'

'Trust me,' mumbled Mae. 'It's not good for anything.'

> Bubblee: When are you galloping home for dinner?

> Farah: Bubblee … rein it in.

> Fatti: Don't pay attention to them.

By the end of the day, Mae was in such a bad mood that she'd muted the WhatsApp group and was, for a moment, tempted to leave it altogether.

'Damn her!' exclaimed Barry as everyone was leaving.

'What happened?' Mae whispered to Leanne.

'Henrietta, what else? She's only gone and left.'

'Why?' Mae asked.

Leanne gave her an appraising look. 'You ought to be glad it's not you, what with your family coming and you getting out of your costume when it wasn't break time. She complained about you, didn't she?'

What was this? Military service?

'You bloody kids. No sense of responsibility – a bit of tough love and you crumble. You'd better not make me regret this,' he said to Mae.

It seemed that Henrietta had made an official complaint about Mae's lack of professionalism and Bri told Leanne who told Mae that Barry said he'd rather have someone with a sense of humour than a wet blanket who cried every five minutes.

'Now whose arse will you be?' he barked at Mae as if expecting her to answer.

'I can just walk around and be one on my own,' she replied, jokingly. 'I'm really good at that.'

Barry just shook his head, threw packets of pick 'n' mix to everyone and stalked off, mumbling something under his breath.

'Thanks, guys,' Mae said when she got home that evening to tell them what happened. 'My boss was really happy about my family just hanging around.'

'What's the big deal?' said Farah. 'We were just bumming around.'

Bubblee and Farah laughed and Fatti wasn't doing a very good job of hiding her own amusement.

'Ugh, just go and look after your babies,' said Mae.

The sisters quietened down.

'Sorry, Mae,' said Fatti. 'We didn't know it'd cause trouble. We just wanted to see you in your new job. You're hardly around any more.'

Mae looked at the three of them. Did they have any idea what was going on in her life? Did they even ask without being sidetracked by babies and dates? Any time Mae wanted to say something she always felt that their lives were too busy for her. That they wouldn't understand.

'Not as if being at home makes a difference anyway,' she replied, feeling the anger bubble inside her. 'I was here for weeks and it's not as if anyone cared what I was up to.'

The sisters fell silent.

'In case you haven't noticed, raising a family and having a career isn't exactly easy,' replied Bubblee.

Mae looked at her incredulously. 'Yeah, I really see you looking after Zoya, going off on dates every five minutes.'

'Mae …' said Fatti.

Mae looked at her, her tears now surfacing. 'Not even you, Fatti. Even you're too busy.'

She bit back the tears that had threatened to fall and gave a small laugh. 'Anyway, whatever. You guys can do whatever you want, but don't spoil the one thing that's actually getting me through being home again.'

Not even Bubblee had time to respond as Mae marched upstairs and collapsed into her bed. For a moment she wondered what they must be saying, whether they were sorry or angry, but either way, Mae found she didn't really care. She looked at her phone – no message from Ji Su. The whole thing still confused Mae. She questioned her feelings. Tried to understand what they had been. If she had that time back with Ji Su, in her room, would she have done things differently?

Would she have carried on kissing her? She didn't think she would have. But then what had it meant? Mae rummaged through her bag and took out the envelope that had her university results, staring at her failure. That was how she fell asleep.

Chapter Ten

It was nine forty-five when Mae woke up. For a moment, she forgot where she was, what had happened and why she felt so disorientated. Her eyes felt sore and her head was hurting. Then the memory of last night came back, her stomping up the stairs and crying herself into a dreamless sleep. Why had she argued with her sisters? Because of work.

Work.

'Oh God!' exclaimed Mae, tumbling out of bed confused as to what to do first. She ran to the bathroom, got ready as fast as she could and sped down to the amusement park, looking at the time on her phone every two seconds.

'Oh God, oh God, oh God, oh God.'

She was so late. And after Barry had told her to make sure he didn't regret keeping her when Henrietta had complained.

'*Oh God.*'

Mae parked up and ran towards the booths where Leanne and Bri both shook their head at her. Leanne tapped on her wrist.

'Tut, tut,' she said as Mae rushed past. 'No pick 'n' mix for you tonight.'

'Is he really mad?'

Leanne shrugged. 'He's always mad. You've probably just pushed him over into a rage. Thanks.'

Mae walked tentatively into the hut as he looked up at her.

'Oh, nice to see you,' he said. 'Kind of you to join us.'

'I'm so sorry. I don't know what happened. I swear I'd set the alarm but it didn't go off.'

'The alarm. So it's the alarm's fault and not the fact that you're not responsible enough to put it on before going to bed?'

'My fami—'

'I don't want your damn excuses. Just go and get into your horse.'

Mae nodded and went to get the costume when he said, 'It's already out there.'

'What?'

'The. Head. Is. Already. Out. There.'

'You've got a replacement?' asked Mae.

'No, the costume's come to life and doesn't need you any more. *Of course I've got a replacement.* Now, do you want to waste more of my time in here and really make me want to fire you, or will you go out and *do your job*?'

Mae didn't wait around and rushed out of the hut. She walked into the amusement park, past the dragon boat and teacups and looked around the merry-go-round.

That's where they tended to stay in the morning before swapping with the Perky Pig at the A-MAZE-MINT area. There was the horse's head, having a picture taken with a child as Mae hurried up behind. Except this time, she could tell whoever was in there was about a foot taller than her.

'I'm here,' she exclaimed.

The horse turned to her. 'You're late.'

His voice came out deep and authoritative, which was pretty rich considering he was wearing a horse's head.

'Yeah, thanks, I know that,' Mae replied, getting into her costume.

He stopped to hi-five a group of teenagers who walked away, laughing.

'Not going to make this into a habit, are you?' he asked. 'Because a horse needs its back half.'

'Isn't this your first day?' said Mae. 'Chill out.'

'Jobs aren't easy to come by, you know. I don't want to get fired just because you can't tell the time.'

Who was this guy?

'I'm actually the most punctual one here so no need to give me a lecture. Jeez.'

'It wasn't a lecture, just a statement,' he replied.

'Sounded like a lecture to me,' said Mae getting behind him to slip the material over her head. She got in and realised that because he was so tall she wouldn't have a broken back at the end of the day. 'Well, at least I don't have to bend over completely.'

Ugh. Mae shook her head at herself, wanting to laugh because it was kind of funny too. He paused before she felt something shake. Then she realised it was his shoulders that were shaking when he let out a laugh.

'Sorry,' she said. 'Slip of the tongue.'

'You're all right,' he replied.

'I'm Mae.'

'Abdul-Raheem.'

'Shut your face,' she said. 'You are *not* Muslim.'

'I am.'

'*No way*. I never meet Muslim people around here. That is mad.'

Perhaps it was the fact that she couldn't see him, or that he couldn't see her, or that she was so surprised he was Muslim that she rolled out a catalogue of questions: where do you live? Where are you from? Why are you doing this job?

'You ask a lot of questions,' he said. 'Turning left.'

Mae trotted to the left. 'Not much else to do in this costume, is there? Plus, I still can't get over the fact that you're Muslim.'

He paused as a family wanted to have a picture taken with Happy Horse.

'You never said why you're doing this job,' said Mae. 'It's not exactly top choice.'

There was a moment's quiet before he said: 'No. But you've got to be grateful for what you get.'

Mae scoffed. 'You're talking out of your arse.'

'You're talking into mine.'

Mae laughed and began to get curious about what this Abdul-Raheem guy looked like. Was he Bengali? Maybe Pakistani or Indian. She liked the sound of his voice; it was soft and stern at the same time. It wasn't easy to see in that costume but she could tell he was broad-shouldered. Mae shook these questions from her head. Who cared what his origins were, anyway?

'So, you're grateful to be a horse at an amusement park? Sets the bar low for your life's expectations, my friend,' she said.

'I don't have expectations.'

'That's silly. Everyone has them.'

He paused again. 'The only things I expect are of myself and what I can control. Making sure I make the best of whatever God's given me.'

'Oh,' replied Mae. 'Well, that's very mature of you. How old are you, anyway?'

'How old do I sound?'

'About eighty.'

He laughed. 'Got the soul of around that age. What about you?'

'Nineteen.'

'Yeah, you sound it.'

She nudged his back with her hand as he laughed again. 'Shut up.'

'Don't worry. It's all right. Shows that there's still lightness in the world,' he replied.

'I'm light, am I?'

'Well, right now you're dark, but otherwise I can tell there's a lightness to you. Nice when people don't take themselves too seriously.'

'All right, Mr-don't-be-late-to-be-a-horse's-arse.'

'Don't have to be tardy to be light,' he replied.

Mae heard the screaming of excitable children. The music of carousels and roller coasters. The whirring of machinery and pinging of machines and for the first time since she was in this job, didn't want to hurt someone.

'You're not too hot, are you? Hungry?' he asked. 'Here, I've got some almonds.'

He put his hand behind him with a packet Mae could hardly see. 'Mmm, exciting.'

'They're good for you.'

She went to take the packet as their hands brushed together.

'Thanks,' she said, handing the packet back, trying to ignore the feeling that brush evoked.

She didn't even know what he looked like. Had it felt the same when she had touched Ji Su?

'So, you don't like things that are good for you?' he asked.

Mae sighed. 'I used to be a health nut. I mean, a *proper* nut. I'd be the one with a bag of carrots and hummus while my family ate all this fried stuff. Can't believe how boring I was. Then I went to uni and realised what I'd been missing out on.'

'I don't believe that you could ever be called boring,' he replied.

'Ha,' exclaimed Mae. 'Trust me. There's nothing to me. Who goes to uni and makes no friends at all?'

He paused and Mae wished she hadn't blurted that out.

'You don't have any friends?'

'Well, I did. One. But we had a falling-out,' replied Mae.

'Oh. Sorry, it's time to walk towards the fountain,' said Abdul-Raheem. 'Tell me if I'm walking too fast. But carry on.'

Mae followed him, having little choice about it, hurrying up to make sure she kept step with him.

'Nothing really. Just that it's hard, isn't it? Doesn't matter.'

'Go on,' he said.

Mae felt herself get hotter. She hated talking about this, especially to a stranger, but his voice was so kind and soft just then, and maybe it helped that they couldn't actually see each other.

'Sorry,' she began. 'Sounds like I'm whining.' She took a deep breath. 'It's just that I never knew how hard it'd be to be who you are at home, just somewhere else. I thought you carried who you were wherever you went, but it wasn't like that. I dunno, I just found it hard to speak to people.'

'You?' he asked.

'Yeah, *me*.'

'I find that hard to believe, but you're right. Every situation brings out a new version of ourselves, one we didn't even know existed.'

Mae thought about this and how true it rang for her. Just like the situation with her sisters last night – she never knew she could be angry at them in such a way. She thought about her uni results and ended up just blurting out, 'Like the fact that I didn't know it was possible to fail your first year at uni?'

Was failure just another version of her personality?

'Is that what happened?' he asked.

'Yep. Bet I don't sound so smart now, do I?'

'I never said you sounded smart,' he said. 'I'm joking, I'm joking,' he added before Mae could say anything.

'Thanks a lot,' she said.

'Smart people fail all the time.'

Mae scoffed.

'It's the ones who give up who have really failed.'

He paused, as if allowing time for Mae to absorb his words.

'So, you're like, wise, are you?' said Mae.

'Just older,' he replied.

'How much older?'

'Almost a decade.'

'So you really are eighty,' said Mae.

'Don't make me kick you with my hooves.'

'I could whip you with my tail.'

'You've got a lot of front for a girl who's a horse's arse,' replied Abdul-Raheem.

Mae laughed as they went back and forth with equestrian-related jokes. After a good ten minutes of this Abdul-Raheem broke the flow.

'You shouldn't worry about uni, you know. Making friends and losing them is a part of life, but you'll find your feet as and when you're meant to. Trust me. I don't even know you and I can tell you'll be just fine.'

Mae's eyes prickled with tears at the unexpectedness of his words and the sincerity and certainty with which he spoke. It reminded her of Ji Su.

'Thanks,' was all she managed to respond with.

After a few minutes she said: 'How do you know, though? That it's all going to be fine?'

'Faith,' he replied. 'I've always known that God has His plans. All right, maybe not always, but once I learned it and embraced it, living became a lot easier.'

'Was it hard?' she asked.

He paused. 'It wasn't easy. But no need to go into that.'

'I guess I don't think about faith that much,' replied Mae. 'So, you're religious?'

'I don't like that word. People use it as if it's a bad thing or something to be wary of. But I believe in God, pray, fast, and try to be good to people. That's the main thing, really. To be kind to whoever comes your way.'

'Hmmm. Yeah, I guess so.' They were both quiet for a

while when Mae added: 'Isn't it weird the things you're able to say to people when you can't see them?'

'There's a comfort in not showing yourself. But everyone's got to do it sooner or later.'

Mae became aware of lunchtime drawing nearer, of having to come out of the costume and finally seeing the face of the man she'd just poured her heart out to. Each passing minute made her increasingly nervous and she wasn't sure why. What was she thinking, talking to him as if they'd known each other for ages? *Chill out*, she told herself. *It's no biggie. He's just another guy I work with.* It just so happens that he's also Muslim and also knows more about my life in the past year than any of my sisters.

'Thank God,' he said. 'Lunchtime. I'm starving. You?'

'Hmm? Oh, yeah.'

'You want to get lunch? This time we can talk face to face rather than arse to face.'

'Sure,' Mae replied, sounding calm while her hands trembled.

She lifted the costume from her face, disentangling herself from the horse's legs, her shoes getting caught in the hooves. Mae tried to pat down her hair, pinched her cheeks, brushed down her clothes just in time for her to see a rather large forearm slip from underneath the horse's head only to go back in again. *What?* Her heart beat faster as he took off the horse's head as if in slow motion, only for Mae to see a man with a bright smile, which she'd have appreciated if she hadn't been surprised by the colour of his very dark skin.

'Hi,' he said, tucking the head under his arm.

'Hi,' she replied, swallowing hard.

'Not what you imagined I'd be?' he asked.

Mae felt a flush of embarrassment. 'No. I mean, yes. *No*.' She shook her head. 'I didn't think anything.'

'We know that's not true. Everyone always thinks something when they meet someone they click with.'

Mae was taken aback by the honesty of his statement.

'Is that what we did?' she asked.

'Am I a disappointment?' he said with a smile on his lips, as if he were enjoying this.

Why couldn't the ground open up and swallow her whole?

'*Well* …' she began.

'Oh, really?' he replied, only looking as if he was half amused.

'*No*,' she exclaimed. 'I was joking. What about me?' she added, looking down at herself. 'Do you think I look like an actual horse's arse?'

Abdul-Raheem took a minute and considered her.

'Oi,' Mae exclaimed, pushing him.

'Come on,' he eventually replied, laughing. 'You and I both know you look very, very well.'

She felt a flush of embarrassment at the compliment, but she knew she liked it. Was she one of those girls who needed compliments? Mae had never considered it before, but she couldn't deny the warm feeling it gave her.

'Whatever,' she said. 'Are we having lunch or what?'

'Up to you,' he said.

His face was so kind and open Mae thought it matched exactly the person she'd opened up to.

'Obvs,' she replied. 'My treat. For all your good listening.'

Abdul-Raheem refused the deal all the way through their burger and chips and drinks, Flake ice cream and Slush Puppie. He'd already paid when Mae went to the bathroom and she thought, was that just two random people getting to know each other as friends, or is that what a date felt like?

Chapter Eleven

Mae didn't get a lot of sleep that night. The idea of seeing Abdul-Raheem the next day filled her with both anxiety and a new feeling altogether. What was it? She couldn't quite put her finger on it. When she got home that evening everyone was over for dinner. God, this lot got together a lot. Had it always been like this before she went to university or had it got worse? Either way, no wonder she never had time to make close friends, her family was always just *there*. Mae went into the kitchen under the guise of getting a drink, but really just needed a break from the constant chattering.

'Hey,' said Ilyaas.

'Oh, hey. How's it going?'

She'd been looking out of the window into the garden, where the summer sun was dimming but cast a pale light over the lawn and flowers.

'All right,' he replied.

Mae leaned against the kitchen sink as a peal of laughter came from the living room. Adam had burped.

'Escaping from the baby circus?' said Mae.

Ilyaas managed a small smile as he shrugged. 'I don't get them.'

'What? Babies?'

'No. Adults. Like, all babies do is eat, poo and sleep but they're all over them as if they're, like, you know … interesting.'

Mae nodded, but her thoughts kept drifting to the day she'd had. *You're talking out of your arse. You're talking into mine.*

'What's so funny?' asked Ilyaas.

'Hmm? Oh, nothing. Just work stuff.'

Ilyaas nodded.

'I'm sharing the horse suit with someone new,' she said. 'He's tall so at least I don't have to walk around like the hunchback of Notre Dame.'

'He?' said Ilyaas.

Fatti then walked in and looked at them both. 'What's going on in here?'

'Hiding out with my young friend,' said Mae. 'Sorry, not *hiding*. Retreating into the shadows.'

Fatti looked at Ilyaas, who'd gone stony-faced and looked at the floor. 'You all right?' she asked. 'You didn't eat much.'

He simply shrugged as he left the kitchen.

Fatti let out a sigh. 'I don't know how to get through to them.'

'He's all right,' said Mae. 'A bit hard to break but once you do he's a nice kid.'

'Try being a stepmum to him,' Fatti said, her voice clipped. 'Sorry. It's just, there's a whole summer of this.'

She took a seat at the breakfast table and put her head in her hands. It was the first time that Mae felt nothing for her sister, not even a drop of sympathy, and it surprised her. This was Fatti, after all, the one she'd do anything for, who would do anything for her.

'You'll get through it,' Mae managed to say. 'Hey, a new guy started at work today.'

'Yeah?' said Fatti, picking up a breadstick and nibbling on it.

'We now share a horse, thank you very much. It's actually well funny.'

'Oh.' Fatti looked over her shoulder, squinting as if to hear something. 'Aima ... wonder what she has to say now.'

Mae sighed, threw her can of Coke in the recycling bin and walked out.

> Farah: I'm sorry, but if I were Ash I'd be having strong words with that girl

'*Shut up*,' said Mae, flicking her phone back on to her bedside table.

She just about saved the phone from falling to the floor. For the past twenty minutes her sisters had been engaged in a WhatsApp conversation about Aima. Aima who was spoiled. Aima who was passive-aggressive.

Aima who was rude and obnoxious. Aima, Aima, Aima. Sure, she was an annoying brat but her sisters perhaps weren't aware that they too were quite annoying with their respective lives and all their complaining. Mae looked up at the ceiling and thought of Abdul-Raheem. She closed her eyes and remembered the way he'd lifted the horse's face off his head and her surprise at who he turned out to be. Why should it have been such a shock? It was just because she'd expected a Bengali, Indian or Pakistani and instead she got someone whose family were from Ghana. Anyway, what did it matter? Why did she feel embarrassed? Nothing happened between them. Nothing *could* happen between them. But, why not? The idea dropped into her head like a rock as her eyes sprang open. Mae propped herself up on her elbows, feeling confused and shocked. The thought had been brewing in her head. She'd shrugged it off because of its impossibility but it had grown into such a beast that not only could she not ignore it, she couldn't get over it. *Who cared if he was black?* She tried to shift the rock, push it this way and that, hammer at it to try and crack and destroy it, but it refused to budge or break. Mae wasn't racist, for God's sake.

'Er, hello?' Mae said to herself, looking around the room as if for confirmation. 'I'm *brown*. I can't be racist.'

This was just the type of thing that would have her sisters roll their eyes at their parents when they said anything casually racist. Or would they? Mae was certain that Bubblee would, but she wasn't sure about Fatti and Farah, they were both so traditional. It was hard to change the way her parents and that generation thought, but her generation had no excuse. Up until that moment Mae believed herself to be a part of a more enlightened way of thinking, except she realised that she hadn't actually given it much thought. *Any* thought, in fact. She wondered about all the crushes she'd had. They had been mostly white but that was because there weren't that many non-white people around when she was growing up. That was just maths. Then she thought about her first year at university. Any attractions she might've had were for men who were either white or brown. It wasn't even as if she didn't find black men attractive – she did. She'd appreciate a good-looking man whatever the colour of his skin, but whenever she'd thought of having a boyfriend he'd always been Bengali in her head, and in that moment she couldn't say why that was, other than that's what she was used to seeing around her.

'Ugh,' she added to herself, flopping back into bed. 'Maybe I *am* a racist.'

But more than that, it made her realise that her feelings for Ji Su really were platonic. If they were anything else then would she be feeling *this* way about Abdul-Raheem? Mae's head hurt. So many feelings! She looked at her phone again, this time checking on Ji Su's WhatsApp status. It was just the type of thing she'd have been able to talk to her about. But it wasn't just that; she missed *her* in general. Her perspective of things, her insight into situations. Mae missed her friend. And there was nothing she could do about trying to get her back.

The following morning Mae woke up, annoyed with herself. Her annoyance was only made worse when she saw her parents bickering in the kitchen, looking on her mum's iPad for a gazebo for the garden.

'No, Jay's abba, that's too expensive.'

'Only the best for my wife.'

'Someone pass me a bucket,' said Mae, getting a box of Frosted Shreddies out of the kitchen cupboard.

They barely acknowledged her they were so engrossed with their gazebo-shopping, so she stopped to consider their faces. Her dad was a little fairer than her mum, but after years of marriage their features had almost become similar – as they say people's do when they've been together for so long. Mae thought about Fatti's husband, Ash, and Farah's dead husband, Mustafa, and she was struck by the fact that everyone was the *same*. Their roots all led back to Bangladesh, the second language they shared, the food they ate, the cultural references they made and for a moment Mae felt nauseous at the sameness of it all. It was just so unimaginative, now that she thought about it.

On her way to work Mae gave herself a talking-to.

'Calm down. Why've you got to be so dramatic about it? Not like he's your boyfriend or whatever. He's just the guy you share a horse with.'

Then she got out of the car and saw him, leaning against the booth and talking to Leanne. His arms were folded, his head bent low as he smiled at something and she wondered why she even saw the colour of his skin. Their eyes met and Mae waved a bit more enthusiastically than she had intended. Leanne watched her approach now as if with new eyes.

'Ready for another day of horsing around,' said Mae.

Leanne rolled her eyes and walked into her booth. Abdul-Raheem straightened up. He seemed almost bashful, which was just as well because Mae couldn't quite look him in the eye.

'*You*,' exclaimed Barry, standing at the hut door, pointing at Abdul-Raheem. 'You gonna stand around and chat all day or do your job?'

'Stand around and chat if that's a choice,' replied Abdul-Raheem.

'Yeah, the choice between having a job or being fired.'

Mae looked between the two, grateful that at least Barry spoke like that to all of his workers, regardless of their colour.

'So,' Abdul-Raheem said.

'So,' Mae replied as they got into their costume.

'You doing anything nice tomorrow?'

'Family,' she said.

'Don't sound too excited about it.'

'You wouldn't either if you knew them.'

He laughed. 'They can't be that bad.'

'Oh, trust me. They're worse. Mum and Dad have started shopping for a gazebo.'

'Are you the Bengali Brady Bunch or something?'

Mae couldn't help but laugh too, which was a good way to distract herself from feeling as if there was even less room between them today in the costume than there was yesterday.

'Sorry. It did sound that way, didn't it?' said Mae.

'Well, if you want to escape them, let's have lunch somewhere.'

'Lunch?'

'Yeah.'

'You and me?'

'That's the idea,' replied Abdul-Raheem.

'But we're not working tomorrow.'

'I could bring the costume with me if you pre-ferred?'

'No, I mean … well, right. No, that'd be weird.'

Why were Mae's words not working properly? Where had her ability to form a sentence gone? It was like university all over again.

'What? Lunch or the costume?' he asked.

'The costume. Obviously.'

'I don't know. Not much is obvious with you.'

'Whatever,' she replied.

'Well?'

She didn't understand why there were knots in her stomach, or why she had to keep swallowing hard, or why she felt compelled to reach forward and touch his arm.

'Yeah. Cool. Lunch sounds good.'

'Good. Great. Shall I come and pick you up?'

Mae had a horrifying moment at the idea of any member of her family seeing someone like Abdul-Raheem turn up at her doorstep. Wasn't he Muslim enough to know *boys don't pick you up from your home?* It'd be unthinkable if it was anyone really, but *him* … They'd probably prefer her to bring home Ji Su and announce that she was a lesbian. *They were all racist.* The fact of it almost made Mae invite him over for dinner but she managed to hold herself back from that particular impulse.

'We can just meet in town,' she suggested.

So, he mentioned wanting to try Zobar's Café and they exchanged numbers because that's what people who met each other socially for coffee and lunch did, didn't they? Once the lunch question had been settled, Abdul-Raheem made a joke about them being the only two people of colour and perhaps they should hang out with some of the others during break time.

'Just in case they think we ethnics band together,' he added, a smile in his voice.

Mae wasn't sure what to make of this. Had he already got bored of her? Did he regret asking her out for lunch? Oh God, did that mean she was actually going on a date with him? As they got out of the costume for their break, she couldn't help but be surprised every time she looked at Abdul-Raheem. As if he'd morph into another body. Except this time she also saw Leanne looking at him.

'Fit, isn't he?' said Leanne as a bunch of them were sitting on the benches by the hut, eating their food.

'Do you think?' asked Mae.

Even though she knew the answer. Of course he was fit.

'I mean, anything looks fit given the turds that work here, but he'd be fit anywhere, I reckon. Especially in my bedroom.'

Leanne laughed as she licked the tomato ketchup off her chip and stared at Abdul-Raheem. Mae wasn't sure if she wanted to be sick or stick the chip up Leanne's nostril.

'Sorry, excuse me,' said Abdul-Raheem. 'Time to pray. Mae, do you want to join me?'

'Huh?'

She looked up at him, towering over her.

'Don't you want to pray?' he asked.

Want to? What she wanted to do was say, not really, no. Mae would pray here and there; when it was Eid, or maybe on a Friday when she was at home and her mum would tell her to get her act together or she'd go to hell, but hellfire never had induced enough fear in her to listen to her mum. She had to hang on to herself. Part of her knew that by going with Abdul-Raheem she'd just be doing it to impress him, but if she was going to pray then she wasn't going to make a mockery of God and do it for a man.

'No. Thanks,' she said.

This was it. Now that he knew she didn't pray he wouldn't want anything more to do with her. He'd move on to another person who shared his religious values and forget all about her, the thought of which made Mae depressed.

He smiled. 'All right. See you in a bit.'

'Religious,' said Leanne, shaking her head and now diving into her pecan nut ice cream. 'Knew he was too good to be true.'

As Mae watched Abdul-Raheem walk away, she wondered whether Leanne might be right.

At the family dinner that night Farah had said at least three things about Bubblee never being at home with Zoya and Mae realised that if anyone had probably gone on a date with a non-Bengali, it'd have been Bubs. Mae had tried several times to corner her in the kitchen but someone was always walking in or out, interrupting. It was when Farah said it was Bubblee's turn to change Zoya that Mae followed her upstairs and into their parent's room.

'What?' said Bubblee, realising her younger sister was behind her.

'Nothing.'

Bubblee popped the buttons off Zoya's Babygro as she got all the nappy paraphernalia ready.

'Aren't they the cutest legs you've ever seen?' said Bubblee to Mae.

'Yeah. Cute.'

'Farah goes on as if I don't see the new facial expression she's pulled, or that her hair's grown a bit …'

Mae looked at Zoya's patchy head but decided not to say anything.

'Hmmm,' said Mae. 'Farah.'

'Exactly.'

'The dating still bugs her then?' said Mae.

'That's an understatement.'

'Have you actually met anyone, though? Someone you like enough to go on more than just a few dates with?'

'As in someone I might actually bring home?' said Bubblee, almost laughing.

'Yeah.'

'You've got to be kidding me. I'm having fun, but I don't have time for a relationship – not with work, and baby here. Anyway, what kind of a man could even deal with this set-up?'

Zoya thrashed her legs around as Bubblee grabbed both her ankles in one hand so she could wipe her bottom. 'Zoyaaaa. No, that's not nice, is it? We have to have a clean bum-bum. No one wants a dirty bum-bum, do they?'

Mae saw the opportunity to ask her question. 'But, like, maybe if you dated someone who wasn't Bengali, he'd be all right with this.'

Bubblee patted down the nappy to make sure it was fastened properly and stared at the wall in front of her for a moment.

'Men,' she said, finally. 'They're all the same really. I mean, sure, there might be one or two who'd be okay about it, but I'm not betting on finding one of those.'

'What if you did?' Mae asked. 'And he wasn't Bengali?'

'Who cares about him being Bengali or not?' said Bubblee. 'I can't even believe you're asking me that question. Who are you? Farah or Fatti?'

Mae smiled and felt closer to Bubblee than she had in a long time. 'I know, I know. It's just … sometimes we have more prejudices than we think we do.'

'Not dating or marrying someone because of the colour of their skin makes you, in my book, the worst type of person,' said Bubblee.

She threw the nappy in the bin, screwing her nose up at it as she did so. Mae suspected the look had more to do with the subject matter than anything else.

'So, if you met a white or black guy who was everything you wanted, then you wouldn't care?' she asked.

'Black?' said Bubblee. 'My little Mae, it's one thing not being a racist, but it's another thing giving the parents a heart attack.'

'Huh?'

Bubblee picked Zoya up and kissed her cheek. 'There's enough drama in life to have to add to it.'

Having babies really did change a person. This was

the same Bubblee who'd use any given opportunity to rock their parents' sanity. All someone had to do was mention Jay not washing his own dishes for Bubblee to start quoting Simone de Beauvoir and start going on about the injustices of being a woman, brown *and* Muslim. All the hard edges of Bubblee seemed to have softened and while it did mean the family got a bit more peace, Mae also felt something had been lost.

'So, what?' said Mae. 'Just give up on happiness because some old people think they know better than you?'

Bubblee looked at her for a moment. 'No. That's not what I mean. Just that, if you can avoid bringing drama into life, then that's probably better.'

There wasn't much else to say when their mum walked in and she and Bubblee began talking about Zoya's sleeping patterns. Mae looked between the two of them, amazed how the bond of motherhood could bring two people, so frequently at loggerheads, together. Mae thought about what Bubblee had said and shook her head. What if she didn't want to avoid drama though? Wasn't that living? What if she actually really wanted it?

Mae chose the outfit she was going to wear the following day with great care. She'd have liked to wear her cargo trousers and a T-shirt, but it made her look even younger than she already was so opted instead for a pair of loose-fit jeans, a red short-sleeved top and a pair of tan sandals. She didn't quite have the nerves for breakfast because she was sure it'd come right back out and so inspected herself in the mirror for a while. The top was quite baggy, hiding her love handles, but she tucked it in to her jeans to give herself a nicer shape. The hair was another matter. It was short and straight and usually gave her no pause for thought, but today she wished it would do something different. She made a little puff with her fringe, pinning it back with a kirby grip, and it gave her face an open look.

'Make-up,' she muttered, looking through her five make-up items.

Every time she looked at her lip gloss now she couldn't help but shudder, recalling the incident on the train, but she steeled herself and applied the raspberry-coloured gloss to her lips, curled her thick eyelashes before putting on her mascara and touched up her face with some blush.

'Hmm,' said Mae, looking at the mirror. 'Subtle but effective.'

She grabbed her bag and her dad's car keys and went to say bye to her parents.

'Where are you going?' asked her mum, looking at her up and down. 'With your abba's car?'

'Out.'

'Out with who?'

'A friend.'

'What friend?' asked her mum.

'From work.'

'What's her name?'

Her?

'Oh my God. Is this twenty questions? I'm late.'

'Just because you're now at university doesn't mean you don't tell us what you're doing or who you're seeing. Isn't it, Jay's abba?'

Her mum looked at her dad who was too busy flicking through the iPad. 'I think this one's too big.'

'*Jay's abba,*' said her mum.

His head shot up, looking at Mae. 'You look nice.'

'Ask her who she's seeing. And why are you taking your abba's car?'

'It's okay, it's okay,' said her dad.

Mae let out a sigh of relief before saying bye and leaving the house. As she sat in the car a smile escaped her. For the first time since being around Ji Su, Mae realised that this was what it must be like to actually have a life.

She reached Zobar's Café before Abdul-Raheem and she was glad for it because it gave her time to compose herself; tell herself this wasn't a big deal and to just be cool. Normal. Except when she saw Abdul-Raheem walk through the door, people doing double takes, all her composure fell away.

'Hey,' she exclaimed as she waved at him and got up, knocking over the sugar that was standing in the middle of the table.

He came forward, grabbing a serviette and cleaning the granules as he laughed.

'Oops,' said Mae. 'Soz.'

He sat down opposite her and Mae noticed people were looking over at them. What was their problem exactly?

'No worries,' he replied. 'As long as you don't bring this behaviour to work.'

Mae could feel her hands get clammy and she wished they'd turn the air conditioning up in this place, even though it was on pretty high.

'So,' he said. 'Did you tell your parents who you were seeing today?'

The question caught her off guard. Why did it matter? And no, of course she didn't tell her parents.

'Was I meant to make an announcement?' she said, trying to keep her tone light.

Abdul-Raheem picked up a menu and scanned through it. 'Do you know what you want?'

Mae also picked up the menu but felt his eyes on her. 'Veggie fajita will do me, I think. And chips.'

'Good idea. Can't have lunch without chips.'

Abdul-Raheem fell into easy conversation with Mae about what he'd been up to that morning – gym – and hanging out with some friends last night. He mentioned waking up for fajr – morning prayers – and Mae played with a napkin, wishing they could move on from conversations about prayers.

'And now I'm on a date with you,' he said.

The surprise on Mae's face must've shown because he laughed.

'Just wanted to clarify that,' he added. 'Unless you don't want it to be, of course, and that's fine too. But I'm too old-school to pretend and act cool about something like this.'

'Oh,' said Mae.

Mae may not have dated a lot, or at all, but she'd heard enough stories to understand that it was a bit of a minefield. No one knew what the other was thinking, and of course everyone was too busy playing it cool to ask. People got *ghosted* and *zombied* and were you just friends who messaged all the time, or did it mean more because who messages all the time when it's just platonic? Are they passing their time until someone better comes along, or are they just too scared to admit how they feel because what if you've friend-zoned them without them realising? Mae stuffed three chips at the same time in her mouth.

'Well?' he asked when a few moments had passed because Mae had got lost in her reverie.

'Well, what?' she said, her mouth still full.

'How do you feel about that?'

She chewed on her food, trying to buy herself some time. 'I think we should get more chips.'

He looked at his plate of penne pasta. 'Right. I get it. It's fine.'

'What, no,' Mae exclaimed, almost knocking her Coke over. 'I didn't mean it like that. I mean, yeah, I would quite like more chips, but that's not the point. Not that I'm making a point. If I was then I'm not sure what it would be but it's not what you think. I don't even *know* what I think—'

'Whoa, Mae, Mae, Mae,' said Abdul-Raheem, putting down his fork and looking at her. 'You're going to choke if you don't pause.'

Mae took a deep breath, and for some reason Abdul-Raheem looked like he might laugh.

'I get it might be a lot to take in. I mean ...' he paused, looking almost embarrassed, 'I don't know if you've had any relationships before or what you've been through, so maybe this is different. Or maybe not. I don't want to assume anything. And I know I'm a bit older than you, but I don't know ... how often do you meet someone who you just click with?'

He took a sip of his orange juice.

'I guess not often,' she replied.

'If it's too much, don't worry. We can just be friends.'

'Why are you so nice?' she asked.

'Am I?'

'You know you are.'

'All right. You got me there,' he replied.

He twisted his glass of orange juice around, staring at it as Mae waited for more. Abdul-Raheem seemed to hesitate.

'Do you really want to know?'

'Why you're nice?'

He nodded.

'Well, yeah,' she replied.

Although it had been a rhetorical question, now she really did wonder, because as far as life went, there weren't many nice people around. Not least men, she thought, thinking about the man on the train, and the guy at the club. She still shuddered to think about it.

'It's probably best I tell you, anyway.'

Mae leaned forward. What was with all the mystery?

He took a deep breath, looked her in the eye and said: 'I used to be in prison.'

Mae paused and found herself leaning back, without meaning to. 'Oh.'

'Yep.'

There was a long silence. The chattering of other customers in the restaurant. A baby crying. Alicia Keyes singing from the speakers.

'Prison?'

'Yeah.'

'God.'

He let out a small laugh. 'Yeah.'

'When?'

'Eight years ago now. Since I've been out, that is. I was in there for five.'

'Months?'

'Years. On and off.'

'Oh.'

He nodded. 'I know. I started young. Did stuff I wasn't proud of.'

'Like?' she asked, almost without thinking. 'Sorry, I mean, you don't have to tell me. Not if you don't want to talk about it.'

'Does it matter to you?'

Mae knew she should lie and say that if it was in the past then obviously it didn't matter. But she kind of felt it did. How could it not?

'No judgement,' she replied. 'If that helps?'

He took a deep breath before finishing the rest of his orange juice and asking for another, as well as ordering more chips.

'The truth is I fell in with the wrong crowd. Grew up in a rough neighbourhood and it was just easier to do what everyone was doing – drugs, petty thefts, that kind of thing. But the small things stack up, don't they? And once you get caught, you get trapped in the cycle. Pretty hard to come out of it.'

'Yeah,' said Mae, leaning back again. 'Always is hard to break cycles.'

That was definitely something she could relate to. Still, it was hard to imagine someone with a smile like Abdul-Raheem's doing any of that stuff. He looked so polite and, aside from that, *was* so polite. He lifted up the sleeve of his T-shirt to show a silvery gash at just the top of his arm.

'Got stabbed there when I was eighteen and out on parole. I've got another one on my stomach.'

Mae flushed, partly because she wasn't sure whether she wanted to see it because it was a stab wound, or because it was on his stomach. She kind of wanted to lean over and feel the wound on his arm for herself.

'God,' was all she could manage to repeat.

'I could go into detail,' he said. 'But maybe another day. Think that's quite a lot to take in already.'

'No kidding,' Mae replied. 'But you didn't answer my question. How'd you get to be so nice?'

'Kind of a cliché, really. Went in not really thinking about God and ended up reading *Malcolm X*. All the stuff he went through and at *that* time. In America too. It made me think: why am I so angry? What right do I have? Got a roof over my head – even if it does belong to the council – food on the table and I realised I'd never been grateful for anything in my life. Then I read at the end – when he goes for Hajj – how it didn't matter if you were a man or woman, rich or poor, black or white – it was all the same in the eyes of God. When you spend your life being angry because people see you differently, and you know that there's one being, at least, who doesn't care about any of that, just the deeds you do for yourself and others ... well, it kind of changes you.'

'So, what? Now you're nice to people because of God?'

He shrugged. 'Guess you could put it that way.'

Mae took a bite of her fajita that had now gone cold and thought about it.

'And what about when people are bad to you?'

'That's a lot harder to deal with,' he said with a smile. 'Don't know if I've got a handle on it yet, but I'm trying.'

'Hmm.'

Mae was busy absorbing this information and almost forgot Abdul-Raheem was in front of her.

'What do you think then?' he asked.

'Bit impressive, isn't it? To get yourself out of something like that.'

'I don't know. It's one of the reasons I moved to a quiet town rather than living in the city. Fewer temptations. Now I think I'd be fine anywhere, but still ... you have to think ahead. Have a plan.'

This just reminded Mae of the fact that she had no plan. That she wasn't even thinking about thinking ahead.

'I don't mean to be rude or anything, but ... why the hell are you a horse during the day?' she asked.

He leaned forward. 'Because I'm obviously Batman at night.'

Mae rolled her eyes. 'Loser.'

'Okay, fine. I know. But jobs aren't easy to come by. Especially when you're a black man with a criminal record.'

Imagine if Abdul-Raheem knew what her own reaction had been when she first saw him? What her family would think if they ever knew she was on a date with him. It seemed so weird that the colour of anyone's skin should matter and that Abdul-Raheem seemed so content. She guessed that's where gratitude came in.

'Let's face it,' he added. 'You weren't exactly jumping for joy when you first saw me.'

Mae felt her face flush so much she didn't know where to look. '*What? No*,' she exclaimed, her voice a few octaves higher than usual.

Abdul-Raheem raised his eyebrows. 'Don't worry. You're all right. I'm used to it.'

'Bu— wha—, no, it's no—'

'Listen,' he interrupted. 'It's not the best feeling in the world. But you've lived in a village your whole life, you're young, and so I get it. And don't think I don't know there's as much racism within Asian communities as there is in the big bad white world. It'll be in any community, really.'

Mae wanted the ground of the café to open up and swallow her whole. *Actually* whole. How could she have been so awful?

'No, it's just you never come across black or brown people around here. I was surprised, that's all,' she said, trying to compose herself.

He merely took another bite of his pasta. She was lying and he knew it and the silence between them felt like something was shifting, and not in the right direction. After what felt like ages, when Abdul-Raheem hadn't looked at her and seemed ready to rush through the rest of the lunch, she spoke.

'Okay, yes, you're right.'

He looked up.

'I'm just so embarrassed. I don— You don't— What I mean is … I'm *not* racist.'

'We all have prejudices in us,' he replied, putting his fork down. 'Every single one of us. That's the way human beings work, but the most important thing is recognising it and then doing something to change it. Like, I don't know … being on a date with me.'

Mae threw a chip at him, grateful for the fact he was smiling, that he didn't get up and walk right out. That he would give her a second chance. That's when it hit her that she *wanted* a chance. How the hell did that happen? Had it been like this with Ji Su? Would her feelings for Abdul-Raheem change the way they had for her ex-friend? This time though, she didn't feel uncertain – nervous yes – but not unsure.

'All right, fine,' she said. 'If that's how I've got to prove it.'

He smiled as the waiter brought his orange juice and another batch of chips.

'No,' said Abdul-Raheem. 'The only way you prove it is if you come out tomorrow as well.'

Mae didn't even think twice before saying yes.

Mae found herself expressing interest in her parents' choice of gazebo, Adam and Zoya's eating and sleeping patterns and even Aima being a brat. And she did it all with a smile as she nodded away in understanding, actually feeling sorry for them all caught up in their dreary lives when she was dating a man who adored her. It wasn't cheesy adoration that was all chocolate and flowers either (though that's not to say they weren't a part of it). He did things that Mae didn't think would matter until she realised how much she quite enjoyed them. Like him going out into the rain for her, just when they were about to go home, because she realised she'd forgotten her jacket. Or, if they shared some chips or dessert, he'd always let her have the last bite. Telling her that he knew he liked her even before he saw what she looked like, and that when he did see her he couldn't believe his luck.

'Sap,' she said, hitting him on the arm.

'I know you love it, but let's pretend that's what you really think.'

The problem was that after work, there was only so long she could stay out without her parents being suspicious. On their days off Mae would lie and say she was doing some extra shifts at the park or she knew her mum would start asking even more questions than she already was. Like: *Is that a new perfume? You're wearing make-up today again? Why are you in such a good mood?* Which was incredible because it meant that her mum must've noticed that Mae hadn't been in a good mood lately, but hadn't even cared to ask why. Except it hardly mattered because now there was a person who *did* care about her moods and stupid things like what she had for dinner, and which one was Bubblee, and how were her niece and nephew doing? Mae found herself telling him about her small annoyances, how her family were kind of self-involved right now, the drama between Bubblee and Farah and Fatti and her stepchildren. She asked him questions about his life before he'd converted to Islam but he didn't seem that keen to discuss it.

'What's past is past. I want to move forward.'

Which sounded sensible, though Mae also felt that sharing the past could help with moving forward. It was one day, before lunch and a film (because late nights were out of the question), that they were sitting in his car, outside his house, and Mae wondered when Abdul-Raheem planned to kiss her. What was the protocol here when it came to someone who was religious? She'd never have imagined being with an observant Muslim but now that she was, it was kind of annoying not having any sort of physical relationship, apart from holding hands or a hug.

'My dad's been on my case to visit him for a while so I might go and see him next time I have a few days off,' he said.

'Oh. Okay. That sounds good.'

Even though she'd got so used to Abdul-Raheem being around, what would she do when he wasn't there?

'He doesn't mind you being Muslim?' she asked.

'Minds more about me being a horse.'

Mae laughed. 'Yeah but then you'd have never met me.'

Abdul-Raheem turned to her. 'That's exactly what I said.'

'You've told him about me?'

'Of course.'

'Oh.'

She looked at her hands for a minute. 'How come you've never invited me into your house?'

He paused. 'You want to see it?'

She shrugged.

'We'll miss our film.'

'Or we could just watch one at yours.'

'I don't really have a TV,' he replied.

'Oh my God. How do you live?'

'Prefer to read, or do other things to engage the mind.'

'Fine. We can read a book together,' said Mae.

He took a deep breath. 'I'm not sure that's a good idea.'

For the first time since she'd known him, Mae wondered whether he might be a serial killer or something. What was he hiding? Because if you're being weird about someone coming into your home then there had to be a reason for it.

'Why not?' she asked.

Abdul-Raheem scratched his neck. His arms bulged at the sleeve of his T-shirt and Mae felt something flutter in her stomach. She was used to this fluttering; it happened whenever she saw him, but there was something about being outside his house, a quiet space where they could be together, alone, that the fluttering became more like a drilling. He raised his eyebrows at her.

'Why do you think?' he asked.

'You're a murderer?'

'What's another reason?'

She shrugged. He took her hands and stroked the inside of her palm with his thumb. She wondered if he could feel the vibrations from the drilling in her stomach.

'I don't know.'

'Mae, I like you.'

'That's good because I like you too.'

'I mean. I *really* like you,' he said. 'You're just …'

'What?'

'There's no one quite like you. You say whatever comes into your head. You never want to impress people, you eat what you want, you wear what you want.'

If only he'd met the Mae *before* university, obsessed with kale and gluten-free products.

'… and you're happy without wanting to be part of any kind of rat race. You're *fun*.' He gripped her hand tighter. 'And you're beautiful.'

Mae looked away as if she was about to scoff. 'Shut up.'

He took her face in his hand and turned her towards him. 'You are. The most beautiful person at the amusement park, anyway,' he added.

'Even compared to that girl with the bowl haircut who started last week?'

'Maybe not as beautiful as her—'

She hit his arm, but liked the feel of it so much, she didn't remove it. Mae lifted the sleeve of his T-shirt, just like he'd done on their lunch, and looked at the scar again, running her finger over it.

'Sorry you got stabbed,' she said, her voice low, barely being able to look at him.

'Taught me a lesson,' he said.

'What?'

'To control my anger.'

She nodded.

'To be careful of all emotions when they overwhelm you. In case you lose yourself.'

Mae swallowed hard. She liked the idea of losing herself. But then she hadn't yet found herself, so she'd have to do that first.

'And that's why I don't think it's a good idea for you to come inside,' he said, also lowering his voice, his face so close to hers, she'd just have to inch forward to be able to kiss him.

Just as she was about to, he pulled back. Mae was left sitting there, her heart in her stomach and ego somewhere in the car boot.

'Is it me?' she asked, her voice as if she were about to cry.

'What? *No*,' he said. 'Of course it's not you. Trust me,

Mae. There's nothing I'd like more than to be alone with you. I mean, alone, alone. But, it's not a good idea. There are certain ways to do things,' he added. 'I haven't even met your parents yet.'

Her heart, which was already in her stomach, had now shifted somewhere into her intestines.

'I guess so,' she said.

Silence.

'Shall we go then?' she added, looking straight ahead.

Mae was suddenly very keen to get to their lunch and movie and out of this conversation.

'When do you guess that might be?' he asked.

She looked at him, reluctantly. 'You want to meet my family?'

'Of course.'

'Abdul-Raheem, I'm Bengali. What do you think this is? An actual Brady Bunch film?'

She thought the reference might make him laugh, but his face was still and she wasn't sure whether he was upset or angry.

'It's not like I'm allowed to date at all. I could never introduce my boyfriend to my parents.'

'Right,' he said.

She waited for him to say more. 'You get that, don't you? Come on, you might not have been born Muslim but you know what it's like with the culture, don't you? For Bengalis, anyway.'

He nodded. 'Yeah. Yeah, I know. Of course.'

'And don't you think it's kind of soon? It's only been a few weeks.'

Abdul-Raheem's shoulders seemed to relax as he nodded again. 'Yeah, you're right. I get it. We'll see how things go,' he said. 'You'll tell them when you're ready. I know you will.'

Just as Mae was beginning to feel better, she wondered what did he mean: *when you're ready*? Mae couldn't imagine a point in her life when she ever *would* be ready. Was she deceiving him? Abdul-Raheem started the car and pulled out of the parking space, heading towards the town centre as Mae thought about what her parents would say. A black man *and* ex-convict? The very thought made her want to throw up. Would her dad be disappointed or would he actually lose his temper? She couldn't remember the last time he'd done that. As for her mum? God knows what her mum would do. Mae had a feeling that she'd bring the whole house down. With or without a gazebo.

Chapter Twelve

> Fatti: I'm running out of ways to keep two teenagers occupied. Help me. xxxxxx

> Mae: Lock em up in a cupboard!;)

> Farah: Good practice for when our babies are older, though, isn't it? xx

> Bubblee: For God's sake those kids. I'll call you on my break X

Abdul-Raheem, as promised, had gone to see his dad. Because he never went back on a promise. Mae had asked to work on her days off but Barry said he'd be 'done' for worker exploitation.

'That's fine,' said Mae. 'Exploit me. I'm okay with it, really.'

It was no use. She'd have to spend her two days off with her family and so she tried to think where the lesser of two evils might be: with Farah and Bubblee, or Fatti and her new family. In the end she'd decided on Farah and Bubblee. Maybe Mae could get a bit more information from Bubs about this whole relationship thing because no matter how hard she tried, she couldn't shake the feeling of things moving *too* fast with Abdul-Raheem. She had got too used to him being around – a welcome break from her family and thinking about things like uni and where her life was going – but it was getting a bit too intense with talk of meeting families. The very idea made her sick with anxiety and not just because he was black, but because she was so young and they'd only been dating a few weeks.

Perhaps this was Mae's problem: she kept relying on people to distract her from her issues without considering what *they* were feeling. Is that what Ji Su was getting at when they'd kissed? The realisation dawned on her just as she was pulling up outside Farah and Bubblee's place and she wondered what type of person this made her.

She'd have to put these thoughts on pause though as she knocked on the front door.

Unfortunately, not much had changed in their household and Mae found herself in the middle of a parenting-type tug-of-war.

'You have to let her self-soothe,' exclaimed Farah.

'Just let her carry on crying her eyes out?' replied Bubblee, already making her way up the stairs.

Farah grabbed the back of her jumper. 'Who's with her all day? I know what I'm talking about.'

'So, why isn't she *self-soothing* yet? Listen to her. She's hysterical.'

Mae thought that actually, if it was a toss-up between her sisters and nine-month-old niece, her sisters won the hysteria contest.

'Er, guys?' said Mae.

'She's not hysterical,' replied Farah. 'That's how babies cry.'

'I have *not* heard Zoya cry like that before.'

'You would if you were around more,' Farah retorted.

'Guys?' repeated Mae.

'Oh God, you're like a broken record,' said Bubblee.

'The record would change if you changed.'

'*Guys*,' exclaimed Mae.

'*What?*' they both shouted, looking over their shoulders at Mae.

'Oh,' said Bubblee, noticing the pizza delivery man at the door.

'Two thin crust vegetarians?' he said, feebly.

'Sorry,' added Mae. 'I don't have any cash.'

'Ugh,' said Bubblee, stomping down the half-climbed staircase, grabbing her wallet and handing over the cash to the delivery man.

By which time Zoya's crying had calmed down and they could now only hear her whimper through the baby monitor, watching her little body relax as she dozed off to sleep.

'*Thank you*,' said Farah, looking at Bubblee.

Mae wondered whether if she weren't there, Bubblee would've taken the baby monitor and flung it at Farah. As it happened, Bubblee was just incensed enough to exclaim an expletive at Farah and storm out of the room, and subsequently house, slamming the door behind her. Farah looked on in surprise as Mae wondered what Abdul-Raheem would make of this when she told him. Should she even tell him? Why was she constantly needing to unburden her stuff on him?

'Jeez,' was all Mae could muster.

Farah still looked as if she could hardly believe her eyes or ears. 'What the …'

Mae waited for her to finish. 'Well, you were kind of … you know …' she said.

'*What?* What was I, Mae?'

This house had become a minefield and Mae was always a bit hit and miss with where she stepped.

'Like … all I'm saying is that, maybe—'

Farah looked like she might actually commit a murder.

'*Maybe*,' added Mae, 'she's feeling left out. With the whole mothering thing.'

That's all it took before Farah went into how that was her choice, that she was never around, that her art work meant more to her than her family. That this new guy she'd been seeing saw her more than Farah did.

'She has a new man? Like a proper one?' asked Mae, leaning forward, fascinated by this new development in Bubblee's dating life.

'If she cared that much she'd make the time and not be going out with *him* all the time.'

'Yeah, but—'

'She just waltzes into the house, all smug and uplifted with tales of work and dating and what am I doing? Up to here' – Farah lifted her hand above her head to demonstrate – 'in nappies. Trying to run a home and bring up a little human being. But does she even understand how hard it is? She's always wanted everything her way, and this is just typical her – having her cake and eating it.'

Mae sighed. She could've done with some cake. Chocolate gateau maybe? Or even a simple lemon drizzle. She could see Farah's point, but she wondered what Abdul-Raheem would say. He was always going on about seeing things from another person's perspective. But he didn't just say it, he did it.

Farah seemed to deflate as she sat on the edge of the sofa and stared into space.

'Do you know what it's like to lose someone who was practically everything to you? A husband? The love of your life,' she added in a whisper. 'Then have to build that life up again, thinking you'll have the support of your twin sister? But she's just not there?'

Mae sat next to Farah and put her arm around her. Maybe it was because Farah came across shouty all the time, Mae hadn't really thought about how difficult this must still be for her.

'But you're Farah,' said Mae. 'You get through stuff. You *do* stuff for everyone.'

Farah looked up at her. 'Exactly. And now? When I need something from Bubblee?'

Unfortunately Mae didn't have a response to that.

'She wants it *all*, Mae. And what she doesn't realise is that you can't have it all.'

'Maybe not,' she replied. ' But can you blame her for trying?'

Farah just shook her head. 'You're too young to understand.'

Mae scoffed, moving away from her sister. It always boiled down to this, didn't it? She couldn't help but feel annoyed.

'Yeah, and you're too old to be grabbing on to your sister's jumper to stop her from seeing her baby when it's crying.'

She shouldn't have said it, but she was tired of being told she was too young to understand things. It seemed to her, in her family, age didn't necessarily mean wisdom.

'So you're on her side?' said Farah.

Mae got up and opened the box of pizza and took a huge bite. 'No,' she spluttered. 'That'd mean one of you is right.'

'And?' asked Farah, waiting for Mae's point.

Mae sighed, agitated, as she put her slice of pizza down.

'You both had this vision of parenthood, yeah? Only you never told each other what it was, just assumed you'd be living your own version and the other person would be on board.'

Mae took another bite of her pizza as Farah seemed to take in what she'd said.

'But, how many versions of parenthood could there *be*?' said Farah.

Mae shrugged. 'Dunno. I'm too young to understand.'

'I didn't mean it like that.'

'Yeah, you did, but whatevs,' replied Mae. She would not show her sister how offended she was. Instead, she finished her slice of pizza and grabbed another one as she brushed her hand down her jeans. 'I'll be off then.'

'No, stay,' said Farah. 'There's still loads of pizza left.'

Mae bent down, took two more slices and wrapped them up in a napkin.

'I'll take them to go.'

She walked towards the door and turned around to Farah. 'I get you're mad at her. It's not been easy for you, I know. But, you know …' She paused. 'You're not always right about everything.'

'I never said I was,' exclaimed Farah.

Mae looked at her sister and wondered how even adults, with all the things they might've gone through, all that life experience, could really lack in self-awareness. She simply raised her eyebrows at Farah.

'All right then,' said Mae. 'What do I know?'

With which she left Farah to ponder Mae's words of youthful wisdom.

'Oh, thank God you're here,' whispered Fatti.

She pulled Mae in, Adam hanging from her arm, as she seemed to listen out for something.

'What is it?' asked Mae.

'Aima and Ilyaas have been at each other's throat all day and I just ... I just *don't know what to do.*'

'Why's he not at work?'

'Day off,' replied Fatti, shaking her head.

'Can't she go into the office?'

Fatti raised her eyebrows at Mae. 'She's not exactly the work-in-an-office-type.'

Mae sighed as she walked into the living room and Fatti handed Adam to her.

'Now at least I can cook without him screaming his head off. He refuses to be left alone and just wants to be carried around all the time.'

With which Mae was left with Adam who stared at her before he hit her face with his fist. She could hear Aima and Ilyaas argue about whose iPad charger had or hadn't been ruined. So, Bubblee was actually seeing somebody? Mae wondered who it could be. Where he was from. Like, originally. She took her phone out of her pocket with her free hand to message Abdul-Raheem.

Mae: Yo. Hows it goin with the padre?

Mae realised how much she missed Abdul-Raheem not being around. This being in a relationship thing wasn't easy. Out of nowhere you get used to another person and expect that they'll just be there, except they have a life of their own too. It made her realise how friendless she was. Ji Su still flitted into her thoughts but now that Abdul-Raheem wasn't around, she thought about her even more. Mae looked at Ji Su's new WhatsApp profile. She was at a protest, covered in rainbow-coloured badges and ribbons and Mae wished she was there with her instead of holding on to her drooling nephew. People were out there, *doing* things. Things they were passionate about and Mae got a sinking feeling about university and the idea of never going back. But how could she go back? She'd failed. When was she going to tell everyone and what was she going to do with her life? Be a horse's arse for ever? Adam screeched in her ear. Mae went to put him down. She had to think about things, she wanted to be alone and consider what her life was going to be. What it *should* be. Unfortunately, Adam let out a scream, which turned into crying that seriously rivalled Zoya's. Fatti rushed into the room.

'Don't put him down,' she exclaimed.

Mae rushed to pick him up again as Ilyaas walked into the room.

'Oh, hey,' he said, stuffing his hands into his jean pockets.

Fatti rushed back out to see to the food in the kitchen.

'Hi,' Mae replied, bouncing Adam about on her hip in a bid to calm him down.

Ilyaas was staring at Adam and Mae wondered what he was thinking.

'Do you want to hold him?' she asked.

Ilyaas just shook his head. According to Fatti, neither of the children ever wanted to hold Adam and Mae felt sorry for the little bean – to have two older siblings who didn't seem to care about him.

'You should give it a try, you know,' she added.

'He cries a lot,' Ilyaas replied.

'Babies,' she said, sighing. 'It's a bit of a hazard.'

Adam's crying stopped so suddenly she had to be grateful for the convenient timing. Ilyaas looked at Adam, uncertainly, as if he was trying to figure him out as Mae stepped forward and gestured for him to take the baby. He hesitated.

'I'll take him back if he lets loose,' she said.

Ilyaas took his hands out of his jeans pockets and shuffled his feet as he put his arms out. Adam twisted his body towards his half-brother, putting his own hands out and Mae thought she saw the flicker of a smile from Ilyaas as he took him. He rested Adam on his hip, looking at Mae, as if seeking assurance that he was doing the right thing.

'Great,' she said. 'Look at him.'

Adam was holding on to Ilyaas's face and gurgling.

'Ow,' Ilyaas said, with a laugh.

He didn't emit laughter very often. For all the annoyances babies were, they were all right sometimes, weren't they? That's when Aima sauntered in, looking at her phone, and slumped herself on the sofa.

'Careful you don't drop him on his head,' she said. 'Did that to you and look what happened.'

'Shut up,' Ilyaas retorted.

Mae tried to smile at Aima but she was too engrossed with her phone. 'Do you want to hold him?'

Aima looked up for a moment, as if she were actually considering it. 'Nah. Might puke on my new top.'

That's when Fatti walked back in and paused, looking at Adam in Ilyaas's arms.

'Oh,' she said. 'Well, lunch is ready. Sorry it's late. Just going to bring it in.'

Aima sighed and slunk off the sofa, making her way to the dining table, her eyes still glued to the phone. Fatti's gaze followed her, looking nervous, and something in Mae bristled.

'Maybe you want to help bring the dishes in?' Mae said to Aima.

'Oh, no, it's fine,' said Fatti.

Aima didn't look up.

'Aima,' added Mae.

'What?'

'Maybe you want to help bring the dishes in?'

Aima let out another exasperated sigh and pushed herself off her seat to go into the kitchen. The three of them watched her before Fatti followed her in and Mae went to take Adam, suggesting that Ilyaas help as well. He seemed reluctant to let Adam go now, but Mae smiled and said he could have him back after they'd had lunch.

'I've already eaten, anyway,' she said.

'You're going?' he asked.

She did want to go. She wanted to call Abdul-Raheem and hear his voice, tell him about her day, have him ask questions about it. But maybe Fatti needed her more than Mae needed Abdul-Raheem.

'No,' she replied. 'I'm not going anywhere.'

'I can't believe it,' said Fatti as she loaded the dishwasher.

Mae's own hands were free because Ilyaas was holding Adam.

'And Aima actually helped bring the dishes in,' added Fatti.

'The lazy cow—'

'Shhh.'

'The lazy cow,' repeated Mae, lowering her voice, 'should've been doing it all along. Doesn't Ash say anything to her?'

Fatti ran a plate under the sink before she put it in the dishwasher. 'I guess he's too tired to notice. Between work and Adam screaming at night, he just ... I don't know ... switches off.'

'When do *you* switch off?' asked Mae, popping a Malteser in her mouth.

'I'm a wife, mother and stepmother. I don't get to switch off.'

Mae scrunched up her face. 'What is this? The nineteen fifties?'

'Mae, you don't ...'

'What? What don't I do?'

'Nothing,' said Fatti. 'I appreciate you being here.'

'I'd appreciate you finishing your sentence,' replied Mae.

She was getting a little tired of how her sisters babied her, pretending they had life all figured out and she just flitted around having fun, never experiencing the general trials of being alive.

'It was nothing,' said Fatti. 'Forget it.'

'No. Just say what you wanted to,' said Mae, forgetting about the box of Maltesers.

'It's just ... and don't take this the wrong way, because I don't mean anything bad by it. But, you're *young*.'

Mae felt her breathing get faster, her face felt hot.

'What's your point?'

'My point,' said Fatti, wiping her hands with the tea towel and closing the dishwasher, 'is that there are some things you can only really understand when you're in them. Like marriage. And being a mum.'

Mae stared at her sister for a while. She expected this kind of stuff from Farah and Bubblee, but not from Fatti. Fatti was always meant to be on Mae's side, to get her and love her and think she was perfect, no matter how imperfect she actually was.

'Is this what marriage and motherhood does to you?' asked Mae.

'What?' said Fatti, looking genuinely confused.

'Turns you all holier-than-thou.'

Mae saw Fatti swallow hard. 'No. I didn't say that. That's not what I meant. How could I be holier than thou? I haven't washed my hair in a week.'

'Whatever,' said Mae, turning to leave the kitchen.

'Where are you going?'

'Home.'

Which was a lie. She'd just drive around, park up somewhere and wait until it was late enough to not have to endure too much of her parents, but early enough so that they wouldn't ask questions. God, she missed the freedom of university. At least no one was married with babies. At least she was respected as a human being in her own right. Or she would be if she had any friends. Where was Ji Su? Why couldn't she forgive Mae?

'Are you angry with me?' said Fatti.

Mae paused and turned around. 'Yeah. Kinda.'

And she walked out, leaving behind a bewildered Fatti on the verge of tears.

Mae had got into her car and already regretted the way she'd left, but felt, on principle, that it was the right thing to have done. Of all the people to say something like that to her – Fatti? It was the disappointment. The one thread of hope in her family that she was seen as a fully rounded person broke in that kitchen, and Mae felt a desperate sense of separateness from everything. She got her phone.

> Abdul-Raheem: It's going good. He can't wait to meet you.

Mae stared at the message. *He told his dad? His dad wants to meet her?* Her breathing got fast as she gulped and came out of WhatsApp. Isn't this what women wanted? For men to be like, *interested*? But everything seemed to be happening so quickly. Then her phone rang.

It was Abdul-Raheem.

She looked at his name flash on her screen but couldn't quite bring herself to pick it up. Instead she let it ring until he finally hung up.

Was there something wrong with Mae? No. Even she knew that things were moving too fast. They hadn't even kissed properly yet! She knew that this wasn't entirely unusual because he was keen on being a 'good' Muslim, but that didn't mean she didn't want to be kissed, to be able to kiss him whenever she wanted. At least it might begin to feel serious enough to then warrant meeting his dad. Mae was startled out of her thoughts by a knock on her window.

'Hey,' she said, putting down her mobile and looking at Ilyaas.

'Why'd you leave?' he asked.

'Things to do.'

She went to start the car and was about to say bye when he said: 'Can I come with you?'

Oh God.

'You'd just get bored. I was going to go and do some uni reading,' she lied.

He shrugged. 'That's all right.'

He looked at her so desperately she could hardly say no. Mae held in her need to bang her head on the steering wheel, and would have to not think about why she suddenly felt so stifled by Abdul-Raheem as Ilyaas got into the passenger's side. She drove into town and they sat in the same café she and Abdul-Raheem had their first date.

'Where are your books?' said Ilyaas.

'What?'

'Your books? For studying?'

Mae had not thought this through.

'Why don't we just chill out?' she said. 'We can have dessert, if you want.'

'Yeah. All right,' replied Ilyaas, picking up the paper menu. 'I'll have the apple pie.'

The waitress came and took their orders. Mae naturally asked for a side of chips with her chocolate bomb cake.

'How's work going?' she asked.

Ilyaas shrugged.

'You missing home?'

Ilyaas shrugged again. Mae was beginning to understand what people meant when they said they were at
the end of their tether. The waitress came and delivered
their desserts and Mae's chips.

'I guess we'll just sit in silence then,' said Mae, picking
up a chip.

Ilyaas stabbed at his pie with a fork. After him hardly
taking a bite of it, Mae asked, 'If you don't want it, I'll
take it, you know.'

He pushed the plate towards her, his fork still in his
hand. 'What's it like at uni?' he asked eventually.

Mae paused. This question, along with everything else,
seriously hampered her enjoyment of the apple pie. 'It's
great. There's the best doner kebab in town.'

She said it with perhaps more enthusiasm than intended,
and Ilyaas looked at her as if dubious about this answer.

'You know,' she added, 'I guess it's not all fun and
games. Obviously. You're there to study, after all.'

He nodded. 'But, like, what's it *like*? To be around all
those people?'

Ilyaas never seemed to be on his phone the way Aima
was, he'd not ever talk about any of his friends either,
but then it wasn't as if he talked about anything.

'Weird,' she said. 'Especially when you're not used
to being around so many. And when they all seem to
have these amazing lives and you're like, I've spent my
life between my family's living room and my bedroom.'

He let out a small laugh.

'Don't you like people?' she asked.

Mae swore if he shrugged one more time she'd have to shake him.

'They're just …'

'What?'

'My sister's all cool and stuff, isn't it? And, like, she has loads of friends but …'

'But you don't find it so easy?' Mae asked.

He shook his head and looked down at the table again. 'Whatever, though. My high school's full of morons and I can't wait to get out of there.'

'High school's tough,' said Mae, with a knowing nod. 'Life gets better though.'

'Does it?'

He looked straight into her eyes as if challenging her. Did he see through her white lie?

'I mean … yeah.'

'Don't really sound like you mean it,' said Ilyaas.

Mae put her spoon down and leaned forward. 'All right, fine. It's crap sometimes, and might get crappier. But you've got a family who love you and a new baby brother. You're a good-looking kid and Fatti was saying how much Ash loves having you around the office. That you're a really good worker.'

Mae noticed Ilyaas's cheeks flush as he lowered his gaze again.

'It's true,' she said. 'So, at least you know you're making a difference to your dad's work day.'

He looked up at her and went to pull his plate with the apple pie back.

'Don't think so,' said Mae, holding on to it. 'Losers weepers.'

'Whatever,' Ilyaas said, tugging at the plate, laughing, before Mae let it go.

'That's really bad form, by the way. Giving someone your pie and then taking it back.'

Mae licked her spoon before diving in for her chips as he stared at her.

'I'm joking,' said Mae.

'What? Yeah, no, I know.'

'God, I miss those doner kebabs,' she said.

'That good?'

'The best.'

They both ate their respective foods and Mae felt quite fond of Ilyaas. He might not be the most talkative person in the world, but she guessed there was always a story behind why someone was the way they were. She looked up at him and noticed him staring at her. Did she have something on her face? She smiled but he just kept looking at her with such intensity she didn't know what to do. Then her phone rang. It was lying on the table and Ilyaas's eyes flicked towards the screen as Abdul-Raheem's name popped up and her heart skipped a beat. She snatched at the phone. If it was a choice between speaking to Abdul-Raheem and having Ilyaas stare at her then she knew what she was going to choose.

'Give me one sec, okay?' she said to Ilyaas as she slid out of her chair and walked outside the café.

'Hello?' she said.

'Hey, asalamoalaikum.'

'How's it going?' she asked, trying to sound normal.

She had to remember that Abdul-Raheem had all these ideals about meeting families, but it didn't mean she had to go along with them.

'Good. Great. Dad's on good form. How are you? What's going on?'

Before Mae could stop herself she launched into what had happened that day with all of her sisters, how she just needed to be alone, that Ilyaas ended up getting in the car with her and she couldn't say no. Obviously she left out the bits about her panicking about Abdul-Raheem wanting her to meet his dad.

'Take a breath,' he said.

She did as he suggested.

'It's okay,' he added.

'I'm so fed up of hearing crap about my age and how I don't know about the world from everyone. Imagine listening to all that when everyone's being a crappy human themselves, just because they're raising little humans, who, incidentally, do nothing but crap themselves.'

He laughed so loud it made Mae smile.

'What's so funny?' she asked.

'*You*,' he replied.

Mae wondered what she'd been worrying so much about and before she knew it she said: 'I miss you.'

He paused. 'Do you?'

'Mhmm.'

She waited for him to respond. The seconds stretched into what seemed like hours, not a word coming out of his mouth.

'I miss you too,' he said, finally.

'What took you so long?' she exclaimed.

He laughed. 'You kind of surprised me.'

'Did I?'

'Yeah,' he replied. 'I always think that maybe you don't feel as strongly as I do.'

Mae gulped. Maybe he was right, but she couldn't exactly say that, and it didn't mean she didn't feel things for him at all. *She did*. Right then she just wanted to melt into his arms. It hadn't been quite the same with Ji Su. It had been easy because she seemed to have understood Mae, but these feelings that Mae had for Abdul-Raheem were different. It took being in a relationship to realise it and it made her a little sad because it didn't mean she didn't want Ji Su in her life; that she didn't miss her every day. Before she could respond to Abdul-Raheem he said: 'Hang on, there's someone who'd like to speak to you.'

'Hello, Mae? My boy's not stopped talking about you and I want to know when I get to meet you.'

For a moment Mae stuttered. How could Abdul-Raheem just hand the phone over to his dad without warning her?

'Oh, hi. Hello.'

'And he's shown me pictures. What's a pretty girl like you doing with him?'

'*Dad*,' he heard Abdul-Raheem say in the background.

'All right, all right. Calm down. He says I'll get to meet you soon.'

Mae paused for perhaps longer than needed.

'Hello?'

'Oh, hi, sorry, bad reception,' Mae said. 'Yeah. Yeah. We'll meet.'

Why was Abdul-Raheem saying things like that?

'Anyway, I'll give the phone back to him now. It was nice talking to you and don't put up with any of his nonsense.'

Mae barely said goodbye when Abdul-Raheem spoke again. 'Don't mind him. He's always making my life difficult.'

'He seems nice,' was all Mae could muster.

'Fancy coming with me to see him in a few weeks? When I come to visit him again?'

Maybe she wouldn't have minded meeting the dad. Perhaps she'd get an idea for the boy Abdul-Raheem used to be, hear stories about him. Especially the stories that Abdul-Raheem tried to avoid telling. But all this did was remind Mae of the fact that she couldn't introduce Abdul-Raheem to her family and how fast things were moving. This fact sat between them. He knew it, she knew it, but neither of them said anything. Then Mae felt a sense of annoyance. Why did he put his dad on the phone when he knew that she was uncomfortable about him meeting her family? It felt like pressure and wasn't there enough of that in her life?

'Mae?'

'Doesn't sound like I've got much choice, does it?'

'Sorry?'

It didn't meant to come out so harshly but at that moment Mae couldn't help it.

'Like, you put him on the phone just now so it'd seem kind of bad if I don't turn up. Kind of stuck me in it.'

'Stuck you in it?' he repeated.

'Yeah.'

'Didn't know you felt *stuck* with me.'

She took a deep breath. 'That's not what I meant. It's just …'

'What?' His voice sounded sharp. Severe.

'I mean, we've only been going out a few weeks and we haven't even …'

She paused.

'What?'

'We haven't even kissed properly and you're talking about meeting families.'

It was his turn to pause.

'I didn't realise physical intimacy showed how important someone was to them.'

Why did he make it sound as if her feelings didn't make sense? Or that they were stupid?

'I'm not saying that, I'm just saying I want to slow down.'

Another pause.

'Hello?' she said.

'I see.'

'I mean with all the family stuff.'

'Right.'

'It's like, suffocating, you know?'

'Suffocating?'

'Yeah. All this pressure.'

This time he paused for a long time before Mae added, 'You expect me to be where you are, and I'm not.'

'What are you saying, Mae? Do you want to break up with me?'

No, Mae wanted to say, but maybe she did.

'I don't know,' she replied eventually. 'It's just that, listen, you're great. And I miss you when you're not around, but like … oh, it's stupid.'

'Why don't you tell me what it is and we'll see how stupid it is,' he said, his voice having softened somewhat.

'There's the family thing but it's also that … I had this friend, right? Ji Su. And we were so close and then, well, something happened and she doesn't speak to me any more and I felt like I'd lost the one good thing I had, and then you came along and we're so close—'

'I'm not going to ever stop speaking to you,' he interrupted.

'No, it's not that,' Mae added.

It began to dawn on her that what was niggling her,

aside from the family stuff, was this growing feeling that she *was* young and she seemed to need someone around her in order to be normal. But, shouldn't she be able to do that on her own? Wasn't what happened with Ji Su because Mae's confusion had confused their relationship? Perhaps Mae had to learn to find a way out of her messes without being dependent on someone to help her along.

When she tried to explain this to Abdul-Raheem, he didn't quite get it.

'But you said yourself you hated being alone. That you were lonely. And now you want to be alone again? I don't get it.'

He was right, it didn't make any sense, but how could she tell him that the pressure of the two of them wasn't allowing her to concentrate on other things? Wasn't it time for her to get her act together? Think of what she was going to do about uni? How was she to resolve that drama with the drama of her and Abdul-Raheem at the same time?

She tried to explain this to him too but he just went quiet.

'Do you get it?' she asked, desperate for him to under-stand.

'No,' he replied. 'I don't.'

'We can still be friends,' she added. 'Still hang out, you know? I just think I need to focus on stuff.'

He paused. It was going to be just like with Ji Su.

He'd turn around and walk away and Mae was already beginning to regret it. But she had to be bolder in life. She had to take control of things instead of just burying her head in the sand. Although she did wish she wasn't taking her head out of the sand while on the phone.

'Okay,' he said.

'Sorry?'

'Okay,' he repeated. 'Let's just be friends.'

'Really?'

'Listen, I'm not saying I like it, but … if there's one thing I get it's trying to focus on things, and you have important decisions to make in life. I don't want you to feel I'm in the way of it.'

Mae wanted to cry, but this time not out of anger or hurt, out of pure affection.

'Thank you,' she whispered.

'Well, you're still going to be my horse's arse,' he said.

She laughed. 'Yeah. Nothing to be done about that.'

They both went quiet before Mae added, 'You're pretty great, you know.'

Abdul-Raheem paused. 'No. I'm just in it for the long run.'

Long run. She didn't know what to feel about that, but noticed Ilyaas staring at her through the window. She'd been on the phone long enough. She hung up and walked back into the café. Ilyaas looked at her as she sat back down.

'Friend from uni?' he asked.

'Hmm? Yeah. You finished? Shall we go?'

Ilyaas hesitated before he said, 'Yeah, guess so.'

She drove him all the way home, making small talk, so engrossed in her own thoughts about Abdul-Raheem that she didn't bother to wonder why Ilyaas didn't look at her when he got out of the car and mumbled goodbye.

It was still too early to go home and Mae wondered what she could do to take her mind off the fact that she'd just broken up with her boyfriend. That she now had no excuse to figure out what she was going to do with her life. Then it struck her that she knew exactly where she should go, and was surprised not to have thought of it earlier. So, Mae drove towards the stables.

There wasn't anyone around when she got there so she waited for about fifteen minutes before Alison appeared.

'Hello,' she said. She had a tin bucket in her hand. 'I was wondering when you'd come over again. Did you read the book?'

Mae was embarrassed to admit she hadn't even thought about it.

'I got a new job,' she replied. 'At the amusement park. Been kind of busy.'

'Ah,' said Alison. 'At least you found a job. Well done.'

'How's Ginger?'

'On good form, actually. You want to see him?'

'Can I book an hour? Is that all right?'

'Of course,' said Alison, putting the bucket down and walking into the stable.

Mae found it just as tricky to get on Ginger as she had the first time, but she felt more assured when riding through the fields and asked Alison to let go of the reins, if that was okay. She readily obliged and walked next to the horse.

'You know what's nice about this?' said Mae. 'Not being stuck in front of a laptop. It's almost like social media doesn't exist.'

Alison laughed. 'That's probably a good thing.'

'You forget there's more to life than Snapchat or whatever,' replied Mae.

'I've no idea what you're talking about.'

That, to Mae, was one of the single most amazing things she'd heard. Who didn't know what Snapchat was? Crazy.

'I prefer to live in the real world,' added Alison as Mae stared at her.

'Yeah. Guess that's better.'

It occurred to Mae that she hadn't really done a lot of social media in the past few weeks at all. Maybe it was being with Abdul-Raheem, maybe it was because it reminded her too much of the train incident. She wasn't sure, but either way she didn't really miss it, which was odd. That was meant to be the way her life was headed. The hour finished a lot quicker than Mae would've liked, but this time she managed to get off Ginger without stumbling, too much, to the ground.

'See you again soon, boy?' she said, stroking Ginger's neck. 'I kind of love him,' she added, looking at Alison. 'Looks like he feels the same way.'

Chapter Thirteen

The following day there was nothing Mae wanted to do more than to go to the stables. But first she picked up the book that Alison had given her. Mae realised that it was an old children's book and though it was simply written, it was just what she needed and she found a lot of it interesting. After she finished it she went to the stables and booked in another ride with Ginger.

There was something about the open air that just made Mae forget all her troubles. It was her and Ginger and no other worry or thought occurred to her. When she returned home she saw a message on her phone.

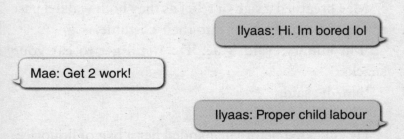

Ilyaas: Hi. Im bored lol

Mae: Get 2 work!

Ilyaas: Proper child labour

Back in the mad household her annoyance with Fatti resurfaced and was only made worse by the fact that

Mae was actually helping her by being friends with her stepson. And yeah, he had a sense of humour and he wasn't a bad kid, but she didn't really like the way he'd been staring at her. It was kind of creepy.

The following day Mae struggled not to let her nerves get the better of her when getting ready for work. It'd be the first time she'd seen Abdul-Raheem after their phone conversation. She hadn't heard from him for two days and already felt weird about it.

Then, outside the booths, she saw him and he smiled at her.

'Hey,' he said, looking down at her.

'Hi,' she replied.

'We're not going to let this be awkward, all right?' he added.

'Oh, thank God for that because I've had enough awkward moments lately to last me a lifetime.'

He smiled again. 'Time to saddle up.'

Mae breathed a sigh of relief as they both walked past the teacup ride and got into their costume.

'I'm hungry,' said Mae. 'Do I still get to eat your snacks?'

'No,' he said.

'What?'

He chuckled before he handed her a bag of liquorice.

'I went to the stables again, you know,' she said.

'Oh yeah? How was it?'

'I love Ginger.'

'Yeah, horses are really majestic animals.'

'Unless you're dressed as one,' she said. 'And I didn't look so majestic trying to get off Ginger, but you can't have it all.'

She heard him laugh and that's how they spent their day at work, just as they always had done. It almost felt too easy and Mae wondered whether she should trust it. Perhaps that was too cynical of her – she should be grateful that Abdul-Raheem was still talking to her, being his usual self. Mae wanted to give him a hug but guessed that was off-limits now.

At the end of the day, everyone gathered at the entrance as Barry handed out their goody bags. Abdul-Raheem gave his to Mae. She was about to walk to the car but then turned around and forgot herself. She went and gave him a hug so tight he lifted her in the air.

'Thanks for still being my friend,' she whispered.

She left his embrace and noticed Leanne looking at them and sighing.

'Always,' he replied.

The rest of the week at work was much the same. Though sometimes Mae would bring the snacks.

'So?' Abdul-Raheem asked. 'How's the focus going?'

'Well, right now I'm stuck being an arse so not able to focus on much else.'

'Don't think I don't know you're using jokes to avoid answering the question.'

Mae sighed. How did he get to know her so well?

'I ... well, I don't even know where to start. What am I meant to do with my life?'

'You could start by telling your family what happened,' he suggested. 'They might be a lot more supportive than you give them credit for.'

Mae scoffed. 'You'd think life in prison would've made you a little less optimistic.'

She felt him reach back and flick her arm with his finger. She grabbed it and laughed as she held on to it, his arm out of use because of it.

'Try being a horse without an arm,' she said.

'Yeah, dunno how horses live without arms,' he replied.

'Oh. Oh yeah.'

Mae let go of his finger.

'Listen,' he said after a few moments. 'Why don't we go out on our day off? Dinner or something. Your treat since we're no longer dating.'

Mae swallowed hard. Was he trying to get back together with her? But then he knew where they stood and it did sound so much better than having to spend it with the family.

'Dinner might be tricky,' she said. 'Family.'

'Are you rolling your eyes?' he asked.

'Oh my God, how did you know?'

'Psychic.' He paused. 'Listen, I get that going out at night's difficult, but Mae, you're at university—'

'Actually, technically, I'm not,' she interrupted. 'Remember?'

'My point is, it's normal for people to go out for dinner. You're an adult and you've got to make them see you as one.'

It was true. What did her parents know about what she'd got up to when she had been at uni? Why did she have to stick to this weird no-going-out-in-the-evenings schedule when she was at home? Everyone went on at her about being *young*, well she'd have to make them see her as an adult.

'Yeah, okay,' she said. 'God, isn't it break time yet? I'm so hot in this stupid thing.'

A ray of light hit her as Abdul-Raheem took his horse's head off.

'Yep, it sure is.'

The day they were meant to meet for dinner, the weirdest idea got into Mae's head. What if he invited her into the flat now they were just friends? She imagined them sitting on the sofa, the lights dim, and the effect of what a nice night out and them actually being alone might have. She felt her stomach flutter at the possibilities but had to remind herself they were *just* friends. That it had been her decision.

It was at around two o'clock that her phone rang and it was Bubblee, panting down the phone.

'We need you to look after Zoya tonight. Please,' Bubblee added, almost as an afterthought.

'What?'

'I didn't realise that Farah was going out to see a friend, and I'm going out too and neither of us can cancel.'

'Sorry, but I also have a life. I'm out.'

'Where?'

Mae paused. 'What's it got to do with you? I'm seeing a friend too.'

'What friend?'

'Maybe ask fewer questions and try to find someone else to babysit. There are like a million people in this family,' said Mae. 'Just drop him over to Mum and Dad's.'

'They're going to an aunt's house and I don't want to lumber Fatti with another baby. She's already frazzled enough with things at home as it is.'

Mae tried not to feel sympathy for Fatti.

'Soz, but not my problem.'

'Mae, *please*. Farah's not been out in ages, and we all know she could do with it.'

'And I bet she wasn't exactly pleased when you'd ended up double booking?' said Mae.

'What do you think?'

'So, you cancel.'

Bubblee paused. 'I really can't. It's work-related and could mean losing out on a serious donation for the gallery.'

Mae took a deep breath. It was just typical, wasn't it? The *one* time she'd agreed and planned a night out with her boyfriend and her entire family was throwing a spanner in the works.

'Please, Mae, I'm seriously begging you. I'll do anything to make it up to you.'

'Just organising your life better would be great.'

'You'll do it?' asked Bubblee.

'I didn't say that.'

'But, Mae, it's an emergency.'

She had to pause and think about it. Mae had picked out the perfect thing to wear, how she'd do her make-up and hair – she'd even shaved, though she refused to ask herself why she'd done that. The more care she'd taken to choose her clothes, the more she realised how much she was looking forward to spending quality time with Abdul-Raheem, without having to be in a costume in the scorching weather.

'Why do I have to cancel for you guys?' she said.

'I know, I know. I'm sorry, but if there was another option I'd use it. Just this one time. *Please?*'

Why was it so hard to say no when Bubblee asked like that? Mae couldn't believe it.

'Fine. Whatever. You'd better leave me some nice food in the fridge, you know.'

'Oh, whatever you want,' exclaimed Bubblee. 'Thank you, thank you, thank you. Be over at half six, okay? I've got to go now. *Thank you.*'

Before Mae could say, 'I wish I could say it's no problem,' Bubblee had already put the phone down.

'And you'd better not be lying and meeting your new man instead,' Mae added, into the phone, knowing full well that Bubblee had gone. 'Ugh.'

> **Ilyaas:** Hear ur babysittin Z.

> **Mae:** yeh its gonna b gr8 fun.

> **Ilyaas:** u want me 2come ova n help?

> **Mae:** Ru mad?? Y wud I put u thru that?? Thnx 4 offer tho. Pray I make it 2 the otha side.

There was nothing to do but tell Abdul-Raheem. When he picked up the phone she went into quite a dramatic rant about the fact that it was typical of her family, that her sisters had better appreciate what she was doing, that it was the last time she was going to babysit, because, *hello, she had a life.*

'Hello?' she said, when nothing but silence came from the other end of the line.

'I'm here.'

'Oh. I'm so sorry, but shall we try again next week?'

'Then what's it going to be?' he asked.

'What's what going to be?'

'What excuse?'

'It's not an excuse,' said Mae. 'It's not like I'd rather be changing nappies.'

'Really?'

'What are you on about?'

Abdul-Raheem paused. 'I might have no right to say this any more but your family always seem to come before anything else. You want to make changes in your life? Maybe that's where you should start.'

What? Yeah, they plagued her life, but that wasn't because they came before everything else; it was just the way it was in the family.

'You don't understand,' said Mae. 'You know what it's like between Farah and Bubblee right now. There's no way Bubblee would have asked Farah to cancel and Bubs couldn't cancel – her work is her life.'

'What about your life?'

'Why are you making this into a thing?' said Mae. 'It's not like we're boyfriend and girlfriend any more.'

'I didn't realise our friendship meant less to you,' he replied.

Oh God.

'But you're right. We *are* just friends, so maybe I've no right to be mad. I'm not mad,' he added. 'I'm just … disappointed.'

'I'm sorry,' she said.

That was worse than him being angry.

'No, don't be sorry.' He paused. 'Just think; you finally made a decision to think carefully about what you're going to do with your life – you broke up with me because of it – you want to be an adult.' Another pause. 'What kind of adult has to lie about her days off?'

It was his tone that caught Mae off guard. He wasn't accusatory or mean. Just right.

'It's not easy when you're Bengali,' she replied.

'How many times are you going to use that as an excuse?'

'It's not an excuse, it's a *reason*. You might not be Bengali but you're a Muslim, don't you get it?'

'What? A grown woman sneaking around? Not being able to go out for dinner with a friend? No, I don't get it. I think it's ridiculous. Come on, Mae. You're at university—'

'Not really.'

'Exactly. You're smart and funny but have you thought about what you want to study? What you're going to do?'

Mae's head was swimming around with too many things. How had this conversation gone from simply cancelling dinner to assessing Mae's choices and her life?

'Why are you making such a big deal of this?' she said. 'Chill out.'

'I'm chilled,' he said. 'It's not my life here. But think about it, you haven't even told your family about uni yet. You don't tell them anything, but everything you do revolves around them.'

Didn't he know that she wished they were more involved in her life? That they actually took an interest in what was going on in it?

'Tell them anyway,' he replied. 'Make them listen to you.'

'What, like strap them down, lock the babies away and fix every other problem that each of them has, just to tell them about mine?'

'*Yes*,' Abdul-Raheem said. 'Maybe don't lock up the babies because there are laws about that, but yes, do that. *Make* them listen. Why don't you think your life is as important as theirs?'

'Ugh.' Mae put her forehead in her hands. 'They all have families. Babies. It's always more important.'

'That's a load of crap. You know it, I know it. *They* might not know it, but you should tell them what you think of the fact that their lives always seem more important than yours.'

'It's … whatever,' mumbled Mae.

'No,' he said. 'It's not whatever. You have a chance to make something of yourself, Mae. To actually *go* to uni. I'm not saying that you can't make something of yourself without it, but if you want that experience then you need to hold on to it, make sure you make it happen. Do you know how much I wish I had the chances you do? How I beat myself up for not saying to hell with other people, I'm going to make this work? I whatever'd my way through life, but then I converted and began to learn that sometimes the harder something is, the more it's worth.'

'So why are you working in an amusement park?'

She said it without thinking, but it was true, wasn't it? He was lecturing her on life and he was a twenty-eight-year-old in a horse's costume.

'Because I'm saving up money to go back to school.'

'Oh,' was all Mae could manage. 'You never said.'

'You didn't ask. Anyway, it's going to take a while and, well, I'm embarrassed of the things I'm having to do, just to get another shot.'

Mae picked at some dirt on her jeans. 'Sorry.'

'Don't apologise to me,' he said. 'I've got a dad who's supportive and I've been around people who've had it far worse than me. I should be grateful that I'm able to actually graft. So, I don't want to hear sorry from you. I want you to *do* something about your own situation.'

But *how*? Mae got the sentiment, and she felt sheepish that someone like Abdul-Raheem, who'd faced so many more obstacles in life than she had, was telling her to get her act together. If Mae had felt some sense of control she wouldn't have failed university in the first place, though.

'All I'm saying is I wish that you saw that it's your life. It's part of the reason I'm not angry or so upset that you broke up with me. I thought you were going to change things, but it doesn't look like you are. Your family should be helping you to get where you want, not putting obstacles in the way.'

Mae gave a wry laugh. 'Is that what they're there for?'

'They should be,' he replied. 'And if they're not, then, well … the rest is up to you.'

'What? Leave my family?'

'No,' he said. 'But if they're stopping you from being the person you want to be, then it's time you made that stop.'

She wanted to say that that was the whole problem. She didn't know *who* she wanted to be.

Before she left for Farah and Bubblee's house, her parents were in the middle of getting ready to leave as well, her dad grabbing her mum's coat for her. They agreed that Mae could take the car and they'd get a taxi. She hadn't been able to get the conversation with Abdul-Raheem out of her head. They'd ended it being normal enough, but she felt the impact of his words long after she'd put the phone down.

'Well, off I go,' she said to her parents. 'Another day of babysitting.'

She'd have left the house without another word, just trudged on and left her parents to it if only her mum hadn't responded.

'Think of how hard it is for your sisters. The least you can do is help a little. You will know how hard it is when you have a family one day.'

Mae had never been the screaming and slamming door type. It was all kind of dramatic and who could do with that kind of tension? That was Bubblee's domain. But in that moment she felt she might throw the door off its hinges.

'Who the hell told them to have babies?' shouted Mae.

Her parents stopped short. The arm of her mum's coat dangled as she and her dad stared at her.

'No one forced them, you know. They wanted the baby and decided to do this whole co-parenting thing, so why should I feel bad about it?'

'Mae ...' said her dad.

'It's *true*.'

'See how selfish she's become?' said her mum.

Mae couldn't believe her ears, though she didn't know why it surprised her.

'Jay's amma ...' said her dad.

Apparently the only thing her dad could ever do was repeat everyone's name. Mae had always loved him because you couldn't *not* love someone that gentle, but right then she wished he'd step up and be a proper father. Not just a husband who did whatever it took to prevent his wife losing her temper. Why couldn't he put things in perspective for her mum? Why couldn't he show her that she was being unreasonable and why wasn't he doing something other than just staring at Mae helplessly? If it was Abdul-Raheem, he'd never have let someone get away with the injustice of such a comment. No, her ex-boyfriend always tried to do the right thing. Her ex-boyfriend who she cancelled dinner with, who she *broke up* with, only to be called selfish by her own mum. There was too much inside her for her to even have a retort. She wished she could abandon all promises to her sisters but there was nothing for it and she'd have to go. But she wasn't going to say another word to her mum. She swept around, walked out of the house and slammed the door loud enough that even Bubblee would've been proud.

Farah had already left by the time Mae arrived, and Bubblee was too busy putting on lipstick to notice the way Mae's eyes were fixed in a state of concentrated anger.

'There's food in the fridge. Sorry, couldn't make anything special – just leftover bean salad and brown rice. She'll be ready for sleep in about half an hour. Can you give her a quick bath as well, please? But make sure you feed her first. Better get started because it takes ages to get her to eat. Thanks so much,' added Bubblee, giving Mae an air kiss and sweeping out of the house.

Bean salad? Mae threw her bag on the sofa, leaning over Zoya who was lying on her jungle gym.

'I'm supposed to feed you as well as bathe you?'

Zoya looked up at her with Bambi-like eyes, which made Mae's bubbling temperament come down to a simmer. Mae banged and slammed things as she got Zoya's food out of the fridge, warmed it up and sat her in her high chair. Mae sniffed the dinner.

'Mmmm, cauliflower and cheese. That's pretty gross, isn't it?' Tone was everything, she'd heard, so as long as Mae sounded positive and happy she could be talking about killing her whole family and it wouldn't make a difference. *Selfish? Mae?* The words banged down on her again like a two-tonne truck. It was just so unfair. It was one thing to help everyone and not be appreciated, but to be called selfish when no one cared about what was happening in her own life was just too far. Maybe Abdul-Raheem was right. She was beginning to forget the reasons she broke up with him. Why did she feel he'd hinder her figuring her life out? She gave a spoonful of the food to Zoya, who took it in for about a second before spitting it out.

'Don't think you understand the concept of eating, Z. You swallow.'

This time though, when Mae tried to put the spoon in her mouth, Zoya clamped her lips shut and turned her head away.

'Don't listen to me,' said Mae. 'It's delicious really. Look at all those delicious lumps of cauliflower that haven't been blended properly? Mmmm.'

But it didn't matter how hard Mae tried, Zoya refused to open her mouth and got so tired of the entire thing that she started to cry.

'All right, all right,' said Mae, putting the bowl and spoon down. 'What do you want then?'

Mae picked up her phone and called Bubblee to ask what she should feed her instead, except she didn't answer. She rang Farah and she didn't answer either. What kind of parents left their child alone and didn't glue themselves to the phone? By this time Zoya's crying had got louder.

'Why're you crying? I'm not force-feeding you any more.'

Mae left her to her tears and buttered some soft white bread to give to her instead. This, however, didn't produce a more favourable effect – Zoya continued to whine.

'Bean salad?'

It couldn't be bad for her, could it? Mae mashed up the beans and other bits of vegetables to make it more digestible. She managed to get a spoonful into Zoya's mouth without her spitting it back out. It wasn't easy getting her to eat it. Zoya kept smacking at the spoon, shaking her head, banging on the high-chair table and going red-faced, but at least she ate something. Although she did spit in Mae's face, with some of the bean salad's remnants flying into Mae's hair.

'All right then, come on. Up we go for our bath.'

Zoya was still whining even though Mae was swaying her, singing to her, doing whatever she could. She filled the baby tub with water and baby bath as Zoya thrashed her arms and legs on the bathroom mat. Mae needed to have a quick pee. She lifted the toilet lid and just as she was relieving herself Zoya let out a cry so loud Mae thought something had stabbed her. She finished peeing, got up and pulled her trousers up, quickly washing her hands as Zoya's face began to go red. What was wrong with her? She stripped Zoya's clothes off and realised that there was yellow, slimy poo, all down Zoya's back, sticking to the Babygro.

'Ew, gross,' exclaimed Mae, lifting the offending item as far away from her as possible.

She bunched it up and flung it on the floor as her niece's cries got louder. Mae looked around madly for Zoya's rattle that she was sure she'd brought upstairs with her. She saw the handle poking out from under the Babygro, which she threw behind her, forgetting that she hadn't put the lid on the toilet back down.

'Oh shit,' she exclaimed, looking between Zoya still in a nappy and the Babygro that had landed in the toilet.

Not only had she not put the lid down, but she'd also forgotten to flush.

'Oh God. Oh God, oh God, oh God,' she said, as she reached into the toilet, having to put her hand in her own urine to get the Babygro back.

'Ewww,' she repeated as she threw the garment in the sink, Zoya's crying getting even louder. 'Okay, sorry, sorry.'

Mae took off her niece's nappy, wondering how on earth you're meant to protect your hands from getting dirty when a baby's exploded what seemed like a week's worth of food. She turned Zoya this way and that, the poo getting all over the bathroom mat because Mae had forgotten to put down the plastic one for changing. Mae got one baby wipe after another, trying to clean it all before putting Zoya in the tub. The bin was now over-flowing with all the wipes that she'd used. Thankfully, Zoya began to quieten down, still whimpering, but at least not screaming, as Mae lifted her into the tub. Unfortunately, she hadn't quite got all of the poo off as she saw bits of it float to the top of the water.

'Right, well, that wasn't very clever, was it? Why didn't I first wash your bum with water?'

It was too late for regret though since Mae would have to fill the tub with clean water. She had her hands under Zoya's arm, pulling her out of the bath when Zoya gave her a blank kind of look. That's when she threw up the entire contents of the bean salad all over Mae's arms, down her own stomach and into the tub. Mae retched, willing herself not to vomit as Zoya dangled over the tub of filth. Mae looked away from the bits of beans and corn, floating around in the water. She'd make it, she would not throw up. But just as she'd conjured the energy to lift her niece fully out of the tub, Zoya threw up again and Mae couldn't hold in her own bile. She put Zoya down as gently as she could – given the circumstance – on to the floor, no plastic mat to be found, as Mae threw up in the toilet, missing it by about two seconds and half an inch. For a moment, Mae thought the sound of her retching had distracted her niece from her own crying. It was only when she looked over that she saw the lull in crying was because Zoya was too busy doing a runny poo all over the bathroom mat.

'Oh nooooo. No, no, no, no, no.'

Mae wanted to actually cry as she wiped her mouth, dragged her knees over to Zoya, turning her head away from the stench. Just then her phone rang.

'Hello?' she barked, without seeing who it is.

'Listen, I just wanted to say sorry for how I spo—'

But before Abdul-Raheem could finish his sentence, Mae cried: 'Help me, *please*.'

Abdul-Raheem was at Bubblee and Farah's house in twenty minutes. Mae had washed Zoya down with the shower as well as she could and if Farah or Bubblee complained that this wasn't a proper bath, Mae would throw Zoya's dirty nappy at them. When she answered the door she didn't have a chance to check how she looked in the mirror. Abdul-Raheem's expression was enough to tell her it might not be great, but it was apparently amusing.

'Thank God you're here,' she said, almost jumping on him.

She would have embraced him fully if Zoya wasn't hanging on her hip.

'Is this the thing that's got you all rattled then?' he said, looking at Zoya and putting his arms out to her.

Her niece didn't hesitate before reaching out to him, looking up at him as she blew bubbles from her mouth.

'*Rattled?* Are you kidding me? It was like something out of a horror film in that bathroom. It still is,' she said.

'Right,' he replied, handing Zoya back to Mae. 'This way?' he asked, already running up the stairs.

'To the left,' Mae shouted as she looked at Zoya's now calm face.

She gave her milk, took her upstairs into the nursery and put her in her grow bag and into her cot. Mae stroked her head and wondered how something so cute could be so terrible at the same time.

'You're a little piece of ... well. You know what you are.'

Mae planted a kiss on Zoya's head, took the baby monitor and closed the door, leaving it ajar for a little light.

She peeked into the bathroom to see Abdul-Raheem on his hands and knees, wiping remnants of Zoya's vomit and poo from the tiles. He'd hosed down the mat with the shower, emptied the baby's tub, cleaned the adult tub and had also wiped clean all traces of Mae's own vomit. Perhaps it didn't look or sound romantic, but it certainly felt it to Mae.

'Glamorous life, isn't it?' she said.

'Way to spend an evening,' he replied, getting up. 'Cleaned the mat but it'll have to go in the wash.'

'Leave that to my sisters. I think we've done enough already.'

She paused and looked at him, wanting to tell him how grateful she was for him coming, for him just being who he was, but how was she meant to do that when he was no longer her boyfriend?

'Thanks,' she said eventually. 'You know … for all of this.'

He smiled. 'Is she asleep?'

Mae looked at the baby monitor. 'Getting there. All that throwing up must've really taken it out of her.'

Just then there was a ring on the doorbell and Mae's heart skipped a beat. Who could it be? A look of panic must've come over her as Abdul-Raheem said: 'That must be the pizza I ordered.'

'Oh my God,' she replied, both relieved and thankful, because pizza – whilst not being a doner kebab – was real food. Something her sisters didn't think of but her ex-boyfriend did. 'I *actually* love you.'

Turned out that Mae, as well as other things, was vomiting words too.

Abdul-Raheem seemed to stiffen.

'Sorry I—'

'Don't worry. I know that's the baby formula talking,' he joked, washing his hands.

I love you?

The doorbell rang again and he touched Mae's arm as he went to answer it. Mae looked in the mirror at her dishevelled hair and flushed face.

'*What the hell is wrong with you?*' she whispered to herself. 'Did you just tell your ex-boyfriend that you loved him? *In a bathroom?*'

She smacked her face with her hand, wishing that her filter system wasn't so extreme. At university, she was barely able to say two words to people, and at home she blurted out everything that came into her head.

Which was when she realised: she *did* love him.

What did this mean? Should she ask to get back together with him?

'Whoa there,' she said, pointing to herself in the mirror. 'Did any of the baby formula powder get into your head?'

Or was it the simple effect of being relieved that there was someone to help? What if anyone else had come in – say, Barry? Would she have declared her love to him too?

'Not likely,' she said, half troubled and half relieved by this.

Then she tried to picture someone fit. Someone she'd actually fancied, or could fancy – like Dilek's boyfriend, Marcus. Or the cute man at the bar that night she got drunk? Unfortunately, neither of them were conjuring the same kind of feelings.

Ji Su? Yes. She would've told her she loved her, but she wouldn't have wanted to kiss her like she wanted to kiss Abdul-Raheem.

'Oh, this is bad. This is *really* bad.'

'Are you going to come downstairs or talk to yourself in the mirror for a bit longer?'

Mae started at Abdul-Raheem in the doorway. She tried to smile.

'Quite nice talking to yourself, isn't it?' she said.

He just cleared his throat and went back down the

stairs. Mae took a deep breath and would address this like a proper adult: she'd ignore it completely and pretend it never happened. That she didn't feel this way about him because she couldn't go back and forth like this, making decisions and not being able to stick to them. Abdul-Raheem was already sitting at the table, pizza box open, two slices on his plate and two on Mae's plate, as she sat down with him.

'Good weather today.'

'Mae—'

'So nice when it's not raining and spoiling everyone's summer fun, right?'

'Mae—'

'I mean, wouldn't be great to be at work when it's this hot because of the horse's arse and all that but—'

'*Mae.*'

Her heart was beating so fast she wondered if it might jump out of her chest, just like the words 'I love you' had jumped out of her mouth. Abdul-Raheem dragged his chair towards her and took her hands in his. How could someone come to mean so much to another person in such a short space of time? Ji Su drifted into Mae's thoughts and she felt a pang of regret that she couldn't share what was happening in her life. That she didn't know what was happening in Ji Su's life either. How quickly relationships can form and how much quicker they can break. Mae looked at Abdul-Raheem's lovely, open face; the sharp edges of his jawline, the curl of his lashes, the small mark just under his eye where someone had split his skin open with their fist. How could she even *think* about comparing him to the likes of Marcus, the guy at the bar and ... *Barry?* What the hell? He put his hand now to her face, stroking her cheek and Mae wanted to climb on to his lap and kiss him. But she knew she couldn't.

'I don't know if you said that back there because I was cleaning up your vomit, and I know we're not together any more so maybe I shouldn't say this because ... I don't want to confuse you, not when I know you're trying to focus on yourself, but ...' He paused and stared at her. 'You should know ... I love you too.'

'Shut your face,' she replied. 'You do not.'

He laughed. 'Not quite the response I thought I'd get.'

'You love me? Even after I broke up with you?'

'Of course. Only made me like you more. I mean, I didn't like it. I *don't* like it but I can't help how I feel.'

'Really?'

'Really. You're an idiot to not realise it.'

'I *am* an idiot generally, so I guess that makes sense,' she conceded.

'Don't worry, I know you have things to focus on and however you might feel, that focus is what's important.'

'Yeah, but ...' Mae lowered her voice.

He leaned in a little closer as their legs intertwined. She put her hands on his thighs, sure this time that her heart *would* jump out of her chest. She closed her eyes, feeling the closeness of his face to hers. Then the doorbell rang.

'Huh? What? Who?'

It half felt like Mae had woken up from dreaming. Surely the doorbell couldn't have rung? But before she could even answer that question to herself someone was pressing it repeatedly.

'What the …?'

Abdul-Raheem looked concerned. 'Wait here.'

She pulled him back because what if someone the family knew saw him? Her parents would find out and then all hell would break loose. She rushed out in front of him, but in this one-sided tussle of hers she didn't hear the keys in the lock, her back was turned.

'Stay inside,' she said.

Did he look offended? 'What? Mae, it could be—'

But Abdul-Raheem wasn't able to finish his sentence. His eyes were fixed on something behind Mae. Something told Mae that she shouldn't look back, but she felt the outside air waft in as she turned around, and there, standing in the entrance was her entire family.

Chapter Fourteen

Mae let out a barely audible expletive.

'Quick,' exclaimed her mum. 'Call the police.'

'What?' said Mae.

'What are you waiting for, Jay's abba?'

Mae looked at her dad who seemed to see that Abdul-Raheem wasn't actually a burglar. Abdul-Raheem, who had raised his hands and was already defending himself by trying to assure her mum that he wasn't robbing them. Not in the way that Mae's mum thought, anyway.

'I don't think he's a burglar,' said Bubblee, standing next to her mum.

'What do you mean? Look at him.'

This was so much worse than Mae could ever have imagined. She looked at Abdul-Raheem's lowered gaze, as if holding in all the anger and pain as he clenched his fists.

'*Mum, he's not a burglar,*' exclaimed Mae, louder than she'd intended.

She looked at all her sisters' faces, her gaze resting on Fatti looking worried and nervous. What was Fatti even doing here?

'Then who is he?' demanded Mae's mum. 'What are you doing alone in the house with a-a … *kala fwa?*'

Her mum looked at Abdul-Raheem from top to bottom and Mae only wished that he hadn't been there to witness the look on her mum's face. She swallowed hard.

'Mae,' came her dad's voice; stern, commanding. A tone he hadn't used in many years. 'Answer your amma.'

'He …' she began.

In that moment Mae had two choices and she wasn't sure which one to make. The words seemed to be lodged in her throat. She wished they'd stop watching him like that. She caught his eye and never had she seen him look so disappointed.

'He's …' she began again.

What was he? He was someone she loved but she couldn't say that, could she? It was just too much.

'Ugh,' came a familiar voice. 'He's her *boyfriend*.'

Her family seemed to part like the Red Sea as Ilyaas came into view. What was *he* doing here? And how did he know anything? Her mum and dad were now both looking at her, Bubblee looked worried, Farah confused, Fatti like she might faint.

'Inside,' her dad barked. '*Now*.'

'Listen, Mr Am—'

'You don't speak,' said her dad, not even looking at Abdul-Raheem. 'You can leave.'

Abdul-Raheem stood tall. Much taller than anyone

else in the passage, but it didn't matter how much he seemed to loom, Mae wanted to bring him into her arms.

'I think I'll stay, if it's all the same to you,' replied Abdul-Raheem.

Her dad's eyes narrowed, his eyebrows creased. He looked like he might hit something, or *someone*.

'Mae. Tell him to leave. Now.'

She turned to Abdul-Raheem. 'I think you should go. I have to … I need to explain this to them.'

It didn't matter how much she tried to lower her voice, she knew they could hear.

'*Explain*,' exclaimed her mum, grabbing Mae's arm and dragging her into the living room. 'What do you think you're doing, hmm?'

'Mum, calm down,' said Bubblee, following them both. 'And let her go.'

Mae felt tears prickle her eyes as she heard Fatti in the passage. 'I really think you should leave. I'm sorry.'

'I need to make sure she'll be okay.'

'That's not your job,' said her dad. 'You understand?'

'Abba, *please*,' said Fatti. She turned to Abdul-Raheem. 'Listen, you need to go. This isn't about you.'

There was a long pause. 'Of course it's about me.'

The front door shut and Mae realised that she didn't even say goodbye to him.

'What do you mean, "let her go"?' said her mum to Bubblee. 'Letting her go has turned her into *this*.'

'Mum,' said Farah. 'You'll wake the baby.' She looked

around the room as she said to Mae: 'You were meant to be looking after Zoya, you know.'

Seriously? Farah went and got the baby monitor to see Zoya sleeping peacefully. That clearly wasn't enough though as she left the room and went to check on her. Fatti had come and sat next to Mae, looking up at her mum.

'I don't think shouting's going to work.'

Before her mum could say anything though, her dad was leaning over Mae, pointing his finger at her. 'You will *not* leave the house unless you're with one of your sisters, okay?'

'But—'

'You will quit your job,' he added.

'I can't jus—'

'And you are *not* going back to university,' he added.

Mae looked at her dad as if she hardly knew what he was saying.

'Hang on, that's a bit extreme,' said Bubblee.

'You, be quiet,' said her dad. 'You started this by going to university, showing her the way. Is this why we gave you money? To study just so you can then go around with boys?'

'Bu—'

'I don't want to hear any "but". That is *final*.'

The room filled with silence as Farah walked back in. Their dad closed his eyes, pressing his hand against them.

'Your silly auntie called us at the last minute to cancel

258

because she wasn't feeling well,' said her mum. 'Who does that to their guests? So we decided to go to Fatti's house instead and see the baby. We're sitting and eating and the answering machine comes on with Ilyaas.'

Everyone looked towards him now, lurking between the living room and passage. He looked at the ground.

'And what does he say? "Didn't know Mae was allowed company when babysitting."'

Mae thought she might get up, lunge at Ilyaas and actually kill him.

'No,' interrupted Farah. 'She wasn't.'

'Oh, shut up, Farah,' said Bubblee.

Farah stared at her sister as she went red in the face.

'I said, "What company? What are you talking about?"' continued Mae's mum. 'Then your sister picked up the phone and her face looked like someone had died, so I took the phone from her. And he told me.'

'What were you even doing here?' asked Bubblee, looking at Ilyaas.

'What does it matter?' their mum exclaimed. 'Thank God he was here to tell us.'

Mae couldn't believe it. It was no accident. This whole thing could've been avoided. No one would have had to see Abdul-Raheem in the house with her. Their moment together needn't have been interrupted. And she wouldn't have had to see him look so hurt. The way her dad had spoken to him. The way her mum thought he was a burglar. Mae felt a flush of acute embarrassment at her whole family, the way her sisters had just stood there and let her parents say all those things to him.

'A *kala fwa. In the house*,' added their mum. 'You have no respect for your family.'

Mae looked up at her as if she couldn't quite believe her.

'Would you *stop* calling him that,' she exclaimed.

Everyone looked at her.

'He is not just a *kala*.'

'Then what is he? Hmm?' said her mum, leaning into Mae, her face like thunder.

This was the moment Mae would have to choose: Abdul-Raheem or the indignation of her family. Perhaps it had taken breaking up with him to really see how right he was about them. Everything she did and said meant taking them into account. Her life wasn't her own. And wasn't it time to change that?

'You *know* what he is,' she said, shooting a look at Ilyaas.

'Mae …' said her dad.

'I *like* him, okay?'

Mae's heart hammered. No more excuses. Just honesty.

'And he likes me.'

'Allah,' exclaimed her mum.

'I don't know what the big deal is,' Mae added.

But of course she knew exactly what the big deal was. For the family it was probably the biggest deal there'd ever been amongst them, and plenty had happened over the years.

'This is not how we do things,' said her dad.

'What things?'

'*This things*,' he exclaimed.

Mae refused to acknowledge what he was getting at. She folded her arms and raised her brows. Her dad looked around the room, as if searching for help. He took a deep breath.

'We have traditions for a reason,' he said finally.

'What reasons?' asked Mae.

Her parents looked at her as if she was missing the obvious point in the world.

'Mae, you are young …'

She was going to scream. Actually scream.

'We know what …' he cleared his throat, '*temptations* can happen.'

Oh God. Mae felt her face flush.

'*Abba* …' she said, lowering her voice, embarrassed.

Her dad had never looked so awkward. 'What kind of parents would we be if we didn't protect you from that? Hmm?'

It had never occurred to Mae that they'd wanted to protect her – it always felt too much like control.

'But, Abba,' she replied, unfolding her arms and leaning towards him. 'I'm an adult now. I have to learn to protect myself.'

'Mae,' interrupted her mum. 'You will always be our baby.'

She looked at her mum, surprised by the tears that

had surfaced in her own eyes; the affection she was able to feel towards her mum in that moment.

'You will *not* see him again,' said her dad.

'*Why?*' asked Mae.

Any affection she'd felt slipped away. She looked around the room, noticing Ilyaas staring at her. She'd deal with him later.

'Our girls do not go out with boys,' her dad added.

'No, some of them go out with girls.'

It just came out of Mae's mouth, but it seemed to take her parents a few moments to process what she'd said.

'Not the time, Mae,' said Bubblee. 'Not the time.'

She looked at her sister and hardly recognised her. What happened to her sense of right and wrong? To all the principles she had? Didn't her parents know about all the dates *she* was going on? Mae supposed that Bubblee had changed too much. She was now willing to keep quiet about her private life just to keep the peace.

'You know Abdul-Raheem's Muslim?' said Mae.

Her parents looked confused again.

'I mean, prays five times a day, fasts, is really kind of Muslim,' she added.

They didn't seem to know what to do with this information and simply looked at each other.

'Doesn't that count for anything?' said Mae. 'You're worried about me, yeah?'

Her dad nodded.

'You want to protect me, isn't it?'

Nod.

'Well then? Doesn't he sound like the perfect person to do that?'

Mae had to leave out the fact that she should be able to protect herself, that she didn't need anyone to do that for her. That's what growing up was, surely?

'But he's so dark,' said her mum.

'*Mum*,' exclaimed Farah. 'That's not exactly Islamic, is it?'

It was no use reasoning with her parents. They refused to understand, were too set in their own ideals.

'No, but it's only Islamic when it suits people, isn't it?' said Mae. 'Forget about the fact that he's had a hard life, that he converted in prison, that he's turning it all around *because* of Islam.'

'*Prison?*' said her mum.

Mae took a deep breath.

'You like a man who is black *and* a convict?' her mum added. 'This is the day your parents had to live and see.'

It was the hypocrisy that got Mae. It was one thing that they weren't hearing her; could they even hear themselves?

'Didn't matter when Jay committed a crime, did it?' said Mae. 'He's the reason Mustafa is dead! That's okay though.'

How could they be so blind? Up until then Mae had brushed aside her parents' casual racism, their judgements on others, the way her mum would gossip about family friends' daughters *gone bad*. Like they were a rotten fruit and not a human being. And it was always the daughters who were gossiped about. When it came to the sons, well then, boys would be boys. Sure, it's not as if a black woman would've been met with open arms had Jay brought one home – her parents would've shouted and probably said all the same crap that Mae was having to hear, but they wouldn't have tried to control him. They wouldn't have said that it was for his *protection*. (If anything, Jay's partner would be the one needing protection.) They certainly wouldn't have told him he had to quit his job, that he wouldn't be able to leave the house on his own, that he couldn't go to university. Her failure there loomed over her now as she noticed Fatti fidgeting with her hands.

'Don't you bring your brother into this,' said her mum.

'Jay is doing better,' her dad added.

The sisters all glanced at each other. *Better* wasn't quite the same as *okay*. He was an adult man who was in debt, living with his parents and driving a delivery van because he was incapable of getting any other job.

'No one's going to say anything?' said Mae, looking at her sisters.

'It's not the time for it, Mae,' said Bubblee.

'Not the right time for anything right now, according to you. You'd have been going crazy if you were in my shoes.'

Bubblee didn't respond, which only confirmed the truth of Mae's statement.

'Do you have a problem with him being black?' Mae asked Bubblee.

'What? *No*.'

'But I shouldn't be seeing him?'

Bubblee paused.

'Right,' said Mae, turning to Farah. 'And what about you?'

'Mae, a cultural connection is really important. Relationships are hard enough.'

Mae had to scoff. 'Because a cultural connection was so helpful for you and your husband, wasn't it? Where is he now? Your relationship was dead before he died.'

'Mae!' her dad shouted.

'And *you*?' Mae said, finally turning to Fatti.

Fatti with her kind ways and kind heart. Fatti, who never wished or said a bad thing about anyone.

'I don't have a problem with black people,' said Fatti, looking at Mae, worry etched on her brows. 'But ...'

'But,' said Mae. 'There's no "but" here, Fats. You can't please everyone right now. Because it's not about pleasing people, it's about being ... being ... just being a *nice* person.'

She looked around the room as the simplicity of it dawned on her. Her family weren't nice. How could you be when you had such narrow views? The very idea scared her. Because wasn't she almost the same? If Abdul-Raheem hadn't come along, would she have even given it any thought? Could she have gone through life without realising her own prejudices?

'This girl is getting out of hand,' said her mum, looking at her dad.

'Get up,' he said. 'We're going home.'

'What?' said Mae. 'No, we're not.'

'She can stay here,' said Bubblee.

'You think I want to stay here?' she exclaimed, almost laughing.

Mae stood up and marched over to get her bag.

'Mae, you stop right now or I'll … or I'll …'

But her dad didn't seem to know what the ending of that sentence was.

'What will you do, Abba?' Mae looked him straight in the face.

'You have to listen to your parents,' he said. 'This is God's command.'

'Yeah, well, I think he also commanded that people shouldn't judge people based on the colour of their skin. Maybe I'll listen to you when you listen to God, yeah?'

Mae snatched her bag and grabbed the car keys as she strode past Ilyaas. She stopped.

'I thought you were cool,' she said, looking at him as she shook her head.

He looked as if he were about to say something, but before he could get the words out, Mae marched out of the house, the sound of Zoya's crying now filling the household.

She sat in her dad's car and had to take several deep breaths. Her anger was bubbling all over the place, her heart thudding, her teeth grinding. *Of all the bigoted things*. Her dad's look of disappointment and anger would've made her feel bad if she didn't feel both those emotions tenfold. She looked at her phone and called Abdul-Raheem. It rang for ages but he didn't pick up. Was he upset? Angry at her? Why hadn't she spoken, defended him, when he'd been there to actually hear? Not that she expected a medal for it, because she knew she should've done it sooner.

 Sistaaaas

> Bubblee: Mae, don't make this worse. Just come home. We'll calm Mum and Dad down.

The only people making this thing worse was them, just standing there without one word of support. They were meant to be her backbone, the ones who gave her courage and encouragement. She was the youngest so weren't they meant to be the role models?

'Forget this,' mumbled Mae as she went to the group chat and scrolled down. *Exit group*. Her finger hovered over it. It hadn't been a group for a while, had it? A group means each person has their own importance but Mae hadn't had any since university. Even before university, maybe. She'd always just been young, chilled-out, nothing-about-her's-important Mae. Abdul-Raheem was showing her that she *was* important. That some of the things her family did and said just weren't right. Sometimes you have to speak up and tell a person when they're wrong otherwise how is anything meant to change? Mae realised she'd spent her life either chatting nonsense because 'serious stuff was a yawn-fest' or being silent. Her finger hovered over the button a few more moments, before she said: 'Not any more.' The time had finally come to stop pretending that everything was okay, or that nothing mattered.

Mae has left the group

Chapter Fifteen

There was only one place to go and twenty minutes later Mae found herself outside Abdul-Raheem's house. She rang the doorbell but there was no answer. Mae called his phone again but he still wasn't picking up. Where could he be? She didn't have any of his friend's numbers, or any idea where else he might be. She knocked on the door, calling out his name because maybe he'd gone to bed, though she wasn't sure how anyone would be able to sleep after the evening they'd had. Mae sat back in the car and realised she had no one else to call. No sisters, no friends and no Abdul-Raheem. Never had it mattered to her as much as it did then. What she'd give to be able to speak to Ji-Su. Mae rested her head on the steering wheel. Her phone buzzed and she shot up to see if it was Abdul-Raheem. *Fatti Calling*. Mae declined the call and silenced her phone. They could all sit and worry about her, all come to whatever conclusions they wanted about where she was and whether she was with Abdul-Raheem or not.

'Good,' Mae mumbled.

She hoped they thought the worst. That she was in bed with him right now. She was just annoyed that it wasn't true. Leaning her head back, she wondered where he might be. What if the whole thing had driven him to do something stupid? She'd heard about triggers, and what if he did a one-eighty and got back in trouble? Exhaustion washed over Mae as she closed her eyes, her vision peppered with images of her family, the assortment of looks they wore. That stupid kid, Ilyaas. The faces fuzzed and muddied as she drifted off to sleep.

Mae awoke with a start, not knowing where she was or what she was doing. She looked around the car, confused, and started again at Abdul-Raheem's face, peering at her through the window.

'Are you going to come out?' he asked.

She stepped out of the car and flung her arms around him.

'I'm sorry,' she mumbled into his neck. 'I'm so, so sorry.'

His grip tightened around her waist with these words.

'It's all right,' he replied. 'You're here. It's okay.'

They walked into the house as Mae checked the time on her phone. It was just gone eleven o'clock at night. There were what seemed like hundreds of missed calls from all her sisters. Were her parents still at Farah and Bubblee's house, sitting around, somewhere between angry and worried for her? Good, it served them right for trying to control her.

'So?' he said, sitting down on the bluish grey sofa. 'What happened?'

The walls of the room were white, the coffee table had stacks of books on them, a Qur'an. She noticed a prayer mat laid out in the corner and rosary beads spread out on top of it. One wall had a painting of Arabic writing on it, which she noticed as the first kalimah prayer – the one you say when you convert, declaring the oneness of God and the prophet being the last messenger. There was a small dining table against the wall, a vase of multicoloured tulips in the middle and it made her heart melt for Abdul-Raheem.

She relayed the entire scene to him, softening the more racist parts of it because whatever she knew her family to be, she didn't want to admit it to Abdul-Raheem. She told him that it had been Ilyaas, who for some reason had been outside the house, who had called Fatti to tell her what was going on.

'I see,' replied Abdul-Raheem. 'I guess he has a thing for you.'

'*What?*' said Mae. 'Don't be stupid.'

He shook his head. 'So naive.'

'Am not.'

'Why else would he be hovering outside the house when he knows you're in there? Or call and tell them I was in there with you? Trust me, Mae. Jealousy can make you do some horrid stuff. Especially when you're that young and stupid.'

Mae had to take a few moments to absorb this information. 'Oh,' she said, finally. 'That's weird.'

'Not that weird,' Abdul-Raheem said.

'He's still a little you-know-what.'

'Oh, yeah, that's for sure. But who could blame him, right? You're pretty you-know-what,' he added with a smile.

How could Abdul-Raheem be so calm and collected after all that she'd told him? Why wasn't he in a rage about them all?

'They're your parents,' he said, eventually.

'What's that got to do with anything?'

He took a deep breath and held her hands. 'Everything. Listen, don't ask me what I think of them – you can probably guess.'

She could – she was thinking the same – but it still didn't make it easy hearing it from someone else.

'But, they're your parents. They're going to be protective and think that they know best—'

'But—'

'Even when they don't,' he added. 'And in this case, they really don't. But they don't know that. It's a lifetime of what they've known and how they've been brought up.' He paused. 'Your sisters didn't exactly seem to be on your side either. The younger generation's meant to know better, but they don't always, do they? We all mess up.'

'What are you saying?'

He squeezed her hands. 'I'm just saying to have a little patience with them.'

'Let them order me about, so that I quit work, can't go out *or* go back to uni? Though I suppose the last bit is out of my hands.'

'Is it?' he asked.

Mae shrugged.

'I'm not saying any of that stuff. You're here, aren't you? They know they can't control you and you should be able to show you're independent, but just … try and understand where they're coming from.'

She pushed his arm. 'You're too nice, you know. Makes me even madder they judge you without knowing you.'

'It's how it goes in the world.'

'All right, can we go a day without the philosophy?'

He laughed.

'I was worried about you, you know,' she added.

'Me? Why?'

'Dunno. Thought maybe … the way Dad spoke to you …'

'What?'

'Maybe you'd, I dunno, gone off the rails again.'

Abdul-Raheem looked at her for a moment before bursting into a laugh. 'Mae,' he said, putting his hand on her face, 'I've heard and seen a lot worse since my days of crime to let something like that flip me.'

'Oh.'

Mae flushed in embarrassment. Of course it was a ridiculous thing to assume. He looked down at her and she felt the pace of her heart fasten.

'I didn't want to leave you, but ... I knew that if I stayed any longer, if any more was said, I might have lost my temper and God, I've spent years trying to get a hold on that. I'm sorry I left.'

'Don't be,' she replied. 'I had to have it out with my family. Where'd you go, anyway?'

'Just driving around to cool down. Called my dad.'

'Oh my God, you told your dad?'

'He helps me put things in perspective.'

'So, now he knows I have a racist family?'

'I mean, he knows you're South Asian. He didn't have high hopes.'

He said it with a smile but it was depressing how true that was.

'And, you know, it's usually less about the colour of someone's skin and more about the unknown,' he added. 'No one trusts anything they're not used to.'

She looked at him for a moment before he took his hand away and stood up.

'Perhaps you should go home now? Your parents are going to be worried.'

'I don't care. And I don't want to,' she replied, looking up at him.

She stood up too and hooked her fingers into his front jean pockets.

'Mae ... This isn't a good idea,' he said, lowering his voice.

'Why not?'

'Because we're Muslim, for one.'

She shrugged, stepping closer to him. 'So? Why does that have to mean everything?'

He looked down and paused. 'And we're not boyfriend and girlfriend any more, are we?'

He held her wrists and placed them gently by her sides.

'I want to stay,' she said. Then she lowered her head, pressing it against his chest. 'And I want you to be my boyfriend again.'

He looked down at her. 'Really?'

She nodded. 'I meant what I said in the bathroom – romantic setting that it was.' She looked up at him. 'I do love you.'

He took her face in his hands and kissed her on the forehead. 'I love you too.'

Then she wrapped her arms around him and felt him tighten his grip around her waist.

'Can we go to bed?' she asked.

He sighed deeply.

'I still don't think that's a good idea.'

She loosened her hold. 'Why? It's not like I'm saying "let's have sex". I want to just lie down with you.'

'Yeah, me too. But not everything in life is about what you want.'

'Bit boring,' she said.

'Maybe, but I don't believe in doing whatever you feel like doing. One thing can always lead to another.'

'What about what *I* feel like doing?'

He took a deep breath. 'Don't make this harder than it is, Mae. If you want to stay, you can sleep in my bed and I'll take the sofa.'

Why was everything about Abdul-Raheem so reasonable? She felt annoyed, yet she didn't feel she had the right to be because, technically, as a Muslim she guessed he was right. Mae just didn't want to do what was right. She wanted to do what she felt like doing and right then she didn't feel like either going home or staying in a bed without Abdul-Raheem. Of the two options, though, his bed annoyed her the least, so she told him that was fine. Mae curled up in his bed, feeling the tiredness of that evening come over her as she looked up at Abdul-Raheem putting a glass of water on her bedside table.

'Sleep well,' he said.

Why couldn't he just get in next to her?

'Alone. Great,' she replied.

He put his hand on her forehead before bending down to kiss it. Mae moved her head and caught his lips instead. She pulled him in closer, feeling the pressure of his mouth on hers, thinking that this feeling was better than she'd even imagined it. It was a few moments before he pulled back and took a deep breath, opening his eyes.

'Mae, you can't do that. You have to respect my wishes.'

With that he switched off the bedside lamp and closed the door gently behind him, leaving Mae with the awful feeling of a person who's too selfish about what they want to care what another wants. She *wanted* to respect his wishes. But as she looked up at the ceiling, trying to reason away her own desires, she wondered: if she was always worrying about the wishes of all the people in her life, what happened to her own?

Mae's embarrassment was only amplified in the light of day the following morning. There were more missed calls from her family. Semi-hysterical messages. A very loud voicemail left by her mum. Walking into the room, Mae saw that Abdul-Raheem had put out breakfast things on the table. She could hear something being cooked in the kitchen and went in to see him at the stove, making scrambled eggs.

'I can make fried eggs, if you prefer?'

'No,' she said, shuffling on her feet.

'Sit.' He leaned forward and pressed his lips against her head. 'I'll bring it in.'

She sat at the table as he asked from the kitchen how she'd slept, if it was too hot in the room, that he'd put out a spare toothbrush for her in the bathroom. All this small talk made Mae feel worse.

'How are you feeling?' he asked, finally sitting down opposite her.

'Not great.'

'You should probably go home and show your parents that you're alive.'

Mae was about to take a sip of her orange juice when

she looked at him. 'You know, I do have my own moral compass. You don't have to make me feel bad all the time.'

'I wasn't trying to make you feel bad.'

'I know I'll have to tell my parents I'm alive at some point, but I'll do it when I want. Not when you tell me to.'

He put his fork down. 'Fine.'

They ate the rest of their breakfast in silence. She waited for him to apologise, but he'd started talking about random things, work, the weather – *the weather, for God's sake.* Did he think she was being immature? Unreasonable? Did he honestly think that being rational was going to win her parents over? He began to clear up the plates as if the night before hadn't happened and Mae couldn't understand how measured he was being. It didn't feel natural. What would Ji Su have done in this situation? Mae was pretty sure she'd have torn up the place, told Mae to stay with her for as long as she wanted, that no person had the right to tell an adult what to do, not even a parent.

'Well, I guess I'd better go then,' she said, picking up her keys.

'Yeah,' he replied.

Why wasn't he telling her to stay?

'I'll see you later,' he said.

'If I don't get locked up before being shipped out of the country.'

'Don't joke about that.'

'Well, crazier stuff happens,' replied Mae.

He paused. 'Maybe, but not to you. Not that.'

She'd been hoping for more but they were now hovering at the door. Wasn't he going to bend down and give her a kiss at all? Or even a hug?

'Yeah, well. Better not or you'll have that on your conscience,' she said.

Nothing.

'Message me to let me know what's going on,' he simply replied.

Mae stepped outside into the warm summer morning and paused. 'Listen … Are we still …'

'What?' he asked.

'We are together again, aren't we?' she asked. 'You haven't changed your mind?'

He gave her a big smile. 'Are you crazy?'

Then he pulled her to him and kissed her on the lips.

The kiss had fortified Mae. As she pulled up outside her parents' house she wasn't sure what she was going to say. She walked inside, greeted by the sounds of her parents shuffling from their seats and calling out her name. She decided to just ignore them and made her way up the stairs.

'You come down and tell us where you've been,' exclaimed her mum.

To which Mae just slammed her bedroom door and

got back into bed. Unfortunately, she'd forgotten to lock it and so both her mum and dad barged in, demanding answers from her.

'I'm an adult,' she said. 'I don't have to tell you where I've been.'

'We are your parents,' her dad said.

What a disappointment it was when the person you probably loved most in the world ended up being someone so different to what you thought they were. To what you wished they were. Would she and her dad ever joke about her mum again? Would they ever share a secret look or laugh? Why did having one relationship have to mean changing another?

'I'm going to sleep.'

'You will listen to us,' said her mum.

Mae sat up, throwing her duvet to one side. 'You know what, Amma? No. I won't. Not right now because I'm tired and all I want to do is sleep. If you want me to walk out of the house again and disappear for another night, then I can do that. So you either let me sleep, or I leave.'

Her parents looked at each other, unsure, confused as to how the tables had turned, so that their daughter was now angry with *them*. They must've sensed something in what she said.

'Don't think we've forgotten this,' said her mum. 'We will talk when you are up.'

With which they left the room.

There was less talking and more talking over each other, including some shouting. Mae tried to think about what Abdul-Raheem had said about the whole honouring your parents stuff, but if he'd been in the room, her parents not listening to one thing she was saying, he'd have changed his mind. They kept going on about respect and tradition and culture and none of it even made sense. What did that have to do with the colour of a person's skin?

'A single girl should not be alone with a man,' exclaimed her dad.

'Hang on, is this about me having a relationship or him being black?'

At first, they looked horrified and offended by Mae using the term 'relationship'. Then they glanced at each other, unsure of how to tackle two evils with one response.

'Good Bengali girls do not have … *boys* as their special friends, Mae,' said her dad.

'Who is going to marry you now?' said her mum.

She looked ready to have a fully fledged panic attack.

'Maybe Abdul-Raheem will.'

It came out, just like that, and for a moment Mae thought she'd given her dad a heart attack. His eyes seemed to glisten as he stared at her. She leaned forward.

'Abba?'

There was a long pause as he shook his head at her as if he didn't even recognise her, and it opened up a pit of anxiety in Mae's stomach.

'I am no longer your abba.' His voice cracked, sounding thick and heavy.

He stood up slowly, as if he might stumble and fall, holding on to her mum's arm. Mae watched him stagger out of the room, wiping a stray tear as he left.

The impact of his words left Mae unable to form any of her own. She couldn't stay in the house. Her mum called out to her to stop, that she couldn't leave the house, the same old stuff about respecting your parents' wishes, but Mae couldn't breathe. She got into her dad's car and began to drive. Where to, she didn't know. *I am no longer your abba.* Even if she had murdered someone she didn't think he'd ever say such a thing. He probably would've forgiven her for murder. She gripped the steering wheel harder.

'Ridiculous,' she whispered, stopping at a red light, biting back her tears.

Her dad's face, the way he walked as if he might collapse, his own tears.

'*It's so ridiculous,*' she shouted to no one at all.

The light turned green and instead of going straight, Mae wiped the tears from her face, took a sharp left and knew exactly where she was headed.

'Mae,' said Fatti, opening the door. 'Thank God. Mum said you came back.'

'Where is he?' said Mae, unable to look at her sister. What was the use of being a supposed kind person when your principles slipped just to protect your parents? When your principles were just plain *wrong*.

'Who?'

'You know who,' replied Mae, striding into the living room. 'Ilyaas, that's who.'

'Listen, Ash's spoken to him.'

Mae whipped around coming face to face with Fatti. 'Spoken? *Spoken*? Had a quiet word and said that was a little naughty of him? Though probably not that naughty because, let's face it, what I did was outrageous, wasn't it?'

'Mae, calm down. What's happened to you? You're not acting like yourself.'

'*Me*?' Mae scoffed. 'I'm not acting like myself? That's rich, Fats. All of you lot stuck up your own behinds with your babies and your families and your life and I'm the one who's changed?'

Fatti stared at Mae with her nervous look and pained expression and for a moment Mae wanted to tell her that it was fine. That it wasn't her fault. Fatti would be feeling guilty, but Mae couldn't bring herself to do it because she'd be lying and she'd had enough of that.

'Ilyaas,' Mae called out, rushing up the stairs. 'Ilyaas!'

'Mae, you'll wake the baby.'

Right on cue, Adam started crying as Mae flung Ilyaas's door open. He was sitting on his bed, leaning against the headboard as he looked up, headphones in his ears. He took them out, a look of panic coming over his face.

'I hope you're happy,' she said.

He didn't speak.

'Because what you did there shows exactly the kind of person you are, and let me tell you, it's not great.'

Ilyaas lowered his gaze, mumbling something.

'What?' said Mae.

'I'm sorry.'

'I can't hear you.'

'I said I'm sorry,' he repeated, looking up.

Mae thought she saw tears in his eyes. What was up with all the crying today?

'Yeah, well, sorry's not going to fix stuff, is it?'

'Mae, he really is sorry.'

She turned around to see Fatti, holding Adam.

'Fats,' said Mae, half exasperated. 'You need to stop trying to be the perfect stepmum, because trust me, *he* doesn't deserve it. And I don't think the other one does either. But then what do I know? I'm only your sister.'

Mae pushed past Fatti, only to find Aima standing at the top of the stairs. Aima looked her up and down, giving her a mocking smile as Mae pushed past her too, running down the stairs.

'God knows what anyone sees in her,' came Aima's voice as Mae ran out of the house.

The following day Mae left the house early, except she realised that her dad's car keys weren't where they usually were. Without saying goodbye to her parents, she left anyway and would have to take the bus. She hadn't heard from Abdul-Raheem and wondered why he was so quiet now they were back together. She kept telling herself that he wasn't rethinking his decision, but who could blame him if he was? Who would want to be a part of all this drama?

When Mae had got back home after Fatti's, she'd avoided her dad and spent the entire time in her room, angry, frustrated and, she realised, at a loss. Now that anger had taken hold of her, she wasn't sure she could let it go. Every small injustice from the past came back to her and inflamed her further. Every minor comment she might have made as a way of asking her parents and sisters for help or attention, which they'd ignored, was just another sign of them not seeing anyone else's life but their own. The way she'd always been taken for granted because she was *little Mae*. More than that, the one thing that she couldn't quite stop thinking about was being told she couldn't go back to uni, when she *knew* that she couldn't go back because she'd failed it. Then there was her dad saying that he was no longer her abba. Now, in the dark, lying in bed, the words trickled in and settled themselves in the roots of her mind. What happened to a parent's supposed unconditional love? Even Bubblee had never got that reaction and she was meant to be the black sheep in the family. To think that you could be disowned just because of the person you chose to love. Mae had gone to sleep with tears on her pillow and now she was on her way to work, to face excitable children, high on candyfloss and roller-coaster rides. And the boyfriend she had at the expense of her dad.

Everyone was huddled around the hut, as usual, when she approached. Abdul-Raheem was already there, his back turned to her as he spoke to Leanne. A pang of jealousy mixed with paranoia came over her and she realised that when life became unsettled, all your feelings did the same.

'Hi,' she said.

He turned around, holding a cup of coffee. 'Asalamoalaikum.'

Leanne sighed and walked away and Mae lost the energy to muster any annoyance for Abdul-Raheem.

'How are you?' she asked.

'I'm all right. You?'

She shrugged. 'Didn't really sleep.'

He took a sip of his coffee. 'There's a lot of stuff going on in your life.'

Something in what he said made her heart sink. *Your* life. Wasn't it his as well now? Isn't that what relationships were?

'Just mine?' she said.

Even if he'd had an answer it wouldn't matter as Barry came and everyone dispersed to their regular posts. *Why didn't you message me?* she wanted to ask. He'd made out as if he'd be there every step of the way but he wasn't. They both walked in silence, carrying their costumes towards the carousel. Why wasn't he saying anything? Or even looking at her? Was this it? Was he going to finally say they shouldn't get back together after all? She shook the idea from her head. Hadn't he kissed her outside his doorstep? He *loved* her, after all. They got into their costume, everything going dark as Mae could hear crowds begin to stream in, the music of the various rides blaring and clashing, the heat already giving Mae a headache. It was after the third person had taken a photo with them that Mae got fed up.

'So, what? Aren't you going to talk to me?'

Silence.

'*Hello?*'

'Not now, Mae.'

'Right. So, when?'

'When we're not in a horse's costume.'

But Mae was fed up of waiting to talk, holding on to her thoughts and feelings.

'Why are you annoyed with me?' she asked, wanting to hold on to the back of his waist just because.

'I'm not annoyed.'

'Don't lie to me,' she replied. 'You didn't call or message once yesterday when you'd promised and—'

'Imagine if the roles were reversed,' he interrupted.

'What?'

'If I'd done what you did,' he replied.

'What did I do?' asked Mae, at a loss.

He paused. 'Mae, I know it's frustrating but you kissing me like that – before you went to bed … you know it was against my wishes. If I'd have done the same, you wouldn't be so willing to call, would you?'

'So what? You were angry with me? But you kissed me back afterwards.'

He sighed. She wished she could see his face, she was so confused. *Why were they having this conversation in a horse's costume?*

'I know, because I felt I was losing you and … I was annoyed that you made me feel that way. Wouldn't you have been?'

It hardly made sense to her. What was the big deal? He was a man, after all. She recalled that night at the club, how terribly wrong things could've gone for her. But it wasn't as if she'd drugged Abdul-Raheem. It wasn't the same thing.

'I'm a girl,' she said.

He paused again. 'So, that makes it okay?'

'Oh my G—'

'Listen, I don't want to make comparisons here because I know it's not really the same thing, but it still boils down to a matter of respect. You know what my feelings about it are. You know I'm more observant as a Muslim than you are and you crossed a line. And now, instead of apologising, you're making out as if I'm the one in the wrong.'

Why did he always have the ability to make Mae feel wrong when she was sure she was in the right?

'Yeah, well, it's not a great feeling being rejected, you know.'

'Mae.'

She waited for more. 'What?'

'I don't know what you've been told all your life, or why you think something like that when you know how I feel about you. I've told you as often as I can without scaring you too much. Have a little self-belief. All this doubt … where does it come from?'

Mae felt a lump come to her throat. 'It's *not* doubt.'

'Isn't it?'

Of course it was. She couldn't explain it though. A person either believed in themselves or they didn't, and Mae guessed that she didn't.

'I dunno, maybe a bit, yeah. But you know, it's also something I want. To be close to you and stuff. It's normal, right?'

There was a long pause. 'I know. Of course it's normal. And I want that too,' he replied.

He brought out his hand behind him as she took it.

'Are you still angry with me?' she asked, relieved that she was holding his hand again.

'I told you, I was annoyed, not angry, because it's not easy. For either of us, and trust me when I say that it's as hard for me as it is for you. Harder, even.'

She kissed his hand and squeezed it because thank

God she still had him by her side. What would she do if she didn't? How would she be able to cope with her family? Her whole life?

'That's why I think ...'

'What?' asked Mae, suddenly scared that none of it mattered.

He was sensible, after all. A man of faith. He didn't let his feelings run away with him. Maybe he'd weighed up the pros and cons and felt it was better to let Mae go than stay in this. *Why had she kissed him when she knew how he felt?*

He gripped her hand tighter in his, a klaxon sounding in the background, a bunch of children screaming so Mae could barely hear herself think.

God, please no. Don't break up with me. Not now.

'I really want ...'

'What,' she whispered, barely able to speak.

Someone had come up and asked for a photo with the horse. The novelty of this job was really beginning to wear off.

'We love each other, don't we?' he asked.

'Yes.' She gripped his hand tighter. 'Yeah, we do. I do. I mean it. I'm sorry and the whole kissing thing won't happen again, okay? Not unless you want it.'

She could hear a smile in his voice.

'So we really do want to be together?'

'*Obviously*,' she said, a wave of relief washing over

her. 'Or this whole drama with my family would've been a bit pointless.'

'Good. All right. I'm glad.' He paused again.

Thank *God*. Mae breathed a sigh of relief. She'd have to adjust her ways a little, respect him and what he wanted. But she knew she wanted him by her side and the fact that he was here was all that mattered.

'In that case,' he added. 'Let's get married.'

Chapter Sixteen

Time seemed to have stood still and the noises around the amusement park had dissolved.

'Excuse me?' she said.

'I want to marry you,' he said, beginning to get out of his costume.

It wasn't even their break time yet. Before Mae knew it, he was facing her in his T-shirt and horse legs. She couldn't stop looking at the horse's head tucked under his arm.

'Oh,' she said.

The sun was beating down on them, and was it Mae or was everyone extra loud today? Mae felt beads of sweat gather on her forehead. She wiped it with her arm.

'I know,' he replied. 'It seems rushed.'

Seems?

'And we've only just got back together but doesn't that show that what we have is strong? And important?'

Mae swallowed hard.

'I was thinking about it all day yesterday,' he continued. 'How that when you go back to uni—'

'Who said I'm going back?' asked Mae.

Even though the urge to go back since her parents said she couldn't felt a lot more potent, but that was beside the point.

'It would be a real shame if you didn't,' Abdul-Raheem replied.

'For who?'

He looked confused. 'For you, of course. And listen, if you went back then I could move with you and work for a year and maybe even enrol at the same university the following year.'

Mae had a vision of Abdul-Raheem with her at university, the two of them hanging out together, sharing their time and stories of their respective days. She'd have someone to go home to. There wouldn't be the excruciating embarrassment of attempting to talk to people, trying to make new friends and failing. Mae would be spared the indignity of loneliness.

But marriage was for life. And life could be long.

'Right,' she replied. 'Yeah.'

'Yes?' he said. 'You mean it? Because I've come to a time in my life where I'm ready to settle down, to move forward, and I know you're younger than me but I can't imagine not being with you. I thought this summer would be the worst one yet, unbearable considering what I'm doing here, but you changed all of that. And I want you to go to uni too and live your life. Think of what we could make of *both* of our lives. Together.'

A panic rose in Mae's chest. Of course she wanted to be with him. Getting back together was her idea. And everything he said made complete sense, so why was she hesitating? Was it the idea of her family actually disowning her altogether? Maybe it was. Her bravery seemed to be failing her and wouldn't it be a stupid thing not to be with someone for ever just because your family was racist?

'I guess,' she replied.

'Are you all right?' he asked. 'You don't sound sure.'

She looked up at him but before she could say anything, Barry was marching towards them.

'Didn't know I was paying for you to stand around.'

'Oh, sorry,' said Mae. 'I was, er … I was feeling a bit faint.'

Barry looked at her, leaning in closer as if to assess just how faint she was.

'Hope he's not making you swoon in there,' he replied, looking at Abdul-Raheem.

'Sorry, Barry,' said Abdul-Raheem.

Barry merely grunted before he saw Braveheart the Bear running after a group of teenagers who seemed to have stolen his sword.

'Guess we should talk about this when we're not being a horse,' said Mae as they both got back into their costumes.

The rest of the day was a series of stilted conversations about anything that didn't involve Mae's family, their relationship or university.

'What shows are you watching on Netflix?'

'You know I don't really watch stuff. I prefer to read.'

'Oh yeah. What are you reading?'

Abdul-Raheem named some book written by a black woman who converted to Islam when she was forty-three, married with four children.

'Wow,' said Mae.

'You?' he asked.

'I was reading *A Dog's Life*,' she replied. 'About a man who becomes a dog and has to try and communicate, right, with his barks and stuff.' Mae laughed. 'It's pretty funny. But then I went to the stables—'

'Did you go again?' he asked.

Mae hadn't mentioned it to Abdul-Raheem and she wasn't sure why. It felt like something private – just for her – because she couldn't really explain the pull it had without sounding weird and random. She shrugged.

'There was nothing else to do. And you know, I liked it the first time. So, I thought, why not? Anyway, Alison there, she gave me a book about horses, *Heads Up – Heels Down*, so I started reading that. It's a children's book, but still, really interesting.'

'Well, that's good,' he replied.

'Yeah.'

There was a long pause.

'I mean, I read serious stuff too,' added Mae. 'Not just random stuff about horses and books about dogs.'

'That's all right,' replied Abdul-Raheem. 'I don't care.'

'Do you like funny books?'

'I guess I would if I read them, but I prefer to read stuff to do with more social issues.'

'Right, yeah, so do I,' said Mae.

'Mae, you don't have to change your tastes for me.'

'I'm not,' she said, rather more high-pitched than she meant. 'I was reading a book called *Woman Troubles* in uni, about periods and the Suffragette movement and stuff.'

'Good. Though aren't you interested in women's empowerment in Islam?'

Mae hadn't really given it much thought.

'There were some pretty incredible women from the days of our prophet, you know. Our idea of female emancipation is limited to its modern context but there were warrior women, leading people into battles and loads of other stuff.'

'Right. Yeah. Guess so.'

There was a protracted silence.

'Did you see Barry's face when he was walking towards us?' said Mae, mustering a laugh. 'Why does he always look like he's about to have a heart attack?'

Abdul-Raheem laughed. 'He does, doesn't he? Good guy, though. Bark's worse than his bite.'

'Hmm, yeah.'

It was in this vein that the entire day was spent and Mae didn't remember having such painful conversations since her time at uni. It occurred to her that she and

Abdul-Raheem only really talked about serious things; their families and the past. They did joke around, she knew that, but what did they actually have in common? Did you need to have things in common to be together? Didn't opposites attract?

'Should we …?'

'I dunno.'

They both stood by Abdul-Raheem's car.

'We should talk about it,' he said. 'You look worried.'

'No,' she laughed, waving her hand about. 'I'm not worried. Why would I be worried?'

Except that she was and she didn't quite know why.

'Anyway,' she added. 'I should get home.'

'Let me drop you home.'

'Are you kidding? I mean, my parents will have to get used to this but it's still a bit soon. They're … you know.'

He nodded. She was about to leave when he said: 'I asked you to marry me, you know, and you're just going to leave? No answer, no explanation.'

Why did everything have to be so hard? Mae shrugged.

'I don't have an answer. Or an explanation.'

'What do you want, Mae?'

So many things. Everything and nothing at all. She wanted to be with Abdul-Raheem without committing to him for an entire lifetime. She wanted to learn something new and make a go of university, if only she could be herself there, and if only she knew what to actually study – Media Studies just didn't interest her any more. And now that her parents were against her going to university at all, how would she pay for it? She'd have to get a loan. She wanted her family to be speaking to her and accept that she had a black boyfriend without having to justify anything. She wanted her sisters to stop being so selfish and have the same kind of closeness with them as she did when they were younger. But the younger Mae had accepted being the afterthought in everything and this somehow didn't feel right to her any more. Something would have to give, only she wasn't sure what.

'I don't know,' she said.

'Do you want me?' he asked.

She nodded.

He seemed relieved. 'Then? Why are you hesitating? Are you scared of what your parents will say? Maybe do?'

'I don't know.'

His question felt like the logical explanation, but it just didn't entirely ring true. She looked up at him.

'Listen, I just need some time to think about it. I'm only nineteen.'

'I know. But in the end, it's just a number, like they say it is.'

'It feels like a bit more than that,' she replied.

Abdul-Raheem nodded. 'All right then. Fine. Take some time.'

'Are you mad?'

'No.'

'Then?'

He took a deep breath. 'I just … I thought you'd want this too.'

She wished she could say that she *did* want it. But the words couldn't come out. Mae took his hands and squeezed them but he gave her a sad smile before turning around and walking away.

On the way home Mae got off the bus, picked up a doner kebab, and ate it on the rest of the journey home. She'd been left several messages on her phone from each of her sisters. They all probably missed having an on-call babysitter.

Marriage. *Marriage.* The idea made her feel claustrophobic and yet she knew Abdul-Raheem wasn't controlling, the type to tell her what to do or what to wear, so why was she not happy when someone she loved proposed to her? Maybe it was the fact that he'd done it in a horse's costume. No. Mae didn't care about that, though she probably should have. The look on his face doubled up the guilt she had for not saying yes immediately. As she entered the house she heard her sisters' voices quietly settle, but she didn't go into the living room, instead she walked straight up to her room. It didn't take long for someone to knock on her door.

'I'm sleeping.'

'It's only eight thirty,' said Bubblee, opening the door and entering the room.

'Did I say you could come in?'

'If I waited for that I'd be outside for ever.'

'Yeah, maybe you should get the hint.'

Mae had just changed into her pyjamas and began to fold her clothes, pretending to sort through them.

'How long are you going to ignore us?'

'As long as you're all racist.'

'Jeez, you need to stop with that. We are *not* racist. At least I'm not.'

Mae stopped folding her black T-shirt. 'Truth hurts, huh?'

'Okay. Our reaction wasn't exactly … admirable. But it doesn't follow that we're racists. You shouldn't go bandying that word around, you know. It means something.'

'You don't say.'

'You're being a real brat right now.'

Mae turned to her sister and folded her arms. 'And you're being a really bad older sister. The one time you guys should've stood up for me in front of Mum and Dad and instead you just stayed quiet.'

'There was a lot to process.'

'Since when have you ever needed time to process things? And, you know, I was there, having cancelled my own plans just to babysit for you and Farah so you could both have your evenings out and I didn't even get a thank you.'

By this point Farah had come up behind Bubblee.

'I thanked you,' replied Bubblee as Mae looked at Farah.

'You were so relieved I'd agreed to it you'd have said anything in case I changed my mind. What were Farah's words? "You were meant to be looking after Zoya."'

'Well, you were,' replied Farah.

Mae shook her head, wondering how she'd ever got along with her sisters in the past. Had they always refused to see her point of view? Maybe it was because she'd never had a solid point of view.

'Yeah, well, forget that ever happening again. You know, when was the last time any of you asked me about uni?'

Bubblee and Farah paused.

'We do ask you,' said Bubblee.

'When was the last time?'

Fatti had now also come upstairs and stood next to Farah.

'Look through our group chat,' added Mae. 'When have you ever really asked me how it's going, who my friends are, how I'm finding it? And even when you have, you don't wait for two seconds before launching into some story about your babies or whatever.'

'Mae, when you're a mum, then you'll understand what it's like,' said Farah.

Bubblee closed her eyes and sighed.

'Right,' said Mae. 'That's exactly what I'm talking about. No wonder Bubblee can't stand to be around you,

Faar. If becoming a mum turns me into someone like you I'd rather not have kids, thanks. Do the world a favour.'

'Mae,' said Fatti.

'Whatever,' said Mae. 'Leave my room. I don't want to see or talk to any of you. You can all think I'm a brat, or selfish or whatever, but it's not as if you lot are any better. Just because you're mums you think you have this higher purpose and so all that matters is what you do and forget everyone else. Fine.' Mae shrugged. 'Get on with it. You might be great mums, but you can know for sure that you've been pretty crap sisters.'

A strange kind of detachment came over Mae. Anger had fizzled and its after-effect was numbness. She didn't even look at her sisters as she folded more clothes. They all hovered, waiting for more, perhaps wanting to say something, but in the end it felt like there was nothing much to add.

'Mae,' was all Fatti managed as Bubblee turned around and walked out of the room.

Mae closed the door without a second look. As she folded her khaki cargo trousers they blurred so that the room was just a haze. She sat on her bed, trousers in hand, and wiped her eyes. Her phone beeped and she thought it might be Abdul-Raheem as she went to grab it.

> Ji Su: Hey. How are you?

Mae had to take a minute and make sure she wasn't hallucinating. Ji Su was online but Mae didn't respond.

It wouldn't be enough to just message her – how was she meant to be normal over WhatsApp when so much was going on? She might not have known Ji Su long, but she *knew* her and hopefully that meant that the message was her way of saying that Mae had been forgiven, which was good timing because what Mae needed more than anything else right now was a friend. She couldn't stay in the house any longer. Instead of pretending to go to bed she grabbed some of the clothes she'd folded, stuffed them in a bag, along with a few other necessities, and wrote her family a note:

Gone back to uni. Will be back when I'm back. Mae.

They were too busy nattering in the living room to notice her creep down the stairs and place the note in the hallway. She prayed that her dad's keys were hanging by the doorway and there they were. Her mum and dad might kill her, but she'd worry about that tomorrow – in for a penny and all that. She flung her things into the car and was sure her family were too busy to even hear the engine start as Mae pulled out of the driveway.

Mae drove for four hours, stopping once to fill the car with more petrol and use the bathroom. And get some fish and chips. There was a downpour of rain at one point, which stopped as abruptly as it had begun. She didn't even know if Ji Su would be home, but she'd get a room at the Travelodge or something and look for her.

All Mae knew was that she had to get away from home and everyone in it. Even Abdul-Raheem.

In the end, Mae knew she'd been silly driving up on a whim. It was almost one in the morning when she checked into the Travelodge and she messaged Ji Su.

> Mae: Meet me outside r café if u can.

A few moments later her reply came.

> Ji Su: It's the middle of the night …

What had Mae been thinking? A few seconds later another reply came.

> Ji Su: Fine. I'm coming. Be there in 20.

In the meantime, Mae walked around the quiet town, which felt strangely desolate now that it wasn't teeming with students, falling out of clubs and bars. The light of the street lamps fell onto the wet, empty cobbled streets, a few plastic bags drifting around. Mae picked them up and put them in one of the bins. She felt a strange fondness for the place, even as she walked past the club where she'd had the incident. What would it mean if she never walked these streets again? Or, if she walked them with Abdul-Raheem? How would the scope of the place change? How would she change? Being here only made her increasingly aware of how small Wyvernage was, how tiny its life – the roads as narrow as the minds of her family. Eventually, she reached their café and Ji Su was already waiting there. She was in a pair of Converses, zebra-print pyjamas and a white T-shirt, a red shawl draped around her shoulders. Mae hadn't prepared for it. What did she even want to say to her? Now they were face to face, all the things that had happened over the summer clogged up in her throat.

'Hi,' said Mae.

'Hello.'

Mae walked up to her, wondering if she should hug Ji Su, but she was standing there with her arms folded, refusing to move. She had been the one to message Mae, after all. Why did she look so stony-faced?

'I was glad you messaged,' said Mae.

'Yeah, well …'

'Sorry I dragged you out of bed.'

'Bit random. And late.'

'Guess so,' replied Mae.

There was a long pause.

'Well?' said Ji Su. 'Are we going to stand here all day or are we going somewhere?'

'Riverside bench?' suggested Mae.

Ji Su shrugged as they both began to walk towards the riverside. It took around ten minutes to get there and it was spent in silence. If the silence had been awkward then Mae didn't feel it because she was too busy thinking about what she was going to say. By the time they sat on the bench, still damp from the rain, Mae was none the wiser.

'I really missed you, you know,' she said eventually.

Silence.

Mae looked at Ji Su's profile. She was still so pretty, her hair bunched up in a high, messy bun, eyebrows furrowed.

'How've you been?' she asked.

'You know. Busy,' replied Ji Su.

'Saving the world?'

'Failing the world.'

Mae smiled. 'At least you're failing at something worthwhile.'

Ji Su looked at her. 'What are you failing at?'

Mae looked at the dark ripples in the river, feeling the quiet of night-time. 'We'll talk about that later, if you still want to be friends, but first, I just want to say sorry.'

'Please, don't. It's embarrassing,' replied Ji Su, looking sterner than ever.

'No. Not sorry that we didn't go through with anything ...'

Ji Su turned to her and raised her eyebrows.

'Can't apologise for something that I didn't feel at the time,' replied Mae.

Even she was shocked at all this forthrightness, but she was beginning to learn that honesty was better than just carrying on pretending that everything was fine, because that had a time limit.

'I'm sorry I had to lose you as a friend because of it.'

'I just thought … You gave me all the signs, you know.'

'Did I?'

Mae looked back and wondered what the line between friendship and something more than that was. She couldn't lie, she *had* felt something for Ji Su, but in the end it was more to do with wanting to be like her than wanting to be *with* her.

'I guess I did. You're right,' added Mae.

'I've met someone now. At a protest.'

'Really? That's great.'

Mae felt a mixture of happiness for her friend that was tinged with an unexpected pang of jealousy. Perhaps it was because Ji Su had someone with whom she was sharing her day-to-day life; someone other than Mae. Ji Su told her about Leila, showed her a picture of a girl with long brown hair, coming down in waves, a smile with a slightly crooked front tooth and Mae thought what a good-looking couple they made.

'She's very pretty.'

'And smart,' Ji Su added. 'Doesn't take any crap from anyone.'

'Hmm. Sounds like someone I know.'

Ji Su laughed. 'Yeah, well. Arguments aren't that much fun between us but, you know.'

There was another long pause as Mae looked at Ji Su. 'Can we be friends again?'

Ji Su nodded. 'Yeah. I think we can.'

Mae breathed a sigh of relief. 'Thank God for that because that could've been really awks.'

They caught up on other stuff that had been happening, then Mae began to tell her about Abdul-Raheem as she watched Ji Su's expressions change at each turn of her story.

'*He's* holding out on *you?*' Ji Su shook her head. 'What's wrong with people? Men and their whole religious thing. Ugh. It's so last century. Hope you told him where to stick it.'

For a moment Mae wondered what Abdul-Raheem would make of Ji Su. Whatever his opinion might be, she knew he'd be polite and civil.

'No. He's a good person,' said Mae.

'Sounds like a drip. Making you follow his way of life.'

How had Ji Su got it so wrong? She told her that he never forced her to do anything she didn't want, that he seemed to accept her just the way she was.

'Yeah, until you're married and then watch,' said Ji Su. 'Then it'll all be, "I'm your husband, you have to listen to me".'

Mae sighed. 'You know, for someone who's meant to be liberal you're being kind of narrow-minded.'

'What? No, I'm not. I'm just telling it how it is.'

'No. You're telling it how you think it is. You've not even met him.'

'I've met his type.'

Mae paused and looked at Ji Su. 'I'd have thought that for someone who's struggled growing up, you'd get his struggle too.'

'You seem to have made up your mind about him, so why don't you just marry him? Why do you need to ask me about it?'

'I'm not asking anyone.'

Mae looked at the river again and realised how much growing up there was to do in life. That even the people she respected and loved couldn't see how skewed their vision could be.

'All I'm saying is that he's a twenty-eight-year-old man who pretends to be a horse for a day job and refuses to have a physical relationship because he thinks he'll burn in hell if he does. I mean, please.'

Of course, Mae supposed there was nothing untrue about Ji Su's assessment but that was just him on paper; you'd have to know Abdul-Raheem to see how kind and caring he was too.

'*He's* the one who keeps saying I should come back to uni. That I should try to do something I love and try to make a go of it. He wants to get back to studies as well.'

'So, you want to marry him?'

'I don't know.'

'Why not? If he's so great?'

'Loads of people are great,' said Mae. 'Doesn't mean I want to spend the rest of my life with them.'

'Exactly. And you have to ask yourself, what do *you* want?'

Mae knew that. The question had been flitting around her head for however many months now and she'd got no closer to the answer.

'I want some sleep right now,' she replied.

'Yeah. You must be tired.'

They walked back to town, Mae asking about Ji Su's plans in the new term and hearing about the things she wanted to achieve and how she was going to pave the way to work for an NGO after university. Mae's excitement for Ji Su was only matched by her sense of panic for herself. They got to the middle of town where Mae had to turn left and Ji Su right.

'Thanks for meeting me,' said Mae, hugging her friend.

'Well, you did drive all that way. Couldn't stay mad at you for ever.'

Mae turned around and began walking towards the Travelodge when Ji Su called out to her.

'And listen.'

Mae turned around.

'You'll figure out what you want,' said Ji Su. 'If it's Abdul-Raheem, then you'll know. And if you're still unsure then that's another kind of answer too.'

'Thanks,' Mae called out.

'Just … whatever you do, don't change.'

Mae nodded and thought about that as she walked through the town centre. The point was, Mae *did* want to change. She wanted to be a better version of herself and she wouldn't be able to do that in Wyvernage, that was for sure. She turned around, looking at the barren town, and wanted to see it when it was alive again, brimming with people and students. Mae was unsure of many things still, but one thing she now knew: she'd have to return here and finish what she had started. She may have failed her first year at university, but what was failure other than a sign that you just had to try again? This time, she'd just have to try harder.

Chapter Seventeen

Mae set off early to go back home the following day. Now that she knew that she wanted to start university again she didn't want to waste any more time. She'd have to contact uni, ask what to do, how to go about reapplying. Get a loan. More than that, she'd have to figure out what she'd actually apply to do. Mae felt the possibilities of life blossoming before her until she thought about Abdul-Raheem. With each mile that drew her closer to him, her dread seemed to expand and before facing all of that she drove towards the one place that she knew would give her some peace of mind.

Alison wasn't there this time, but a man called George.

'I wanted to see Ginger, if that's okay?' she asked, explaining that Alison knew her and she'd gone for a ride on him a few times.

'Not available right now, I'm afraid,' he said.

'It's okay, I'll wait.'

'Suit yourself,' he said and went back to fiddling between two notebooks.

It was half an hour before Ginger returned and Mae's heart swelled at the sight of him.

'Do you mind if I take him for a ride now?'

'No availability,' he replied. 'I'm here on my own and I can't accompany you. Unless you can ride on your own?'

Mae hesitated for a moment. Things could go wrong, but today of all days, she needed to do this.

'Yeah,' she lied. 'I can.'

'All right then.'

George brought Ginger out and set Mae up. He looked at her dubiously as she put one of her feet in the stirrup, still struggling somewhat to get on to the saddle with any form of grace.

'You sure you can do this? I don't want any injuries,' he said.

'Of course. We're old friends, aren't we, Ginger?' she said, patting his neck.

George led her towards the field as he said, 'Back in forty minutes, all right?'

Mae nodded as a thrill passed through her body at being on a horse, in the middle of a field, all alone.

'Look at that,' she said, barely able to hold back her smile.

Ginger's trot got a little too fast and Mae pulled at the reins, except a little too much because he almost slowed down to a halt. She gripped her legs to the side tighter than she had done before and could feel the muscles already hurting.

'A little to the right,' she said, pulling the reins and she wondered whether it was because Ginger and she were in sync or if it was just riding a horse that felt natural to her. There were nerves, but the good kind. She'd read about the rising trot and wondered if she should try it. It had said that once you got used to it, it was easier than the sitting trot. She pushed her hips up as one diagonal pair of Ginger's legs rose, and sat back in the saddle as the other pair rose. It was easy enough to find her rhythm, almost as if she didn't have to think about it at all – she just went with the motion of the horse, murmuring to Ginger all the way.

'Whoa, boy,' she said as they got back to the stable, George waiting at the gate with his arms crossed.

He'd been looking at her from afar. 'I see the horse likes you, and you did well. How many lessons have you had then, apart from the ones here?'

Mae felt her face flush. 'Not many.'

'You're a natural then.'

Mae beamed as she got off Ginger and jumped to the ground.

'You think? Thanks. Oh, hang on, I have something,' she said.

She left to go to the car and returned a few minutes later, handing the book Alison had given her to George.

'Could you make sure that Alison gets this?'

'Hmm,' he said, looking at it. 'She loves this book. Lent it to you, did she?'

'Yeah.'

'All right.'

Mae went over to Ginger and patted his forehead. 'I'll miss you. But I'll be back.'

'Sure he'd like to go for another ride,' said George.

'Me too,' replied Mae. 'Oh, and can you tell Alison I said thanks.'

'For what?' he asked.

She paused. 'Just thanks. I think she'll get it.'

Mae took another look at Ginger before walking back to her car, feeling ready to do the inevitable.

Unfortunately, the inevitable involved stopping at work where she'd called in sick. Barry was standing outside the hut with a clipboard and pen in hand, his head bowed in concentration and white shirt damp with sweat.

'What are you doing here?' he barked when he looked up to find Mae standing in front of him. 'Thought you were ill. Look okay to me.'

'It was more of an emergency really,' she replied.

He shook his head. 'I had to have that idiot Stuart take over from Leanne at the booth. She's the only one short enough to be the horse's arse.'

'Sorry. Can I go in? I need to see Abdul-Raheem.'

'You two,' he exclaimed. 'Tell him if he's taking a break now then he'd better not try and pull a fast one and take another one.'

Mae raised her eyebrows at him.

'All right, all right. I know,' added Barry. 'He'd give me part of his salary back if he thought he'd taken the mick.'

'Exactly.'

'Fine, whatever.'

Just as Mae was about to walk on, Barry pointed to her and said: 'And don't you go breaking his heart or anything, all right?'

Yeah, thanks, Barry.

She walked through the park, making her way towards the carousel where she and Abdul-Raheem usually stood at this time of the day. There he was, in the costume, and Mae remembered the first day they'd met. How many conversations do you have in life with a stranger where you just never want it to end? In all of Mae's years, how many times had she felt this way? And how many people had felt this way about *her*?

None.

'Mae,' came Abdul-Raheem's voice as he took his horse's head off.

'Hi.'

'Barry said you were ill.'

'Yeah, thanks for checking up on me,' she replied.

Leanne's head popped out from behind Abdul-Raheem. 'You two. Jeez. I'm going for a fag.'

With which she walked away.

'I wanted to but …'

'I guess we should talk,' said Mae. 'Properly.'

He nodded.

'What? Now?' he added.

'Been long enough, don't you think?'

So, they walked in silence towards the staffing area, which was quiet and would be for another half an hour until lunch time.

'I went to uni yesterday,' she began as they took a seat on a bench.

'Oh. Why?'

'Just. I kind of missed it.'

He smiled. 'And?'

'And, I think I do want to go back. I mean, I know I do.'

This time he laughed and grabbed her hand. 'I knew you'd want to go back. This place is too small for you, Mae.'

She squeezed his hand. 'The thing is …'

'What?'

'I want to go back alone.'

She noticed him swallow, his grip on her hand loosening.

'What do you mean "alone"?'

'Like, on my own.'

'So, without me?' he asked.

'No … Well, yeah. I guess that's what it means.'

He let go of her hand and looked at her. 'Why?'

Mae had had several hours to think of how to say all this to her boyfriend but she still hadn't managed to come up with anything that didn't sound ungrateful.

Nothing which didn't make her feel as if she was letting him down. She supposed she was letting him down, and wasn't it selfish to do that to another person, just so you could go and do what you wanted? Even though what she really wanted was for him to come to uni with her as her boyfriend, not husband. In the end though, even that wouldn't be brave, would it?

'Because some things you should do on your own,' said Mae.

'How would I be stopping you? You know I want to go back to university too.'

'I know, but … can't you see it'd be too much? Becoming a wife when I don't even know what I want to study. I don't want this to be over, but … I'd hoped you'd understand,' she replied.

'No, Mae. You wanted to be in a grown-up relationship so tell me in a grown-up way.'

Mae put her hands under her legs.

'I'm so young,' she said.

'That's a load of crap that you've heard from someone else. That's not coming from you. And you weren't so young when it came to us being in a relationship. Not once, but twice. It was *your* decision to get back together,' he added, shaking his head.

'I know but that was before, you know, you asked me to marry you.' She paused. 'It's just so much. And whatever you might think, I *am* young. I've not lived. You've got all these stories and things you've been through and my past is just this bland place. Everything that's happened to me, or anything that I've done, hasn't really been me or mine, it's been me taking part in someone else's story. That someone else usually being one of my sisters.' She looked at his face and how each word she spoke seemed to pain him. But she had to make him understand. 'Even my first year of uni, I didn't really know what to do or how to meet people and it sucked because I realised that I don't really know who or what I am independent of my family.'

Abdul-Raheem sighed. 'But this all sounds similar to why you broke up with me the first time.'

'I guess so. But no. Listen, don't you think, if I go back to uni with you, then I'll just be like, an extension of you? Just like I am in that horse.'

Abdul-Raheem gave a flicker of a smile, which disappeared as quickly as it had appeared.

'You're easy with people,' she continued. 'And they like you and I can just see me being comfortable with that, but that's not right, is it?'

'What's wrong with being comfortable?' he asked, looking down at the floor.

'You know what's wrong with it when you're only nineteen and don't know what you're all about.'

'You say that but you *do* know,' he replied.

'No. You can't tell me what I do or don't know. That's not for you to say.'

Abdul-Raheem shook his head, eyes fixed on the ground. 'We can make it work long distance for a while.'

For a moment Mae wondered if he had a point. There he'd be in the background, someone to lean on and talk to when the day had been bad, or when she just wanted someone to know what she was up to. Mae had to listen to herself. But then wouldn't he just be waiting for her to say yes to marrying him? She didn't want to be tied down to anything – not even an expectation.

'I don't want to rely on you,' she said.

He let out an incredulous laugh. 'As opposed to the past few months?'

'I don't want to rely on *anyone*,' she added. 'You did what you did and I can't forget that, and you know how thankful I am but, like, how can you not get it?' she said, her voice rising.

Abdul-Raheem took a deep breath. 'I get it. I just don't like it.'

'I'm sorry,' she said, looking at the ground too. He was accepting it and Mae began to feel the sadness settle that once this conversation was over, so would they be. 'You're better off without me and my family drama anyway.'

He looked at her. 'Don't do that, Mae. Don't patronise me to make yourself feel better.'

'I'm not.'

'Yes, you are,' he said, getting up. 'Are we done here?'

Was that it? Was he going? Mae thought she'd have a

proper goodbye with him. One that involved some tears and a hug with him wishing her luck and telling her he understood why she had to do this alone.

'I guess so,' she said.

'Take care then,' he replied, not looking at her. 'Hope it all works out for you.'

Mae was left staring at the figure of him walking away and felt a desperate need to run after him. But what would she say? Her mind was made up, she just couldn't believe that she was going to lose him as a friend as well. Just as she'd once lost Ji Su. There was no going back now, not for a third time, and so she had to carry on watching as he walked further and further away from her.

Eventually she walked back to the car park, thinking about her last few words with Abdul-Raheem and how satisfied her parents would be if they found out she'd broken up with him. It only made her feel worse. Before leaving the park she knocked on Barry's door. It was time to tell him that she was quitting.

'Oh, for God's sake,' he said. 'First you lie about being unwell and now you're leaving without giving me any notice.'

The idea of working here another day with Abdul-Raheem and with all the things she had to now do was unbearable.

'I'm really sorry,' she said.

'Yeah, well, sorry's not going to fix my problem. Do

you always go around doing what you want and not taking responsibility for stuff? Thought you were better than this other lot. Go on then, get out of here.'

Mae felt the tears well in her eyes. She wished she hadn't said anything now, but it was too late. She went to leave, putting her hand on the doorknob. This was Mae's problem: instead of dealing with awkwardness, she always walked away from it.

'No, you're right,' she said, turning around.

'Don't want you here any more if I can't rely on you.'

'I'm sorry. I'll stay for a week and that gives you some time to find a new person.'

He stared at her for a moment. 'You're not going to give me that crap about being ill?'

She shook her head and he sighed.

'Fine. Good. Because I've got enough stuff to deal with.'

Mae would have to face Abdul-Raheem again tomorrow, and the day after, but Barry was right, she'd have to deal with her responsibilities. Whatever type of person Mae wanted to become, she'd have to work at it to be the best she could be.

By the time she parked up outside the house it was early evening. She'd spent the day in town, looking at other courses at university, until she'd come across the one course that gave her the same tinge of excitement that she'd felt when she went on her first date with

Abdul-Raheem: as if she was living life and not just a spectator watching from the sidelines. Of course this was what she wanted to do. It was new and exciting and it didn't feel like it would be a slog. She paused for a moment, wondering if this was a little too impulsive – after all, she'd not had much experience with it, but maybe life was about taking chances that felt right, and not just what made sense. She remembered her date with Abdul-Raheem as she went through the application process, thinking about how unexpected it had been, and yet how it finally felt that there was something more to her life than just being an Amir sister. Was this nostalgia?

Mae got out of the car, took a deep breath and opened the front door. Her dad rushed to the passage and stopped as he saw her. They looked at each other for a few moments.

'Couldn't get the train at that time,' she said, handing him his car keys.

'Oh, thank God you are home,' exclaimed her mum, coming up behind her dad. 'What is the point in you young people having mobile phones if you never pick them up?'

Mae just shrugged and made to go to her room. This time her parents didn't stop her. It was later that evening when she could smell the cooking that the doorbell rang and she heard her sisters' voices, along with the cries of her niece and nephew. Never had she wanted to speak to Abdul-Raheem more. She reached over for her phone, looking at the WhatsApp profile pic of him and his dad. If she'd done the right thing, then why did it feel so difficult? If she'd made a decision to not have him in her life any more, then why did she still want him there? She was about to message him when there was a knock on the door.

'Can we come in?' Fatti's head poked through the door as Mae put the phone down and shrugged.

'Guess so.'

Fatti had opened the door to reveal Farah and Bubblee standing behind her.

'You won't all fit,' added Mae to them.

Bubblee and Farah inched into the room as Fatti went and sat on the edge of Mae's bed.

'Where'd you go?' she asked.

'Uni.'

'How come?' asked Farah. 'It doesn't start for another few weeks or something, right?'

Mae sighed and decided there was no point in lying to her sisters any more, even if she wasn't really in the mood to entertain them.

'I failed my first year, was going to quit, but Abdul-Raheem made me realise that I should stick at it. So, I'm applying to do another course.'

Their faces collectively changed as Mae fed them her life update.

'Well, it was him and then Mum and Dad saying I wasn't allowed to go to uni any more. Last thing I want is to be stuck here for the rest of my life,' said Mae. 'No offence,' she added, looking at Fatti and Farah, who had never wanted to leave Wyvernage.

'You never said anything,' said Bubblee.

'Not exactly the kind of news you want to give, is it?'

Fatti put her hand on Mae's leg. 'Listen, we've been talking the past few days and we just want to say—'

'We're sorry,' Farah cut in. 'I mean, the things you said weren't exactly on, but, well, I guess there was some truth in it.'

'Way to give an apology, Faar,' said Bubblee.

'You know what I mean.'

'You've always just been our little sister and we forgot that you're also your own person,' added Bubblee. 'I, of all people, should've seen that.'

'And Abdul-Raheem,' said Fatti. 'We *should* have been more supportive. That's what sisters are meant to do when it comes to facing parents.'

'Serious lack of a united front there,' said Bubblee.

Even Farah nodded.

'Yeah, well, you don't have to worry about that any more because I broke up with him.'

'What?'

'Oh no.'

'Why?'

Mae looked at all of them incredulously. 'Oh, now you care?'

'Listen,' said Bubblee. 'Better late than never, okay.'

Mae didn't have it in her to dig her heels into her grudge, it felt like too much work and not enough positive outcome. So, she told them what she'd done that morning, and how he'd reacted.

'Sorry,' said Fatti.

'He wasn't exactly going to be over the moon, was he?' said Farah.

'Typical man, really, pretends he's supportive until it doesn't suit him,' added Bubblee.

Mae should've felt annoyed at her, but she couldn't help but smile.

'Don't tell Mum and Dad,' said Mae. 'I don't want them to think I broke up with him because they wanted it.'

'Didn't you?' asked Fatti.

'No,' exclaimed Mae. 'As if. I did it because ... you know ...'

'You've got to do uni alone. On your own terms,' said Bubblee.

Mae nodded. 'Yeah. Don't you think?'

Farah folded her arms. 'I don't think you need to second guess yourself, Mae.'

'Well, starting afresh is a nice idea,' said Bubblee.

'Is that why you've now moved on to another man?' said Farah to Bubblee, this time looking amused.

'What's going on there?' said Mae to Fatti, pointing at her twin sisters.

'Okay, fine,' said Farah, putting her hands up. 'I'd become a bore and a nag. I admit it, all right.'

'They're working things out,' said Fatti as Mae let out a laugh.

'It's like coming back to a parallel universe,' said Mae.

'Yes, well,' said Farah. 'Things change, don't they?'

Mae nodded. Just then another figure came up behind Farah and Bubblee.

'We'd better go down and help with dinner,' said Fatti, getting up.

Her sisters left her as Ilyaas hovered at the door.

'What do you want?' said Mae, picking up her phone, pretending to flick through Twitter.

He had his hands in his jean pockets as he looked at the ground and mumbled something.

'I can't hear you,' said Mae.

He looked up. 'What I did … what happened … I'm sorry. It was out of order.'

'Yeah, no kidding,' said Mae.

'It's just …' he looked up at her and Mae was taken aback by the teenage angst on his face. 'I liked you and I got … you know. Like, that thing. Jealous.'

Mae slung her legs over the bed. Abdul-Raheem had been right. Who'd have thought she could have an effect on a teenage boy like that? Hormones. They were weird.

'That's not the way to win a person over, FYI. I mean, that's not the type of person you should want to be.'

He nodded. 'I know. Just wasn't thinking.'

Ilyaas looked back at the ground. Mae didn't want her anger to give way so easily – some things you should hold on to. Because of Ilyaas, things had spiralled out of control, her parents had stopped speaking to her, she'd got back with her boyfriend only to have to break up with him again. But then maybe that's what needed to happen in order for her to try and begin again.

'All right,' said Mae. 'Well, you done?'

She thought he'd leave but he shuffled on his feet before he spoke again. 'Can we be friends again?'

Mae considered this for more than a few moments. What would be the use of having a friend who you can't really trust? But then she wondered what if you could help shape who a person might become? What if Abdul-Raheem hadn't given her the confidence that she now felt growing inside her? (Whatever Bubblee had to say about him being a typical man in the end, no one could deny what he'd done for Mae, and isn't it best to focus on the positives?) Or if Ji Su hadn't been the friend she needed after that horrible event?

'Depends,' said Mae. 'Can I trust you?'

He nodded so vehemently it almost made Mae laugh.

'Okay, well, don't expect me to share my deepest, darkest secrets with you,' she said. 'But, we can start again, I guess.'

'Thanks,' he replied.

He paused again, seeming to be glued to the floor.

'I've got some stuff to do now,' said Mae.

'Oh, yeah, right. All right.'

Ilyaas nodded again and gave Mae an unsure smile.

Mae met it with much more kindness than she felt at that moment, but she thought, given some time, she might be able to smile like that at him genuinely.

She had refused to go downstairs for dinner and was regretting it. She messaged Fatti to bring up some food for her, which she was about to do when Mae heard her mum bellow: 'If she wants to eat, then she will have the respect to come downstairs and face her amma and abba.'

Fatti: Guess you heard that. Sorry.

She did go downstairs, with her head held high, filling her plate with okra curry and rice. Mae managed a salam to each of her parents as they all sat at the table, cutlery scraping against plates, someone asking for more salt, another person going to refill the jug of water. Mae, who was so often left speechless by her errant nerves, was quiet this time simply because she refused to speak unless spoken to. Never had she experienced such a strong command over her emotions.

'Amma, Abba,' said Fatti, wiping her mouth with a napkin. 'Mae's going back to uni next month and we think ...' she glanced around at her sisters as Mae looked confused, 'we think we should all apologise to her about ... you know. Everything.'

Mae's dad's face went pale, as if he was about to throw up. The only thing her mum looked like she might throw up was a stream of lava.

'Yes,' said Farah, decidedly, resting her spoon on her plate.

What was going on?

'And we'll support her in that, won't we?' added Bubblee.

Their mum looked at their dad. 'See? See what's happening? Our daughters are turning against us.'

Ilyaas and Aima looked at each other as Ash cleared his throat. 'Kids, let's put our plates away in the kitchen.'

Ilyaas followed his dad, but it took Ash several tries to get Aima off the table.

'Ugh, why do I have to miss out on anything interesting that happens here?' Mae heard Aima say as they left.

'I have told you, you are not going back to uni,' said her dad.

'No, Abba,' said Farah, looking straight at him. 'She is. And neither you nor Amma can stop her.'

'*Faru*,' said her mum.

Their dad looked around the table at each of his daughters, thinking God-knows-what, before his eyes rested on Mae.

'How can we trust you?' he said.

Mae swallowed hard. 'I'll do what I do, Abba.'

'That is all you can say to me?' he said.

She shrugged. 'I don't want to disappoint you, but you know … you and Amma disappointed me too. I know what it must've been like for you but I didn't think you'd actually be properly horrible. Not when you're going on about religion and stuff on one hand and then doing the thing that actually God hates.'

Her mum and dad's nostrils seemed to flair in unison.

'Sorry, but Abdul-Raheem taught me more about being Muslim than you guys ever have.'

She noticed her sisters exchange glances. Granted, some of his practices didn't exactly tally with Mae's – perhaps they never would – but he could've taught her family a thing or two about kindness.

'Anyway,' said Mae, getting up, when no one spoke. 'Think I'll have an early night.'

She took her plate into the kitchen where Ash was sitting with both his children.

'You're all right, Mae,' was all he said, but Mae could've gone and hugged her brother-in-law when he did.

Mae heard her sisters leave a little later while she was lying in bed, her phone in hand, hovering between her social media apps and wanting to call Abdul-Raheem. It was when she was drifting off to sleep that she sensed some light coming into the room. She opened her eyes and started, not realising it was her mum and dad's figures looming in the doorway.

'You are sleeping?' her dad asked.

She sat up, rubbing her eyes. 'Not really. Almost.'

He stepped into the room without waiting for an invitation and sat on the edge of her bed as her mum came in and switched on the lamp. It took a few moments for Mae's eyes to adjust to the light.

'You are going to uni?' her dad asked.

Mae wasn't sure if it was a question or not but she thought it best to respond in the affirmative. There was no more room left for doubt.

'Yes.'

'With that boy?' asked her mum.

'Jay's amma ...' said her dad, sighing. He paused. 'Mae, it is very difficult for us. The things you have done; the way you were in a house alone with a man.' He shook his head and sighed again. 'But then the world is changing.'

Her mum didn't look too pleased with this observation.

'I have been thinking about what you said. About this boy and his Islam.' Her dad paused, as if unable to bring the words out of his mouth. 'Maybe he is a good Muslim. Maybe better than us. I know the world is changing but this doesn't mean that you have to change with it. Traditions and values are a thing you should hold on to – they are a part of you.'

Mae wanted to roll her eyes.

'You might be too young to understand this, but maybe, when you are older, you will see what your abba meant. Why it's important.'

Her mum kept trying to stick back the wallpaper that had peeled off from one corner.

'But—' added her dad.

'Yes, yes,' interrupted her mum. 'Your abba is going to say that we were wrong about your ... *friend*.'

'And your amma agrees with me, don't you, Jay's amma?'

'All people are equal in Allah's eyes,' said her mum.

'Yeah, but what about your eyes?' asked Mae.

Her dad put his hand on her arm. 'Even old people must learn new things.'

Mae thought she might cry. If she hadn't believed in God before she would've done now because it felt like a miracle. They didn't ask about Abdul-Raheem, whether Mae and he were together, and Mae didn't offer any information either, but this was a step in the right direction, wasn't it? Her dad patted her arm again and held on to it. She couldn't help but grab his hand and squeeze it.

'Are you still my abba then?'

He nodded, looking like he might also cry. 'I will always be your abba.'

'Yes,' said her mum. 'But that's enough now because I am tired with all this apologising and I think ... it's time for us to go to bed.'

She raised her eyebrows at Mae's dad who shot up and cleared his throat, perking up so much he looked ten years younger. Before Mae knew it they'd both dashed out of the room and closed the door behind them. A tear had fallen down Mae's face as she laughed until she could hear them again in the next room. *Ugh*. She got her headphones out and put on her music playlist. Grown-up or not, she was never going to be okay with her parents having sex right next door to her. Before she turned her music on though, her phone beeped:

Sistaaaas has added you to their group.

For the first time in a long time, at least this part of her life felt like it was getting back to normal.

The final week at work was a game of dodgems with Abdul-Raheem. Barry, for reasons unknown to Mae, decided to put her in the booth and let Leanne carry on being the arse to Abdul-Raheem's head. Mae tried to bump into him during break time but he seemed to know she was coming and turn around and go in the opposite direction. Every day, Mae's heart would get heavier at having things left the way they were – how could she keep him on the pedestal she'd put him on when he kept intentionally stepping off it? It was on her last day when Mae was saying goodbye to everyone that she looked for him. She'd pinned her hopes on the final day, sure that he'd come through. As she walked through the amusement park gates one last time, she looked back, just in case he'd changed his mind and followed her out. It was when she looked around that she saw him standing by her car, arms folded, watching her.

'Hi,' she said, looking up at him.

'Hi.'

He leaned both his hands against the bonnet and Mae

felt what a shame it was they couldn't have taken their relationship to the next level. She'd always regret that, even though she had little control over it.

'I—'

'List—'

'Sorry, you go first,' said Abdul-Raheem.

'No, you go.'

He paused. 'I didn't take it very well, did I?'

Mae smiled. 'I mean, it could've been worse.'

'Yeah, well. It could always be worse. But I wanted to say bye. Properly.'

'Do you get it?' Mae asked.

He nodded. 'Yeah. I always got it. I just didn't like it. It's taken me a little while to realise that this is how it's meant to be.'

'You spiritual types …' said Mae.

'It's got to have some uses, doesn't it?' He stood up and put his arms around Mae, bringing her in closer. 'You're going to nail uni.'

She rested her head on his chest. 'Second time lucky.'

'Luck's got nothing to do with it.'

He held on to her arms and drew back as she looked up at him. Bending down, he kissed her on the lips as Mae moved in closer, putting her arms around his neck. After a while, Abdul-Raheem pulled back and smiled at her.

'Had to say a proper goodbye.'

'Thanks,' she said. 'It'll keep me going for a while.'

Maybe this sadness was also a part of growing up, which felt like a bit of a hardship. He squeezed her hands one last time before he let go.

'You take care,' he said.

She didn't trust her voice not to break, so she nodded.

'It's going to be a good time for you,' he added, walking backwards. 'Trust me.'

He turned around as she watched him walk away when she called out: 'Can I call you? Sometimes? You know, as friends.'

Abdul-Raheem turned around again and nodded. 'You know where I'll be.'

Mae sat in her car and looked out ahead of her. She wouldn't be dependent on anyone any more. She'd make a go of things on her own. But it didn't hurt to know that should she need it, there'd be a friendly voice on the other end of the line.

Chapter Eighteen

'Shut your face right up, I got in,' Mae exclaimed as she opened her email.

She looked around and realised there was no one there to hear her. She ran down the stairs where her family was gathered, bickering about how long a baby should be breastfed, when she shouted.

'I got in!'

They all looked up at her.

'Into the zoo?' said Bubblee, bouncing Zoya on her lap. 'Finally locking you up, thank God.'

'Shut up. To my course for uni,' said Mae.

'Mae,' exclaimed Fatti, jumping out of her seat. 'I'm so proud of you.'

Fatti hugged Mae for a lot longer than Mae felt necessary, but appreciated it nonetheless. Farah was also smiling at her and nodded.

'Well done, Mae. See what you can do when you put your mind to it?'

Mae looked at both her parents who didn't seem quite

sure how to take this news. Eventually her dad got up and put his hand on her head.

'May Allah bring you success whatever you do.'

Her mum muttered a prayer under her breath and got up and blew over Mae's face.

'Doesn't matter where you are,' she said. 'You need Allah's protection.'

'Yes, Amma,' replied Mae.

'So …' said Bubblee. 'What have you actually got in to study?'

Mae looked around the room, feeling like she might actually burst with excitement. She took a deep breath.

'Equestrian Psychology and Sports Science,' she practically squealed.

Everyone stared at her as Mae continued to look at them, waiting for their mutual excitement.

'Equesta-what?' said Farah.

Bubblee looked like she might either laugh or cry. 'Horses?'

Their mum and dad looked at a loss.

'My actual God,' added Bubblee. 'She spent the summer pretending to be a horse and now thinks she's going to become some kind of horse whisperer.'

Mae would've thrown the pillow that was on the sofa at Bubblee if Zoya wasn't on her lap.

'That not what it is,' she said. 'It's *so* cool. You get to spend all this time studying their behaviour and working with horses too. And guess what?'

No one could really guess anything when it came to Mae.

'I could even go abroad to Australia or Canada or somewhere for an *international exchange*.'

'Allah!' exclaimed her mum. 'International? Away from England? Away from *home*?'

Her dad patted her mum's leg, telling her to calm down.

'It'd only be like six months,' said Mae.

'*Six months*.'

'Well ...' said Fatti. 'That's ... *great*. Really great.'

'Australia is so far,' said their mum. 'You know how long the flight is?'

'Amma,' said Bubblee. 'It's better than the zoo, which is where I thought she'd end up.'

The conversation went on in this vein for a while, but Mae was too excited to take offence at anything. She even managed to take the trouble to calm her mum down and assure her that she wouldn't somehow get killed by a horse in the middle of the Australian outback. The possibilities to Mae seemed to be sprawling endlessly and she couldn't believe that she was getting a second chance to do something new. It made her realise that maybe there was no end to beginning again in life. She was glad she had youth on her side but when it came down to it, you could begin again however many times you wanted – that perhaps life's adventures never had to end.

Mae went back to her room after a while and started to prepare to leave home again. Sitting on her bed, she got her laptop out and went on to Facebook, searching for that post which now felt like so long ago. The video was still there, the comments going on for what seemed like for ever, but less frequent now. The last comment was dated over a month ago. Mae had tried to ignore the video back then. Then she got drunk and tried to forget it had ever happened, but as experiences go, that was a pretty bad one, wasn't it? Hadn't she learnt that you can't ignore things? That you have to face them, head-on?

She sat down and began to write:

> Six months ago I was publicly shamed for doing something that a lot of women do: apply make-up on the train. I'm not sure why this guy was so offended. Was it because 'women should pretend they don't wear make-up', or because I was South Asian and it annoyed him even more? Why do people expect women to be strong and independent on one hand, while doing everything they can to bring them down on the other?

Mae's thoughts grew momentum and with each sentence she felt her anger come back. A new kind of controlled, straight-thinking anger. She finished her post, adding what had happened at The Crypt, how easily things can spiral if you don't take a moment and step back. She decided to wait a few hours before looking over it again. Mae carried on organising things for university, letting Ji Su know she'd be back.

> Ji Su: Yes! I can't wait! We're going to have so much fun. Hope you're coming back alone but no judgement. Not a lot anyway. Xx

> Mae: ALONE. Thx 4 the support tho. Joke. I get it. Dont hv any room in ur flat 4 me do u? Dorms packed.

It turned out that while Ji Su didn't, she did know someone looking for a flatmate and gave Mae their number. Mae didn't wait to contact them and dropped them a message that very minute. Then she went back to her Facebook post to read it over.

'Hashtag, FaceIt.'

She took a moment, rather happy with this inventive hashtag, before she pressed the 'share' button.

Two weeks later Mae was gathered with her family once more, in the living room, for her farewell party. Her Facebook post had been shared over two thousand times and she'd even got messages from people she went to class with last year. Ilyaas had followed her into the kitchen to give her a present.

'It's just a notebook,' he said. 'For your classes and stuff. Be cool to learn about horses.'

'Thanks,' she said, looking at the abstract cover. 'Yeah, I can't wait. I mean, it's going to be *so* fun.'

'Can I still message you and stuff?'

She looked at his face that had gone a shade of red.

'Yeah. Sure.'

Ilyaas seemed to breathe a sigh of relief as Fatti came in to bring in more drinks.

'You okay?' she asked Ilyaas.

'Yeah. Yeah,' he said, smiling. 'Can I go hold Adam?'

'Of course,' said Fatti.

'Thanks,' he said as he left.

'Progress then?' asked Mae.

'Typical now that they're going back to their mum's, but yes. Aima's still, well, you know … but I've said they should come back for Christmas and guess what? They didn't say no.'

When Mae went to leave, everyone decided to bundle up in their cars and drop her at the station, waving goodbye from the platform. Mae noticed her mum dry her eyes with the corner of her sari. As the train pulled away Mae thought of all the things that she had gone through in the past year. Who she had been and who she might become. She thought of the people that had come into her life, how walking into the stable that day, and Alison giving her that book, had changed the course of her education. She should write her a thank you card or something. Her heart was already hurting less when it came to thinking about Abdul-Raheem, and then there was her family. Still there, not quite the picture of perfection, but then whose was? This time Mae's excitement about the future superseded her nerves, and as she saw her family shrink into the distance, she felt the world open up for her.

ONE PLACE. MANY STORIES

Bold, innovative and
empowering publishing.

FOLLOW US ON:

@HQStories